Brandon poked his head up and saw that the Indians were approaching a mounded hillock that rose about six feet above track level. If the riders reached it as the handcar passed, they could pour arrows and bullets down into it at will.

"Keep pumping!" he yelled to Jack Ryan and released the handles. He took a careful grip on the .38, visualized where in the group the rifleman had been riding—last but one, if he had it right—inhaled deeply, and sprang up and sideways into a crouch, facing the riders.

He took a second that every instinct in him protested against to steady the pistol, the front sight aimed the rider. The Indian's horse would be an easier target, but might not respond to a hit fast enough. Brandon squeezed the trigger, the gun bucked in his hand, and the noise of the report seemed to drive the Indian off the horse's back. One leg flourished briefly in the air as he vanished on the far side of his mount, his rifle turning end over end in the bright air.

At the same instant, Brandon felt a blow in his chest and saw a feathered shaft protruding from his jacket; a yell of triumph came from the remaining Indians and a protesting groan from Jack Ryan.

Brandon rose to his knees, pulled the arrow, waved it contemptuously, snapped it between his hands, and threw the pieces away. . . .

Books by D. R. Bensen

Death in the Hills (Tracker #3)
Fool's Gold (Tracker #2)
Mask of the Tracker (Tracker #1)

Published by POCKET BOOKS

Most Pocket Books are available at special quantity discounts for bulk purchases for sales promotions, premiums or fund raising. Special books or book excerpts can also be created to fit specific needs.

For details write the office of the Vice President of Special Markets, Pocket Books, 1230 Avenue of the Americas, New York, New York 10020.

THE TRACKER #3

→ Death in the Hills ←

D.R. BENSEN

POCKET BOOKS

New York   London   Toronto   Sydney   Tokyo   Singapore

An *Original* Publication of POCKET BOOKS

POCKET BOOKS, a division of Simon & Schuster Inc.
1230 Avenue of the Americas, New York, NY 10020

ISBN: 0-671-73836-4

First Pocket Books printing September 1992

10 9 8 7 6 5 4 3 2 1

POCKET and colophon are registered trademarks of
Simon & Schuster Inc.

Cover art by Bill Dodge

Printed in the U.S.A.

→ **Death in the Hills** ←

1

Like dragons in storybooks," Ned Norland said, "the perfessors tells me they was—big lizards, like to Gila monsters that ramped an' raged all over here in the days afore the Flood."

Cole Brandon listened with interest to the old mountain man's account of what the party of eastern scientists he was guiding was after. Norland, he knew, had been everything from a fur trapper back in the twenties to buffalo hunter, army scout, bullwhacker, trader—whatever occupation the West offered that called for toughness, alertness and a general lack of worry about staying alive. Even though the dinosaurs had been around, alive and dead, a lot longer than the old man, going after them would be a change for him.

Brandon looked past Norland and across the main plaza of Santa Fe. Ned Norland, he recalled, had been through there nearly fifty years ago, when it was the fabled El Dorado at the end of the long trail from St. Louis. Brandon sipped at his mug of ice-cold beer, as good as he could have found in St. Louis, and reflected that Santa Fe had come a long way since the old trading trail days, with a daily newspaper, new brick houses sprouting among the mud-brick cubes that had been the city's characteristic dwellings for a couple of centuries, and now a first-class brewery. Sitting at one of a number of tables set up outside a saloon on the south edge of the central plaza, across from a bustling bazaar of market stalls, he felt that he might have been in a town in Old Mexico or even Spain, except that Spain would not have offered a quantity of blanket-clad Indians and blue-clad U.S. cavalrymen.

It was still a major crossroads of the West, the kind of place where it was not improbable that acquaintances like Ned Norland, finishing off the long haul down from Denver driving a mule team in a train of freight wagons, and Cole Brandon, drifting over from Arizona, would meet by chance.

Chance or not, it's interesting, Brandon thought, that Ned Norland is the one man in the world who knows what I'm doing out here, the only man out here who knows who I used to be. And who I have to kill . . .

"No sooner'd I been paid off an' started studyin' how as to spend my way t' the poorhouse," Ned Norland said, "than this feller in a tall kind of a hat comes up to me an' says he's heared Ned Norland is the best guide that ary drawed breath, an' is knowed fer gittin' herds of the sorriest of townsfolk through the perils of the wild safe and slick as Jonah outer the whale, which I allowed that was all true, an' he hired me on to guide him an' his chums acrost to where the lizards is, out in the sand flats. Big as a house, they was, he tells me, an' now all turnt t' stone. Which is kind o' the way I am feelin' today, stiffened up fer fair."

"Anno Domini catches up with all of us," Brandon said. He considered that in Norland's case it had run Norland down and wrestled him to a fall, since, in his mid-sixties, he looked like a well-preserved eighty or a hard-used seventy.

"Not anno but Ana," Ned Norland said, "not to mention Inez and Luz and them. Was at a *baile* last night and danced them sojers and traders and riffraff inter the shade, till as they foundered like broken horses, while this child footed it fearsome to past sunup, scornin' t' call it quits while there

2

was a lady left game to prance, and any wind left in the band. But maybe you got the right of it, seein' as it's the passage of the years as kep' me from finishin' out the evenin' as used t' be my custom at such frolics."

Whether the problem had been that Ned Norland's vital energies had dwindled so much that six or so hours' constant dancing and drinking had left him unfit for active lechery or that his resemblance to a piece of cowhide left out through a hot summer and a bad winter had grown so pronounced as to repel the hospitable ladies of Santa Fe, Brandon did not see that anything he could say would be welcome.

Ned Norland gulped at his beer and threw Brandon a sour look. "Was gettin' on like a prairie fire with this toothsome filly as had a way of cuddlin' durin' the waltz that'd blow a feller's boiler, an' she ast me some of my exploits and adventures. An' I tolt her about the buffler huntin', an' she rolls her blue eyes at me an' says her mamma tolt her wicked things about the buffler hunters that come through here in the old days, just like I useter, an' she said she thought her mamma knew more than she should about that kinder wickedness, but like mother, like daughter, no? she says with a wink. Well, I took a closer look at them blue eyes, and I kinder traced out how she had a unusual long nose fer a Mexican, prett' much like mine, and a kinder wide jaw, some like mine, and it come to me that I was at more 'n a few *bailes* here twenty-some years back, and it could well have been . . . Anyhow, it put me off, and I closed down that trapline and hooked up with a friendly soul of some riper years, and bountiful of build."

"And?" Brandon said.

"Long nose, strong jaw, and a mamma that had fond memories of the traders that come over the Santa Fee Trail in the days before Santa Ana's war," Ned Norland said morosely. "Now, there was a lot of us, fer true, and enough of the same stock so as we looked alike, but I got around enough whenas I was a kit so that the odds is pretty good that I was cozyin' up to closer kin than I am easy about."

"That's a new problem to me," Brandon said. The law firm of Lunsford, Ahrens & Brandon, back in St. Louis, back in another life, hadn't, as far as he recollected, handled any incest cases, deliberate or accidental. He looked across the plaza to the market and wondered if any of the vibrant, vital young women at the stalls had blue eyes and wide jaws. One wore a scoop-necked orange blouse that glowed like a setting sun and shimmered as she reached up to the bunches of fruit hanging from the latticework roof of her stall.

"And t' me," Ned Norland said. "Without pedigrees an' dates o' birth, an' a almanac to check ag'inst, an' a set o' journals o' my doin's, which there ain't, through my not a-keepin' of such, why, there's no way to tell if a woman between eighteen and forty-five here is or ain't of my blood. Wagh! This child has learnt his lesson the hard way."

"Self-restraint has its advantages," Brandon said idly, looking at the orange-bloused market woman, who was now talking to a hulking, booted man in cavalry blue. Neither of them looked at all restrained.

"No, it don't," Ned Norland said firmly. "That ain't the lesson. The lesson is, no small talk, and don't look at 'em too close, which that is Ned Norland's motter from now. My trouble last night, I looked at somethin' and figgered I knew what it meant, and it done me out of a pleasin' finish to the festivities. I could have been wrong, prob'ly was, but I tolt myself stuff 'bout what I was seein', and what I tolt myself was just fancy and guesswork, and I let it shut off that trail. What you got to do is see things, hear things, smell things, and let 'em tell *you* what they mean, don't tell *them*."

"I think I can make pretty good judgments about what I see," Brandon said. "I've experienced enough, been trained in the law, so that I don't have much trouble in making sense out of things. I figure that's what I've got a mind for, and I propose to go on using it. What the hell!"

Spanish words, howled in horror, slammed into his ears from across the plaza; he looked up and saw the burly cavalryman slamming the orange-bloused vendor in the chest, then ripping the blouse away as she continued to scream. To his enraged astonishment, the other stall-keepers stayed where they were and made no move to protect the woman from the soldier's assault.

Brandon rose from his chair and strode into the plaza toward the market. "Sudden fancy fer fruit?" said Ned Norland, keeping pace with him.

"Somebody's got to help that woman!" Brandon said.

Ned Norland slowed him with a grip on the elbow. "Somebody is. Look yonder."

Brandon saw the soldier assisting the woman, who had fallen back against a corner post of her stall, to an upright position, and handing her back the torn-off portion of her blouse, pointedly looking away in apparent embarrassment as she rearranged it over her bared bosom. Her voice came almost as loudly as when she had been screaming, but its message was clearly different, studded with repetitions of *"gracias."*

Close to, Brandon saw that the soldier was a youth, probably not yet twenty, and either badly sunburned or blushing furiously as he moved away from the woman, who now seemed to consider it more important to embrace him than to keep her fragmented blouse in place.

"Aw, back off, ma'am," the soldier said. *"Por favor,* don't do that, huh? I was glad to help, but *no es ningún* call to carry on and create about it."

Ned Norland nudged Brandon, then nodded downward. Brandon saw, a few inches from the soldier's boots, a crushed shiny brown shape, drastically smeared about the middle, which radiated several jointed legs, but with a segmented, curled tail culminating in a wicked-looking point intact. The tail looked to be almost four inches long, if uncurled.

"Lady ritched up to them fruits hangin' from up top o' the stall," Ned Norland said, "and the damn scorpion run right down her arm and inter her shirt, which she natcherly screams like a painter—'They is a monster amongst my boobies!' is more er less what she says—and this upstandin' young defender of his country done what he had to to git it out from there and send it to jine the silent majority."

"Oh," Brandon said. "I didn't understand what she was

5

yelling. I don't know much Spanish." He turned and began walking back to the table they had left on the far side of the plaza.

"Nope," Ned Norland said. "But yer trainin' in the law and gener'l experience give you a instant idee of what was occurrencin' all the same. Clear, plain, sensible. Jist dead wrong, is all."

Brandon reseated himself at the table and reached for his beer. So I was, he thought. And in what I'm doing, being dead wrong is a good way to be dead.

He glanced around and saw that there was nobody within earshot, leaned forward, and said, "Coming through Colorado, did you smell anything that had something to tell you about Gren Kenneally?"

2

In the fall of 1873 train robberies were still a novelty, with
the James brothers' first enterprise only a few months past.
The plundering of the Chicago, Rock Island & Pacific
express forty miles north of St. Louis would in any case have
been sensational, with the mail car looted and two men
killed, but the robbers, reported variously as ten to a dozen
in number, had assured their place in crime history by
hiding from pursuers in a stone farmhouse, holding the
inhabitants hostage, and, at nightfall, covering their escape
by firing the house and slaughtering the hostages.

Attorney Cole Brandon, absent from his family's country
place on business that kept him in the city, had been rushed
to the scene with a rescue party, arriving at Mound Farm in
time to see his wife, Elise, her father, Berthold Ostermann,
and her aunt Trudi carried out dead from the blazing
building. Very little made sense to Cole Brandon for some
months after that, but by the time the universe had settled
into some kind of comprehensible order again he had
abandoned the shards of his settled life and profession and
was launched on a mission of exterminating every man of
the ten or a dozen who had ridden and killed with Gren

7

Kenneally that day. So far, in just over a year, three were dead, two by Brandon's hand and one by his own greed. The man he most needed to see dead, Gren Kenneally—monstrous heir of a vast criminal clan, seasoned wartime guerrilla and postwar bandit—flickered like a will-o'-the-wisp ahead of him, seen and notorious in San Francisco, but vanished before Brandon tracked him there. The latest word he had, but all too probably stale, put Gren Kenneally in or passing through Colorado, and Ned Norland, if any man could, would know if any track or scent or other sign of the quarry remained. He waited for the answer to his question.

"Nothin'," Ned Norland said. "Mebbe a whisper in Denver o' some worse 'n usual lobo that 'd tore out a few throats a while back, but nothin' to say 'twas Gren more 'n anyone else. Gren you'll come acrost when it's time, 's how I see it. Men don't run on steel tracks, like as the trains to, but there is tracks we don't see, an' yours an' Gren's is set to meet someplace along th' line. Last I saw you, you'd counted coup on two that rode with him—any since?"

"One, in Arizona," Brandon said, and he told him of the Kenneally accomplice who had passed as a mining-town saloon keeper and pursued his lust for gold to a death in an abandoned mineshaft. "His own doing, not mine."

"But there's one the less," Ned Norland said.

"And six or nine to go, depending on whose count you take," Brandon said, "and no track or sign to follow."

"Without you git a inventory, you won't know whereat to stop," Ned Norland said. "Pervided you c'n work out whereat to start ag'in. That girl in Kansas you told me of, stuff she's sent you no help?"

Brandon shrugged. "Some hints in the past, that report about Gren heading for Colorado, nothing fresh." The establishment of his amateur "detective bureau," the aspiring restaurant magnate Jess Marvell and her sidekick, the highly changeable Rush Dailey, had been a bizarre scene in the early days of his mission. Their paths had crossed in Kansas, and Jess Marvell, taking Brandon for a detective, had offered her and Rush Dailey's services for a fee, promising alertness to the whole flood of reports and rumors that washed past the hotel she then managed. The results so far, Brandon had to admit, had not been considerable, but there was always the chance that something significant might turn up, especially now that Jess Marvell was trying to start her own line of railroad station restaurants and would be traveling extensively across the frontier. Also, and this he preferred not to inquire into at all closely, he did not want to lose all contact with Jess Marvell.

Ned Norland fished what looked like a four-inch piece of tarred rope from a pants pocket, thumbnailed a match into a sulphurous flare, and lit the cigar. Acrid smoke drifted to Brandon.

"Now," Ned Norland said, "with the rest of these fellers it ain't a matter of tracks meetin', like it is with you an' Gren. That's to happen, so it is, but the others, them's like it was with me an' the beaver an' sich. I have kep' body and breath together comin' up on fifty year through trackin' and shootin' and trappin' critters I didn't have a cowpat's worth of knowledge of to start off with. I ast and I larned and I come to know the ways of the beaver and the buffler and the deer and the b'ar. And that seen me through maybe most of the time. The rest of it, there weren't no sign, nothin' t' go on, jist the way it is with you now."

"And those times, what did you do?" Brandon asked.

"I let whereat I was tell me," Ned Norland said. "The mountains, the woods, the cricks, the shape o' the place, you let them things speak to you, you open yer ears wide—and I ain't jist talkin' about them flaps aside yer head, *sabe?*—and you listen. And you look around about, same way, with more 'n your eyes. And likely you don't hear nothin' nor see nothin', but it comes to you it's time to git on towards the sunset or sunrise or the pole star, towards a far mountain or a meadow jist yonder, and you do that. And if so be as a magpie flies crost yer path er some other sign be made, why, you pays attention to that, too, and you does what it strikes you it calls fer. That kind of time, when there ain't nothin' else t' go on, you got to trust to your own medicine, and to what is tolt you by what's around you."

"Well, that's . . . ." Brandon began, but he stopped before

he came to "nonsense." If listening to the spirits of the wild like some Indian medicine man was how Ned Norland had survived more than forty years of danger from starvation, volatile-tempered Indians, chronically murderous grizzlies, stampeding buffalo, county-wide prairie fires, precipices, boiling springs, house-high snowdrifts, canned food, range wars, bandits, and the host of more or less mortal perils the frontier abounded in, there might be something to it.

"I guess I don't know how to look and listen like that, and I don't have anything you could call 'medicine,'" he said.

Hazed by a cloud of pungent smoke, Ned Norland looked at him. "That time we buried that first one, out in the Injun mound on yer farm, you reckleck?"

"Have to be pretty forgetful not to," Brandon said, remembering James Casmire's dead eyes staring at the burned-out roof of the kitchen at Mound Farm, and the widening pool of red under his head—the first of the Kenneally gang to die, and, as it happened, the first man Cole Brandon had ever killed.

"I don't mean the corpsin' of him," Ned Norland said, "which I would not have expected you to overlook, but what you dug out of the mound whenas we was plantin' him."

"The coin or whatever," Brandon said.

"Right. Old-timey chief's lucky piece, it coulda been. You still have that?"

"Yes," Brandon said. "Think so, anyhow. It's somewheres in my valise, last I saw."

"I tolt you then, that could be strong medicine," Ned Norland said. "Snake eatin' its tail one side, wolf t'other, that meant somethin' powerful whenas 'twas made. And it was that chief's or whoever's, and buried with him in the long-ago, back in the time of them stone lizards for all's I know, and then as it might be handed on to you by him the same hour as you made yer first kill. Wagh! A do-funny like that, it's got medicine boilin' over and runnin' down the sides. You fetch it out when you gits back to yer digs, and study it some and see what it has to tell you. Might could be it'll find a way t' let you know where to git on to next."

"I think those dinosaurs your professors are after are a lot older than that," Brandon said, drawing on something his memory dredged up from a long-ago issue of *Scientific American*.

"Then I won't be lookin' for any fresh sign," Ned Norland said, grinning at Brandon through the smoke cloud.

Brandon, either tired of or uneasy about the futile speculation on how to choose his next destination out of a near-limitless range of choices, asked Ned Norland about his new job.

"Be interestin' to see the critters that roamed the earth afore the Flood," he said. "There was one as I expect come down from Canada, Torontosaurus they calls him." After some description of the provisions he had made for the fossil search party he said, "But this child's gettin' to feel about as old as them lizards, and it ain't the stiffness from dancin' I'm a-talkin' of. Brandon, you ain't got no notion of what 'twas like when I come out here in the twenties. Nothin' t' speak of beyond the Missouri, till you got down here t' Santa Fee, maybe a thousand mile o' nothin' but the wild. And away north, nothin' till as you got t' the sea, just a world o' mountains and woods and prairies and game, and only a few Injuns livin' in it the way the fish lives in the sea er the b'ar in the woods. But now it's like St. Louis, houses and folks everywhere a man looks."

Brandon, having spent days of unbroken solitude in the saddle traveling south to Texas, and experienced the unpeopled mountains of Arizona, considered this view somewhat overstated; but it was true nowadays that you could get from almost anyplace in the West to almost anyplace else a lot more easily than the young Ned Norland had, and also true that there were a lot more places to get to, with towns springing up like mushrooms since the war.

"'Fore I got here this time, bullwhacked with a train of freighters, down from Cheyenne to Denver City," Ned Norland said. "Jist about got used to both o' them places, since they been there a few hand-counts o' years, though growin' and stinkin' like skunk cabbage. But in between, where there used t' be beautiful open land and mountains, up there by the Poudre River, why, it's towns all the way, every twenty er forty miles another one."

He paused, as if to contemplate the teeming metropolis, covering the countryside like a mulch, that he had just described. "Now, in thirty-four or so, jist after the market fer beaver went all t' hell—no, I'm a liar, 'twas even later, a year or so after the Mex War, jist about only yestiddy"— twenty-five years ago, by Brandon's reckoning—"that I spent me a year up in thereabouts, summer to summer, trappin' and huntin' and fishin' and enjoyin' the delight-some company of three Injun ladies, to the which I was lawful married for the time, so there warn't nothin' disre-spectable about it. 'Twas what they call a park, flat space with mountains around, not a big one like South Park, but a bitty place, five mile er so east t' west, twicet that and some north t' south, and easy passes 'twixt the mountains north and south. Medders and woods a-runnin' with any kind o' game you could fancy, and streams the fish fair jumped out of at you. It was the freest and best time I ever had, what that garden in the Bible woulda been like if there'd been three Eves, and no fruit ner sarpints into it. And if so as I got to feelin' crowded there, why, I'd up with one of the missuses and git off to a littler place o' the same kind, ten miles and some up in the hills, that had a lake like a blue jewel into it, and we'd have ourselfs a vacation from the rush of ever'day life. *Gracias.*"

The sight of Ned Norland's empty mug raised from the table had brought a waiter over with a pottery pitcher of beer from which it was quickly refilled. Ned Norland re-emptied it by about a quarter, set it down, and continued. "But we come through that selfsame place a few weeks back, though I'd never have knowed it but fer the way the hills sets. Now it's a damn town, with streets and stores and houses and folks a-doing business, and the godly reprovin' the wicked, and the wicked at their wickedness, and both kinds figgerin' how t' git the last nickel out o' the woods and fields and hills. A place that's been the way it was since the time o' them old stone lizards, turned into a *town,* jist like back in Ohio er so. Spargill, it's called, fer no damn reason I know er care t' know, and puffed up with its own glory, the which ain't apparent to none but Spargillers, and a-lookin' fer the comin' of the railroad as if 'twas Resurrection Day. Right where . . . well, nemmine that, but none of us was able to walk stiddy fer about a day . . . right at a spot as holds fond and tender memories fer me, there is now a newspaper office, with a flatbed press a-crankin' out so many lies about the bigger and better Spargill t' come that it might as well be a gas works." He grinned briefly. "Feller that runs it, though, he's runnin' hisself ragged, doin' all the work, the feller that wrote er invented stories fer him havin' drunk enough to be tellin' the truth whenas he wrote up the plague of alligators and spiders infestin' the town and crawlin' all over innocent folks. Not that they minded him bein' a soak, but the spiders and alligators made the town look like a trashy place t' live."

"There's still enough empty space for the men I'm looking for to get lost in," Brandon said.

"Not so," Ned Norland said. "Ain't no sich thing as empty. There's always the air, the water, the grasses, and all of 'em keep a trace of what's been through, if so as you c'n pick it up. If you're to find them you're after, then it'll work out so if you let it. What you do is, you go to a kinder place where the game you're after would fit in—where there's the kinder forage and shelter he likes, where he'll fit in amongst the trees and sich, so's he ain't noticeable." He emptied his mug and stood up. "Luck to you, Brandon," he said. "Next as I see you, I'll tell you about my adventurings amongst the stone dragons, and you can tell me how you counted coup on a Kenneally or some. Jist git you on to the right place—and when he comes along, why, you jist drop him."

"There's lots of places that are the right kind of place but aren't *the* place," Brandon said.

"If you pick it the right way, it will be," Ned Norland said.

The foot-and-a-half-thick adobe walls of the ancient hotel building kept the air in Brandon's room comfortably cool even in the white-hot afternoon that drove all of Santa Fe

13

indoors for the siesta. He lay on the bed and studied the dark beams embedded in the whitewashed ceiling, turning over every scrap of information or speculation he had about Gren Kenneally and his accomplices to murder. There were not many, and none of them seemed any more useful than another. The Kenneally family stronghold was in the Ozarks somewhere, and for nearly fifty years they had been living by outlawry—some of them, most notably Gren, achieving a brief respectability during the war when their skill at murder, arson, and thieving had made them valued by guerrilla leaders such as Quantrill. Their web of influence spread widely and nearly invisibly, as Brandon had found when Kenneally money and power had procured the acquittal of Casmire, the only gang member captured after the Mound Farm massacre—freeing him, as it turned out, to die under Brandon's gun months later in the burned-out kitchen at Mound Farm.

The detective Jack Kestrel, back in Texas, had said something about some part of the Kenneally gang moving out to the Neutral Zone between Texas and the Indian Territories, to take advantage of the fact that no legal authority whatever existed there. But that was only a rumor, and there wasn't even a rumor that Gren Kenneally had headed in that direction upon his departure from San Francisco. Just the out-of-date report of his intention to head for Colorado. And there was an equal vacuum of information on any of the others who had ridden with Gren Kenneally. Brandon had, following the sketchiest of clues, encountered two of them so far, one in Texas and one in Arizona, but of the rest he knew not even a name.

The writing table next to the window held a scatter of maps and booklets—guidebooks, train and coach schedules, town prospectuses, anything that seemed to describe or depict some area of the frontier. He had studied them for hours, looking for some indication of the "right kind of place" Norland had talked of, where a Kenneally gang member might choose to go to ground for a while. The result had been a total blank. Idaho seemed as likely as Nebraska, California as Texas, Colorado as New Mexico. Anything he chose to regard as a good starting point—say a new boom town in its early lawless stage—would suggest that its opposite, an established city with plenty of riches for plundering, would be more likely; and the other way around.

Looks as if you'll have to rely on the kind of instinct that crazy old mountain man talks about, Counselor, he told himself. But it's a damn uneasy business, relying on what amounts to chance.

Yet chance had played a major role so far, he admitted. The letter found in the effects of Curly, the dead cowhand who had ridden with Gren Kenneally, had finally led him to Arizona; and he had found Curly only through the most tenuous train of chance, depending in fact on a hotel being hauled across the prairie to where he would find in it a whittled wooden flower, twin to one that a Kenneally had left in the ruins of Mound Farm. And what but chance had put him and Norland at Mound Farm when Casmire was searching it for loot Gren Kenneally had concealed there? That meeting had given Brandon first blood for his family and sealed his decision to exact the last drop.

And now Casmire was buried in the old Indian mound that gave the family farm its name. With any luck, he hadn't been discovered yet, and Attorney Cole Brandon was still, as far as St. Louis was concerned, on an extended voyage abroad to recover from his loss, not wanted for questioning about a corpse discovered on his property. He recalled the tension and effort of the hasty nighttime burial . . . and the clink of his shovel hitting something metallic as he dug.

Brandon rose and rummaged in his valise, finally fetching out a folded square of paper. He unfolded it and tipped what it held out onto the table.

A year of being out of the earth and folded in the dry paper had rubbed away some of the object's dull coating, and a faint gleam of metal showed on it here and there. It looked like a large coin but was probably ceremonial rather than monetary, since the ancient Indians did not, so far as he knew, have a minted currency. On one side, more clearly visible now than the last time he had looked, was the raised figure of a four-footed animal with a long head and sharp nose, low to the ground. It looked, as much as anything, like a wolf on the scent of its prey.

Around the other side, like a wreath, ran a sinuous, thick line like a meandering river, a snake with its tail inserted in the opened jaws of the wide head. A still-adhering crust, or perhaps corrosion, blurred some object stamped or carved in the center of that face of the coin.

"Might could be it'll find a way t' let you know where to git on to next," Ned Norland had said of the medallion. Fine, Counselor, he told himself, but how's it going to do that? Toss it—but heads do what, tails do what? And what's heads or tails on this one, anyhow—both the snake and the wolf or whatever have both.

The coin glinted in the shaft of sunlight that came through the window, then fell to the table. It landed on its side, wobbled a bit, then rolled unsteadily among the papers, finally leaning lazily to a stop. Brandon stooped to see if it was wolf-side up or snake. Wolf, as it turned out, and resting on a railroad guide covering northern Colorado and lines leading into Denver. The guide was open at a map showing a dense array of cross-hatching, representing impressive mountains, with one thick line coming from the right, or Kansas, edge of the map and ending at Denver.

Brandon lifted the coin from the page, then stopped. It had covered an area somewhere above Denver, a space on the map clear of the cross-hatching, denoting a rare level space. In the middle of the space was a small dot, next to which was printed, in the smallest size of type used on the map, SPARGILL.

After what seemed to him to be quite a while, Brandon told himself that Spargill, going by what Ned Norland had said of it, would be as good a place as any to try—fairly new town, expanding, lots of people trying to make money. A Kenneally could be there as well as anyplace else. If he'd thought about it a little more, it was just the sort of place he might have pitched on. Come to think of it, likely he'd done just that, only not known it, and had pitched the coin toward the Colorado rail guide by sub-surface intent.

No need to think for an instant about Ned Norland's

insistence that the long-buried coin held powerful "medicine" to guide him. Brandon refolded the creased paper around the coin and returned it to the valise. In his fingers it seemed somehow heavier than it had been. The shaft of sunlight had moved across the room and now fell on his face. He blinked against the strong light and wondered that he felt a sudden chill, not warmth.

3

"Well, now," Abner Willson said. "Two years on the police beat for the *Dispatch,* a season on the Inskip, Kansas, *Trumpet*—not bad experience."

Brandon had to agree that it was not, and wished that he could honestly claim it—or, for that matter, that the *Trumpet* blew elsewhere than in his imagination. The cow town of Inskip possessed, when he had spent a few days there, no newspaper whatever. But as he could bluff enough about wild times in Inskip, and had been swamped with anecdotes about St. Louis's lowlife by a *Dispatch* reporter he had defended in a bigamy case, he felt that he could make the claim at least convincing. It was beginning to seem that it was convincing enough to land him a job with the Spargill *Chronicle & Advertiser;* Abner Willson, editor-in-chief and publisher, and also circulation manager and pressman, appeared favorably inclined toward him, or at least toward Calvin Blake, the name he had decided to operate under.

"But that's three years," Abner Willson went on, "and you look to have been of working age some longer than that." Hunched in the high-back chair behind his battered, paper-strewn desk, his long-nosed face topped with a coarse shock of black hair, he had something of the look of an intelligent crow as he threw an inquiring glance at Brandon.

"Well, there was the War, of course," Brandon said. "And the fact is, took me a while to see that journalism was what I ought to be doing."

"Huh," Abner Willson said. "And once you saw that, and had the luck to get on the *Dispatch,* you threw that up after a while and headed west."

Brandon sighed. "Everybody out here's got some reason for not being where he used to, Willson, and it's been my observation that nobody else looks into it much. Whether I got on the wrong side of some politician with too many friends, or on the right side of a lady with a bad-tempered husband, or anything else, I'm out here now, and looking for a spot. You want to go on talking about that, or should I sling my hook and get on to the next town and see if the sheet there can use me?"

He felt safe enough saying this. From Ned Norland he knew that Willson's one-man reporting staff had drunk himself out of the job, and the fact that the vacancy hadn't been filled in the two weeks or so that it had existed suggested that candidates were not thick on the ground. Also, he suspected that his totally false hints at his reasons for leaving St. Louis might tickle Willson's bump of curiosity, and that the job, if he got it, might be safe until Willson felt satisfied that he knew the truth of the matter.

Abner Willson raised one hand, palm toward Brandon. "No, no, Blake, no need for that. You're right, out here things are different, and who did what when back in the States don't matter that much. You have to learn to size someone up, judge if he can do the job, then stand ready to back the judgment. You care to deliver yourself of any obiter dicta on the practice of journalism as you would propose to indulge in it here, brother Blake?"

"Load the story with local names till the Plimsoll line don't show, and make sure they're spelled right," Brandon said promptly. "Like giving you both the Ls." He had seen the editor-publisher's name in print only once, on a copy of the paper he had glanced through before coming to the office, and thought it was a neat touch to demonstrate his powers of observation. Unless, of course, it was a misprint, in which case he would look like a more than ordinary fool. "Beat the drums for local enterprise and products, low-rate the next towns and their papers every chance you get, and boost like mad for the railroad to come in."

"With informing the public on vital matters and carrying on the great tradition of Ben Franklin and John Peter Zenger coming in second and third, and not especially close," Abner Willson said dryly. "But you're right, Blake. If you'd spouted any of that line, you'd be on your way with a limp handshake by now. An idealistic reporter's more trouble than a raving drunk. You don't seem like either, and whatever you've done, you've got the look of a man who can listen close and probably spell right, and what the hell else is there to it? What d'you think of Spargill?"

"Tame sort of place, but prosperous," Brandon said, recalling what he had seen of its main street from the jolting, antiquated coach he had ridden on the last leg of the trip up from Denver. "Only half as many saloons as in a cow town or mining town this size, and them not doing much business in the middle of the day; street clean, no bums and not many dogs, fair number of respectable-looking ladies doing their errands and not looking nervous about it. Didn't see anything that looked like the edges of the red-light district, but that could be some away from the center of town. Looks like a place where people are looking for ways to make money more than raise hell. The big story here's the one you're not going to print, how the town council or aldermen or whatever bunch runs the show is getting a rake-off from the public works and such that are making Spargill rise like bread dough."

Abner Willson looked at him sharply. "You've heard gossip?"

"No," Brandon said. "But that's the way it works most times." It certainly had worked that way in St. Louis, and a fair portion of Lunsford, Ahrens & Brandon's practice had been concerned with keeping municipal malefactors unindicted and, unofficially, persuading them to such modesty in their depredations that no public end would be served by replacing them with newer, hungrier servants of the people.

"And so it does here," Abner Willson said. "Thing is, it's what you could call honest graft. The town council's got people on it from every kind of interest—mining, farming, timber, cattle, and the town businessmen—and they work things so that the folks they represent get what they need. And since they know what's going to happen, why, they're in a position to get their money in or out ahead of time, according to need, or to see to it that a contractor who's getting town work is properly grateful. And the only thing you're wrong about is that it ain't the big story, for those who don't know about it already wouldn't get much excited if they did. Spargillers figure nobody'd go into government unless they did well out of it anyhow. So don't go bothering to follow the tainted trail of corrupt practices to their source and turning out reams of copy about whited sepulchers, 'cause nobody'd bother to read it."

"You're talking like I'm working for you," Brandon said. At Abner Willson's nod, he went on. "When do I start?"

"Think you have," Abner Willson said. "You've got a hook on what the town's like, now you can go up and down in it, seeking whom you may get some colorful copy out of. Take an armful of old issues so's you don't accidentally write the same stuff we ran last week, which is clear and present danger in small-town papers. Oh, and watch out for—"

He was interrupted by the jangle of the cowbell tied to the front doorknob that announced visitors so that their wishes might be seen to—or, the newspaper life being what it was, gave a vital warning of the incursion of an enraged reader in time for the staff to escape or take shelter.

"Mr. Willson," said the young woman who stood in the doorway.

Abner Willson goggled at her for a minute, then said,

"Ah . . . well, I . . . yes," as if he had just come to realize that he was in fact being addressed by his right name. To Brandon, the girl, wearing a blue cotton dress and a sunbonnet small and decorated enough to pass as a hat, seemed pleasant-looking enough—short, dark-ringleted, plumpish but by no means fat or even chubby—but Abner Willson might as well have been confronting Venus in all her radiance, or even the gorgon Medusa, as he now seemed to have been turned to stone.

"I came to ask if you'd been able to do something about Pa's drawing," the woman said.

"I . . . well, no," Abner Willson said. "I thought maybe Kern, that has the jewelry store, could engrave it, but he's no good at anything but letters and a decoration that looks kind of like a swan, and he flat refused to try anything with your father's sketch. You ain't a hand at steel engraving, are you, Blake? This is my new reporter, Miss Caldwell, I mean he isn't Miss Caldwell, I know that—Miss Caldwell, this is Mr. Blake, he's the reporter; Blake, this is Miss Caldwell—are you, Blake?"

"No," Brandon said. "No knowledge whatever of engraving, sorry to say." He bowed toward the woman. "Miss Caldwell."

She gave less of a bow, something like an extreme nod, to him and said, "Mr. Blake." With the exchange of perhaps purposely exaggerated formalities, the disordered atmosphere of the moment was somewhat repaired, and Abner Willson pulled his faculties together sufficiently to make a coherent apology for his inability to produce a publishable engraving of Miss Caldwell's father's drawing and to undertake to make every effort to find a way to accomplish this end.

"Though how I'm to do it," he said gloomily after Miss Caldwell had left, "I haven't the faintest idea. Your happening by was a good bit of luck for me, but I can't count on wandering engravers coming through Spargill. The old man has a project that I'm bound to say would make a splash if I could illustrate it, but all I've got is a few advertising cuts that came with the type case, and they're no good. Lord! D'you suppose Julie Caldwell thinks I'm a complete idiot?"

"No, boss," Brandon said. "Likely she thinks you're stuck on her and haven't scraped together the sand to say so."

"Why would she think that?" Abner Willson asked nervously.

"A hermit that hadn't seen men and women together for forty years until that scene would think that," Brandon said. He was trying to think if he had ever in his life addressed anyone as "boss," and thought not; but it seemed to go with the Calvin Blake role, subordinate but independent, the way the reporters he had known liked to think of themselves.

"No wonder I get the jimjams about sparking her," Abner Willson said. "Not much to offer a girl, making a pretty unsteady living running a rag in a half-horse town, nothing much in the way of looks or personality, I don't see that I've got much of a look-in."

"Don't get down about it—surprising what women will overlook if they take to a man for whatever reason of their own," Brandon said kindly.

After a brief moment Abner Willson said, "Thanks for the encouragement, if that's what it was, Blake. Now, what you want to watch out—"

The cowbell at the door interrupted him again. This visitor he hailed with more aplomb. "Judge Gerrish! Good to see you, you're just in time to say hello to a valued addition to the *Chronicle & Advertiser* family, Mr. Calvin Blake. Fresh from adding journalistic laurels to his brow in the mighty metropolis of St. Louis and the colorful cow towns of Kansas, Mr. Blake will lend the power of his pen to promoting the cause of a bigger and better Spargill, and its union with the outer world by the steel veins through which runs the lifeblood of trade, travel, and civilization."

"Hope he has a better hand with a metaphor than you do, Willson. Bad enough you emitted that in your last editorial without quoting yourself in social discourse. Happy to meet you, Mr. Blake, and if you can write a civilized sentence, you'll raise the tone of the paper a hundred percent."

The newcomer was a stockily built man of about fifty, broad-jawed, with a full gray mustache, short, wiry beard and thinning curly hair. He was dressed soberly, with that extra touch of ostentation in details like the piping on his vest that Brandon had noticed as characteristic of senior lawyers and judges. We don't want to seem better than the rest of you, seemed to be the statement, but if you look closely enough, you'll see that we are. Brandon was impressed and had what could have been a pang of homesickness for the courts of St. Louis; Gerrish was a distillation of "judgeness," wearing an air of authority, wisdom and integrity like a garment which, though invisible, was meticulously tailored to fit him comfortably and elegantly.

"Blake," Judge Gerrish said. "I met a gambler of that name some time back, down in Denver. Any kin to you?"

"Not that I've heard of, Judge," Brandon said, suppressing the impulse to say, "Depends what his name was before he changed it."

Gerrish turned to Abner Willson. "This isn't for print just yet, but Parker'll be here in a few days to settle the details of the bond issue."

"Details?"

"The amount, actually," Gerrish said.

"It was seventy-five thousand, last I heard," Abner Willson said.

"Well, it may still be," Gerrish said. "But conditions change, and it may be that the final figure will have to be adjusted."

"Figures like that don't ever get adjusted *downward*," Abner Willson said thoughtfully.

Gerrish acknowledged the comment with a brief wintry smile and said, "There's no point in worrying unduly. The main thing is, Parker'll be here, and the paper will have to see to it that the town makes the kind of show that'll convince him that bringing the tracks in to Spargill will be good business. A good story on Parker and what he means to do, that's what we'll need, then some comments from the good people of Spargill on the benefits they see the railroad as bringing."

"That's John B. Parker?" Brandon said. "The one they call the Killer Elephant of Wall Street?"

"The same," Abner Willson said. "Guiding spirit of the Denver & Transmontane Railroad, running down from the Union Pacific main line. No intention of getting anywhere near as far down as Denver any time soon, but there's a damn good shot at getting it to Spargill, which is good enough for us. Right now railhead's at Split Rock, about thirty miles north, and Parker's working it out whether to lay track on down here. He's done the surveys, but the town'll have to run a bond issue to give him the kind of subsidy he claims he'll need."

Brandon considered that if John B. Parker had a hand in the affairs of Spargill, Spargill was in for an interesting time, from which it might emerge, as some of Parker's associates had, considerably enriched or, as others had, plucked bare.

"May I suggest that Mr. Blake set about gathering comments from ordinary citizens on their hopes for the railroad?" Gerrish asked Abner Willson. "You and I can prepare some detailed information on Parker's plans, which he can later combine with his evident knowledge of that gentleman's reputation to make a lively yet reassuring story. As I infer from the presence of a travel-battered valise next to the door that you have not found lodging, Blake, I recommend that you repair to Mrs. Deckle's boardinghouse two blocks north of here, at the corner of Aspen Street, and hire her second-floor front room, which I notice is now vacant. If your position on the newspaper is insufficient recommendation of your suitability as lodger, a mention of my name should suffice." Like many judges Brandon had known, Gerrish seemed to relish a self-mocking pomposity of speech.

Brandon folded some sheets of foolscap in thirds and stuck them in the side pocket of his jacket, as he remembered seeing his reporter client do, picked up his valise, and left the newspaper office. Gerrish and Abner Willson were still conferring on how to frame the John B. Parker story.

Outside he took a look at the frame building, wondered if any psychic emanations remained from the activities of Ned

Norland and the three Mrs. Norlands on that spot, and wondered yet again just what prodigies of libidinousness they had achieved here.

Brandon squinted up Main Street. From what he could see, the shops and offices along the street were well-kept—mostly painted, no broken or boarded-up windows—and there was a fair bustle of busy-looking people going from one establishment to another, gigs, carts, and light carriages amply present. He felt a welling of excitement that went beyond his hope—still short of full expectation—that somehow he would find one of the men he sought here. A new place, a new name, a new role: No denying it, they had their own savor, and he found himself impatient to become Calvin Blake, to start doing Blake things.

Three buildings along from the *Chronicle* office he found, on a bench outside a saloon, a large man sitting morosely. He looked a little drunk, but not too drunk to talk. Also, he was the only person in sight not seemingly in pursuit of some significant piece of business, and therefore unlikely to object to having his activities interrupted by an inquiring journalist.

"'Scuse me, sir?" he said to the seated man. "Calvin Blake, *Chronicle.*"

"No, I ain't," the man said. "Sut Liebwohl, and the *Chronicle* office's down thataways."

"I'm Cal Blake, and I'm with the *Chronicle,"* Brandon said.

"Damn," Liebwohl said, "I cain't see why you bother to say it. You already know who you are, and I don't give a rat's ass."

"I wanted to ask you some of the benefits you see coming to Spargill if the railroad comes here," Brandon said.

"Benefits. Railroad," Liebwohl said. "What benefits *you* see? You for the railroad comin' in?"

"Of course," Brandon said, realizing that he might have to provide this man with the comments he would then quote in the story. "It'll change the whole town. Freight rates will be a half, a third, a quarter what they are now, and—"

Like a thundercloud swelling suddenly over the crest of a

mountain, Liebwohl seemed to flow upward from the bench, and briefly to hulk in front of Brandon until a pile-driver blow to Brandon's belly sent him skidding on his back in the road, gasping and retching.

Through the dust his descent raised Brandon saw a boot draw back, and rolled aside as it kicked at him. He scrambled to his feet and lunged at Liebwohl, ducking under a flailing arm and landing a blow on the jaw that almost numbed his hand but rocked Liebwohl's head back. He slid aside from a wild swing that could have spread his nose over most of his face, and buried his fist in Liebwohl's gut, eliciting a beer-scented belch of pain.

A fast pivot to one side let Brandon take Liebwohl's pistoning knee on the hip instead of in the groin, and he grabbed the upraised leg and pushed back, following through with all the weight of his body.

Liebwohl toppled backwards, pawing the air, and completed his downfall by trying to kick at Brandon with the foot that remained on the ground. His head hit the raised edge of the wooden plankwalk with a resounding crack, and he went limp.

For an instant Brandon thought he might have killed Liebwohl, but the man sat up and groaned, then leaned over and vomited.

I guess that interview is over, Brandon thought. Maybe I better get some pointers on technique. He looked up and saw that most of the bustling pedestrians had come to a halt and were watching him and the still-disgorging Liebwohl. That was not surprising, but the presence among them of a bulky man with a bright metal star on his shirt was. Chief of police or town marshal or whatever he was, he seemed to display a singular lack of interest in a brief but brutal brawl in his well-ordered town, being content merely to look at Brandon with evident dislike.

"Oh, damn." Brandon turned and saw that Abner Willson had come up to him. "That's what I never got around to telling you. Meant to warn you not to talk to any freighters or muleskinners about the railroad. They tend to be touchy about it."

4

"Very good homeopathic remedy," Abner Willson said, dabbing the arnica onto Brandon's hand, now beginning to swell from its impact on Liebwohl's jaw. "Inspissated or whatever they call it from the herbal extract down to a thousandth of its original strength, yet all the more powerful for it. The internal remedy don't work on that principle."

Brandon sloshed the whiskey around in his mouth and agreed that it was the kind of medication that did not profit by dilution. They were back in Willson's office, having left Liebwohl to see to his own repairs and cleanup.

Abner Willson recorked the arnica bottle and put it into a drawer, but left the whiskey bottle out on his desktop. "Restorative for you, lubrication and fuel for me. Now Blake, I feel bad that I sent you out to beard the lions and you not even knowing there were any. Like I said, I meant to warn you about the freighters and such, but Julie Caldwell came in, and then Judge Gerrish, and so . . . Anyhow, here's what you should know."

The teamsters and bullwhackers who brought into Spargill everything that was not produced there understandably lacked the enthusiasm for the advent of the railroad felt by the majority of the townsfolk. "They'll still have the business of bringing stuff up from Denver and anyplace else to the south," Abner Willson said, "but that's likely to shrink a lot when it's so much cheaper to bring it in by rail from the north. If they don't go out of business, they'll have to cut their rates so there's nearly no profit in it, and they're as happy as a gut-shot grizzly about it."

"Seems to me they should be used to it by now," Brandon said, flexing his hand, which still stung a little, whether from the blow or the arnica he could not tell. "All over the west the railroad's coming in and the freighters are going out."

"True," Abner Willson said. "But what makes it kind of tender here is that it's not all that foreordained. If the DT line don't go south of Split Rock now, that'll be the terminus for at least a year, maybe longer, and the freighters'll have a monopoly for that long. So they've still got some hope of keeping what they've got, and there is nothing like a ray of hope amid the encircling gloom to make a man act like a real bastard."

"I would have thought that fellow with the star would have stepped in to do something about a breach of the law taking place under his nose," Brandon said. "Only notice he took was to look at me as if he was wondering whether to run me in for something."

"Marshal Tooley's got a delicate job in this quarrel," Abner Willson said. "See, it's not just the freighters like that Liebwohl. They're mostly here and gone, then back with the next train. But plenty of the businessmen in town put money into the freighting company, set up Ben Stoddard to have a company right here instead of relying on somebody in Denver or Omaha, and they stand to lose when the railroad comes. And they're taxpayers and voters, so Tooley stays kind of neutral when something comes up that smells of freighters versus railroad."

Well, maybe, Brandon thought. Could be this Tooley's the kind of lawman that glowers at everybody on general principle.

"Maybe you can wait to start asking for Spargill's opinions on the millennium the railroad'll bring until tomorrow.

The freighters'll be on their way again by then, and I'll give you a list of men that have connections to them, so you'll know who not to ask." Abner Willson began to shuffle the drift of papers on his desk, and his voice took on an abstracted note as he seemed to try to arrange them in some kind of order. "What you could do now is get on out to the sawmill and do a piece on how Jim Caldwell's coming along."

"Miss Caldwell's father?" Brandon asked. Abner Willson nodded and squinted with some satisfaction at the papers, then gave a frown. "Coming along with what?"

"You'll see when you get there," Abner Willson said. "Damn, I'm going to have to cut the report on the Methodist social to make room for the saloon ads, and don't you know Mrs. Glyn's going to carry on and create about that? No more 'n half a column on Caldwell, mind." His voice came as if from behind an impenetrable wall of concentration, and Brandon was outside the office and in the street before it occurred to him that his editor had given him no directions to the Caldwell sawmill.

"Pursuing your inquiries undaunted, are you, Blake?" Judge Gerrish turned from the store window next to the *Chronicle* office and addressed Brandon. "I missed your fracas with the opponent of progress but heard vivid, if varying, accounts of it. I look forward to reading the true and objective account of it in the *Chronicle.*"

"Vulgar brawls aren't in our line, I gather, especially when they might suggest that somebody's less than happy about the railroad coming in," Brandon said. "And I'm saving the questions about the railroad until the foes of progress are pretty much out of town, with any remaining ones tagged for me by Willson. He's sent me off to Caldwell's sawmill, but he seems to want to let me find out why when I get there."

"There is a certain thrill in seeing Jim Caldwell's enterprise unprepared," Gerrish said. "I shall enjoy seeing how it takes you, since I'm that way bound myself. It's a pleasant walk of twenty minutes or so."

On the walk, Judge Gerrish regaled Brandon with entertaining anecdotes of the courtroom and other aspects of his law practice; when Brandon, for a moment inattentive to his role, supplied a few of his own, he was obliged to put in a hasty claim to have acquired them while on the police beat in St. Louis.

Within fifteen minutes Brandon could hear the slow but strident beat of the pulse of the mill, a shrill, grinding scream of five seconds or so as the blade ripped through the length of a plank, then about the same amount of silence as the next board was wrestled into place, then the scream of the saw once more. The track led up a steep, wooden hillside that suddenly became an open space studded with stumps, revealing the mill a few hundred yards ahead of them. The domed cylinder of a boiler, like a dwarfed silo except that it was topped with a tall stack, rose above the shed that housed the mill, but no steam came from the stack, and Brandon could see a rapidly moving wheel dripping water on the far side.

"Water power's quite adequate for the work Caldwell gets," Judge Gerrish said, "but he's fitted it out to run by steam as well, if the water should fail. Remarkably clever—ingenious, you might say—and no sense to it. Excellent emblem of how Jim Caldwell operates."

Brandon saw a second shed, lower than the mill's but about as long, off to one side. It was considerably lighter in tone, presumably from less weathering, and therefore also presumably significantly newer, the final presumption being that this was where Caldwell's "project," and with it Brandon's story, was located. Beyond it, across the stream that powered the mill, a swath of bare ground and stumps lay on the steep hillside like a giant, spreading patch of mange. At the furthest edge of the clearing a tree leaned out from the border of the forest and slammed a cloud of dust from the ground as it hit; a couple of seconds later, the thudding noise of its fall came to Brandon's ears. A gleaming pile of fresh lumber, house-high, standing between the two sheds, marked the destination of the felled tree.

"Here's Caldwell now," Judge Gerrish said. A man wearing a carpenter's apron and denim trousers had emerged from the shed that Brandon supposed contained the object of his story and walked to meet them. Brandon could see a resemblance to his daughter, though Caldwell had gone past plumpish to frankly rotund. His face was as animated as Julie Caldwell's, but he had in general a disordered look, tousled hair and a sprinkling of wood shavings and paint smears on his hands and clothing being particularly noticeable.

"Ah, Judge," Caldwell said, "you're just in time."

"For what?" Gerrish said.

"To see where it's gotten to now, of course."

Gerrish looked at him with an air of slight wonder. "If I came an hour later, I'd be just in time to see where it'd have gotten to by then, though, wouldn't I?"

Caldwell beamed. "Just so!" He looked at Brandon and said, "This gentleman's with the railroad? He'll be interested—"

"With the paper," Gerrish said.

"Oh, of course! I should have . . . I must say, I'm disappointed that you haven't been able to attend to that engraving, Mr. Willson. My daughter—"

"This isn't Willson, Jim," Judge Gerrish said patiently. "Mr. Calvin Blake, newly hired as reporter, and sent out to report."

"Oh, dear, you must forgive me," Jim Caldwell said. "I'm a little preoccupied, and the resemblance . . ."

"Is nonexistent," Gerrish said. "Caldwell, you're going to have to pull your head out of that shed and look around and breathe some fresh air. I think the paint fumes are addling your wits."

Jim Caldwell seemed to take the judge's advice immediately by taking a deep breath and shaking his head as if to clear it. He looked at Brandon and said, "Of course, of course, you're nothing like, I see that now that I take the trouble to notice. Willson's taller, something of the look of a stork or crow, and you're . . . well . . ."

"Ordinary," Brandon said. "A good thing in my trade. Makes people readier to talk to you." In the St. Louis days distinctiveness in appearance and dress had been a point of pride with him, and a need in trial work; but the shock of his family's massacre had somehow blurred the clearly stamped Cole Brandon personality, and as he pursued their murderers across the country he found that he more and more had a succession of masks—Brooks the cattle buyer, Bane the hardcase, Callison the gambler—rather than a single, recallable face. A good thing in that trade, too. He wondered if someone who had known Cole Brandon would recognize him in Calvin Blake, and he hoped the question wouldn't be raised.

"Come along, then," Jim Caldwell said, bustling off ahead of them. "You'll naturally be wondering when it'll be ready, Mr. Blake, and you'll see that it won't be long."

"Some new kind of sawmill machinery?" Brandon asked the judge as they followed Caldwell.

"A reasonable guess, which is a mistake when you're dealing with Jim Caldwell," Judge Gerrish said.

A minute later, surveying what occupied most of the length of the shed, Brandon agreed. Gleaming with deep-green paint ornamented with gold-leaf tracery, sending a pungent perfume of drying varnish to them, a splendid railroad passenger car rested on two long wooden rails. Above the dozen gleaming windows red-edged gold lettering proclaimed it to be the property of the Denver & Transmontane Railroad, while a cartouche under the central window gave its personal name as *The Spirit of Spargill.*

"Now you'll agree, Mr. Blake, that a cut of that in the paper, all detailed to show the most intricate features, why, that'd show the DT people that Spargill stands ready to boost for the railroad. Built in Spargill with Spargill labor and Spargill money, as an earnest of Spargill's good faith, hope, and charity," Jim Caldwell said proudly. "I don't hold out for a colored chromolithograph, for that wouldn't be reasonable to look for in Spargill just yet, but a measly steel engraving ain't too much to ask, to my way of thinking. Let me tell you about it."

The story of *The Spirit of Spargill,* as Brandon jotted it down in the informal shorthand he had developed for taking case notes, seemed worthy of the most florid illustration possible. Caldwell, visiting a mining town on the western side of the Rabbit Ears range, had seen the wreck of a passenger car that had failed to negotiate a sharp bend and was smitten with a vision.

"Body was all scrap lumber and splinters, and the tin roof chewed up something awful," Jim Caldwell said, "but the steelwork—body frame, seats, trucks, even the heating stove—was sound. So it came to me then that I could have the steelwork freighted here and build a new car, something that'd—"

"Serve as bait for the railroad," Judge Gerrish said dryly.

"If you want to put it that way," Jim Caldwell said. "Anyhow, I bought it up and freighted it here and dickered with Billmeyer & Smalls, way back in York, Pennsylvania, that's known for building the best passenger cars going, for a set of plans and specifications, and they sent 'em on to me, and I've been laboring at it since, and near done with it now."

"Impressive," Brandon said. "But . . ." Prolonged inspection of the car had given him a sense of oddity about it that went beyond the fact of its existence in this place. He seemed somehow to be further away from it than in fact he was, and the proportions were in some way off. He realized that though the car appeared to be of normal height, or almost, it was distinctly shorter than those he was used to. Moving to the end and looking through the open door, he could see that it was narrower, with a double seat on one side of the aisle and a single on the other. "These plans, are you sure . . . ?"

Jim Caldwell gave him a puzzled glare, but Judge Gerrish laughed. "No, it's not a giant toy train, Blake. I know how it strikes you, but Caldwell's so used to it he doesn't see it anymore. The DT's a narrow-gauge line, tracks three feet apart instead of the usual four and a half, and the cars have to be sized to fit. Most mountain railroads are narrow-gauge, the best way of snaking through these hills, cheaper to lay track for, and the cars can be a lot lighter, so less of a load for the engines."

"You sound like Pa, talking up narrow-gauge like that,"

Julie Caldwell said, coming around the edge of the shed. "I think he's converted you."

"I have to know something of the topic to deal with the railroad people about their coming here, my dear," the judge said. "Also in working out the agreement by which they'll acquire the *Spirit* once the tracks get here; I came out here, in fact, to go over that matter with your father."

"You do that, and I'll show Mr. Blake through her," Julie Caldwell said. "I'm sure he'll be impressed."

Brandon was. The seats were upholstered in green and red, and the hinges, hooks, lamps, and mountings gleamed brightly, and the walls were paneled in woods of varying tones, and the whole effect was sumptuous.

"Colorado wood throughout, Colorado silver for the metalwork," Julie Caldwell said. "Some folks think Pa's hipped on what the *Spirit*'ll do, but he's done a lot of good work on it, and I think he deserves a good showing for it. I really think your Mr. Willson ought to do something about getting a good steel engraving made, even though maybe Pa's drawing isn't all that artistic."

"It isn't that," Brandon said, "just that there don't seem to be any engravers around."

"If he wanted to enough, he could find one," Julie Caldwell said. She looked at Brandon with a slow smile. "Tell you what, I think he'll discover he wants to, and then he'll find himself an engraver somehow. You might tell him that'd be an awfully good idea."

"A good idea!" Abner Willson said agitatedly. "Whatever did the woman mean by that?"

"An awfully good idea," Brandon said solemnly.

"An *awfully* good idea! That's worse, or is it better? Damn, what am I supposed to make of that?" Willson paced back and forth in front of the press, abstractedly hitting at its lever as he passed by it.

Brandon tried to remember just how puff pieces of the kind he was supposed to be preparing read. If he had it right, the main thing was to load it with superlatives and adjectives, pretty much like a summation to the jury when there wasn't much in the law or the facts to bolster the case. *Rarely if ever in the annals of* might do to begin; then came the question, annals of what? As he wrote the opening phrase as clearly as he could manage on a sheet of copy paper he said to Willson, "I would make of it that she knows you're stuck on her, that she doesn't mind, and that if you want a chance, go get an engraver." Maybe *annals of municipal development?* Or *civic progress?*

"You really think so? That she might . . . Well, that's great! No, it ain't, for there's no engraver around, and if that's what she's set on, I'm hip-deep in a bog and no mules handy."

"There's bound to be one someplace, and you can work out a way to find him," Brandon said. . . . *has there been such a . . .*

"Like a magic ring or a dragon's head in one of those fairy stories," Abner Willson said morosely. "Setting me on a quest like some damned princess."

"As I recollect, the fellow that went on the quest generally made it and got the princess anyhow," Brandon said.

"There is that." Abner Willson's face brightened a little. "How you coming with the story on Caldwell's Folly?" He looked over Brandon's shoulder and read, " 'Scarcely ever in the annals of civic development has there been such a.' That's a good start, let me take it from there; I'll paint *The Spirit of Spargill* in such rainbow hues, she'll think she's seeing a four-color poster of it. You get on and get settled in at Ma Deckle's, and turn up here first thing tomorrow."

After he had negotiated with Mrs. Deckle for his board and lodging—the process getting considerably smoother after he brought Judge Gerrish's name into the conversation—Brandon headed for the barbershop for the restoration of a more or less civilized surface. He had been two days on the way from Denver, and the Deckle establishment provided baths only upon sufficient notice, preferably on Saturday nights or afternoons, as the heating of the water and its transport in cans by the hired girl constituted a major project. As he had hoped, the barbershop, like many of its kind, provided a bathhouse behind the main building, and he was able to soap and sluice himself down with steaming water, and dress in clothes which, if wrinkled from being packed in his valise, did not have sixty miles' worth of grit and dust embedded in them.

In the barbershop he settled into the chair, the most comfortable he had been in in some time, and relaxed as the barber adjusted the towel around his neck and began stropping a straight razor.

"You're Ab Willson's new reporter," the barber said, "replacement for Jenkins, that drank himself crazy."

"I'm at the *Chronicle,* yes," Brandon said. "Name's Cal Blake."

The barber laid down the razor, fished with a pair of tongs in a steaming container against the wall, and brought out a towel, which he draped across Brandon's face. As always, there was the initial impression of having received a faceful of superheated steam, and the expectation of cooked flesh sloughing away from the skull, followed by a sense of supreme relaxation.

"As a new man in town, what's your thoughts on the railroad?" the barber said.

"The paper's for it, and they pay me," Brandon said. It was true, but also a reply nonpartisan enough to be prudent when the questioner was about to lay six inches of sharpened steel alongside his jugular vein.

The barber, judging Brandon's face to be nicely simmered, plucked the towel away and began smearing it with thick, pungently scented lather. He heard the door open, a murmured greeting, steps on the floor, and the creak of a bench as a prospective customer sank onto it. "Be good business for me," the barber said. "Passengers coming in from the north that'll want a shave or a trim they forgot to get in Cheyenne or Split Rock, and them that's traveling or excursioning from here'll want to look neatened up before as they go. I'll have twice the trade, I shouldn't wonder."

"Good for most of the merchants, I'd guess," Brandon said, "what with freight rates dropping."

"Good for some, ruin for others," a voice said; the new

customer, Brandon supposed. "Low freight rates means it'll be cheaper to buy some things mail-order from Monkey Ward in Chicago than buy local, and if there's four bits to save on an item, folks in Spargill'll save it, even if it'd bankrupt their grandma."

"Maybe they'd support local merchants even so," Brandon said. "What makes you think they'd grab at a paltry saving like that?"

"*I* damn well would," the customer said.

Brandon preferred to keep his eyes closed when being shaved—tilted back, all he would see if they were open was the ceiling, the too-close face of the barber, and the flashing steel coated with white foam and a coarse peppering of hairs and heard rather than saw two more customers come in.

"Haw," one of them said. "Just saw Marshal Tooley comin' out of Charley Pratt's house, that's up there kind of out of the way behind that stand of trees on the edge of town. What kind of business d'ye expect he's got with Charley?"

"None," the first customer said, "if he's not in the dry-goods store, which is where Charley is now, or was four minutes back. Charley don't usually close up until about half an hour from now."

"Marshal was in here an hour and some back, shave and trim and a good slosh of bay rum to finish off," the barber observed.

"Mrs. Charley'd best have a reason handy fer smellin' of bay rum, then," a new voice, presumably that of the other new customer, offered.

"Marshal Tool, I don't wonder we'll come to call him," the first customer said. "Wasn't it Sarah Hardy, Sam's missus, last week? Seems to be working his way through the business community."

"The married part of it, anyways," the second customer said. "We may be luckier than we think to be bachelors."

"It don't do to think of being married to a woman that'd think Tooley was a prime item," the barber said. "Never be able to trust her judgment on anything."

In the few minutes it took to finish the shave and be once

again steamed with a scalding towel—he declined the ultimate touch of an application of bay rum—Brandon heard enough scandal to fill several pages of the *Police Gazette*, or to sell out an edition of any number of copies of the Spargill *Chronicle*. But no matter if all the names were spelled right, these items would never be printed; even with less than a day's experience as a journalist behind him, he knew that much. For what it was worth, neither Abner Willson nor Julie Caldwell figured in the ribald narrative.

He left the barber's obscurely pleased that Tooley seemed to be a scoundrel. He had not particularly wanted the marshal's intervention on his behalf—hadn't noticed he was there till the fight with Liebwohl was over—but Tooley's glowering look had suggested that he would have been better pleased if it had been Brandon, or Calvin Blake, puking his dinner out in the street, and Brandon was prepared to return any dislike offered.

A lot of lawmen out here had a checkered history, Brandon thought, and the town marshal of today was sometimes the outlaw of yesterday, and quite possibly tomorrow. He made a mental note to find out if Tooley had been in Spargill a year and a half before, when Gren Kenneally and his gang had robbed the CRI&P express and, in flight, destroyed Cole Brandon's family. A long shot, but if he was going to trust to his luck, or the old Indian coin's guidance, or destiny, most of his shots were going to be long.

"What kind of facts?" Brandon said, leafing through the thick book. Though its main title was *The National Encyclopedia of Business Forms,* its scope was a good deal more generous, embracing form letters for all occasions, a guide to etiquette, instruction in the art of versification, rules for games, and "miscellaneous tables for reference," which so far had included key dates in Prussian history, square mileage of oceans, seas, bays, and lakes, the value of thirty foreign currencies down to the *itzebu* of Japan (thirty-seven cents), and a method for estimating crop yield by framing four sticks together and setting them over whatever was growing.

"Any kind of fact that'll take up two column inches," Abner Willson called from the composing table, where his hands darted machinelike between the type case and the galley forms. "The old *National*'s a godsend to a paper like this. You can always find something that'll fit any space and interest the reader about as much as the real news. A while back, when things were slow, or anyhow when Jenkins, the man that worked for me, wasn't up to bringing in what news there was, I took to running the sample letters, invitations and acceptances, proposals of marriage and rejections, references for housemaids, and so on. Meant to provide instruction, but the readers took them for a kind of novel, wanted to know what happened next, did Mary Anne get the job and so on."

"Here's something on the velocity of sound and light," Brandon said. "'Sound moves about thirteen miles in a minute. So that if we hear a clap of thunder half a minute after the flash, we may calculate that the discharge of electricity is six and a half miles off.' Goes on to say that if you shot a cannonball at the sun, it'd take twenty years to get there."

"That should do it," Abner Willson said. "Bring it over, and I'll set it." Brandon put the book on the table and watched as Willson, scarcely seeming to look at the type case, snatched letter after letter from it and slid them into the form, the lines of lead slugs filling up the space with astonishing speed.

"There's a section in the book of Latin phrases in common use," Willson observed. "Tried a chunk of them once—regretted it. Managed to leave an n out of *Annus mirabilis,* that's 'year of wonders,' when I set it. Judge Gerrish was the only one that noticed, thank God, and he laughed himself sick, mainly because the next one was *a posteriori.* I didn't see what the joke was until he told me. Oh, hey, maybe I ought to explain—"

"No need," Brandon said, chuckling. "I get it."

Abner Willson blinked. "Do you? Well, now. Maybe you should chum up with Gerrish, he's about the only one in Spargill that's got a leghold on the tongue of Caesar."

Brandon cursed himself mentally for not seeing that Calvin Blake, as Willson knew him, was unlikely to find Latin errors amusing. No reason a newsman shouldn't be educated; it was just that they didn't tend to be, and Brandon's effectiveness depended in large part on being an ordinary or typical example of the part he was playing for the moment. "Have you and the judge worked out the story you're doing on Parker?" he asked.

Abner Willson nodded toward a galley form filled with type at the far side of the composing table. "All written and set, making John B. look like a combination of the best features of Robert Fulton and Prince Albert. Have a look."

Brandon wandered over to the galley and peered at it. Lines of dully gleaming letters, or rather mirror images of them, shone up at him. Reading from right to left, and reversing the letters in his mind's eye as he went, he saw that the story began with "Among the Titans of the Age," after which point his interpretive faculty rebelled, presenting him with "trehe aer none ot cmoprea," and he abandoned the effort.

"Never mastered the trick of reading from the form," he told Willson. "The typesetters on the *Dispatch* used to josh me a lot about it, but I had to wait till I saw my stuff in print before I knew it came out right. When's Parker due here?"

"There's no definite day. My guess would be tomorrow," Abner Willson said. "He'll have to get the bond stuff settled with Gerrish, who pretty much speaks for the town council, and he can't wait much longer to do that if he's going to get track laid here any time soon."

"Want to bet on that, that he's coming tomorrow?" Brandon asked, looking past Willson and out the front window of the *Chronicle* office. "Say one Japanese *itzebu?*"

"Probably not," Abner Willson said. "You don't have the sound of a man hazarding a true wager." He turned and, like Brandon, saw Judge Gerrish approaching the front door, followed by a burly, red-faced man in a splendid, if dusty, traveling coat and tall plug hat, displaying the small eyes, long nose, and big ears that newspaper cartoonists had exaggerated tellingly in their caricatures of the Killer Elephant of Wall Street. Parker in his turn was followed by three men. As the last of these approached the *Chronicle*'s door Brandon stiffened.

The first time he had seen that mournful face was a year and a half ago, when a detective employed by the railroad had come to inform him that his family was being held hostage at Mound Farm and had companioned him in the discovery of their murder. Jake Trexler, his name was.

And now Judge Gerrish held the door open as John B. Parker, a jaunty-looking young man wearing a derby, and a more florid man with deep-set eyes and a soft hat entered the office. Jake Trexler came in after them, looking around the premises for a heartbeat or so before his eyes locked on Brandon's.

5

Thanks for not letting on you'd known me with another name," Brandon said.

Jake Trexler looked at him wryly over the rim of his glass. "If you're introduced to a man giving his name as John Jones, it don't do to say, 'Ain't you in truth and in fact Tom Smith, lately of Urbana, Illinois?' You could be wrong, which is bad, or you could be right, which is worse. Lots of times a man's name don't follow him across the Missouri, for good reasons and for bad. So long as the alias ain't used to the hurt and detriment of the railroad, it's no concern of mine." He sipped at his whiskey and eyed Brandon. "I will say, though, I didn't look to see you out here. Last I saw you in St. Louis—late in 'seventy-four, wasn't it?—you looked about ready to let the hawser slip and drift on downstream and over the falls. I can understand how you'd feel so, what happened to your family and all, and I'm glad to see that you didn't go that way. Which leaves open why you're here and who you are, if you'd care to go into that."

Trexler's tone was mildly curious, not intrusive or inquisitorial. Brandon considered what edited version of the facts it would be prudent to give him. There were few customers in the bar, and he did not expect that their conversation would be overheard.

He had experienced a heart-stopping moment of dismay when Trexler entered the newspaper office and saw him. When Gerrish performed introductions all round Trexler's face did not change at hearing attorney Cole Brandon presented as newspaperman Calvin Blake, and Brandon's pulse resumed its accustomed pace.

When it became clear that the conference Judge Gerrish had arranged involved Gerrish, John B. Parker, Abner Willson, and Jack Ryan—the jaunty young man in the domed hat—Brandon seized the chance to offer to interview Jake Trexler on his experiences in fighting crime on the western railroads. Judge Gerrish recommended the Chapultepec Bar, a block off Main, as being the most conducive locale in Spargill for interviews. To Brandon's relief, the other nonparticipant in the talks—the florid man, who turned out to be an artist hired by the railroad, Nelson Vanbrugh—chose not to join them but to "perambulate and let the *genius loci* inspirit me and, in the fullness of time, lend accuracy to my brush. Also, I need to work the cramps out of my ass after that miserable ride from Split Rock. I am a painter, not a jockey."

After some thought Brandon said, "You had pretty much the right of it, what you thought about me back then. The family dead, and that fellow they caught let off at his trial—"

"Casmire," Jake Trexler said.

"So it was. Well, with all that, I was pretty deep in the dumps, and nothing did any good. And, in fact, I did kind of let go of life. No point in being a lawyer anymore, no point in being in St. Louis, no point in being Cole Brandon. So I cut loose and set myself adrift, seeing where I fetched up."

"Warner, the man at the Nationwide Detective Agency you did business with, writes me now and then," Jake Trexler said. "Told me a year and some ago that you'd gone on a trip to Europe or someplace."

"'S what I said I was going to do," Brandon said. "Folks

find that easier to understand than . . . well, just going where the river takes you. You see, Trexler, what I came to understand when I couldn't take being me any longer was that there wasn't any reason not to be anybody or anything I fancied, for as long or as little as I cared to be. And out here that's something like normal. People are changing jobs, names, all the time. Look at me. I'm a newspaperman now because I say I am, and I can keep on being that *as long as I can do the job,* that's the thing. In the West, a man is what he can do, not what he's been funneled to or brought up to all his life. I have been a gambler, Trexler, and a kind of hotel bouncer, and good at both, and it looks as if I'll be a pretty fair newspaperman. And whatever else I'm going to be later on, probably I'll be good enough at that, too. And maybe, after I've been enough different men and done enough different things, I'll put in some more time as Cole Brandon, and maybe make a better job of that than I did the first time."

You surpass yourself, Counselor, he told himself. Every word the truth and nothing but the truth—but by no means the whole truth, in fact a damned big hole in the truth. Nothing about tracking and killing Gren Kenneally and all the rest being what's behind all this, nothing about the three dead so far and the one I'm here to sniff out and kill. But no actual lies told; it's a wonderful thing to have the ghost of a conscience, isn't it?

Trexler shrugged. "None of my business, so long as none of your whoevers commits any crime to do with a railroad, like I said. Right now I'm kind of off my track, keeping an eye on this Parker, but the railroad detached me to him as a kind of bodyguard, so here I am."

"Parker's not a railroad executive?" Brandon asked, in some surprise.

"John B. Parker is making this trip in his capacity as general manager of the Occidental Contract Company, which is constructing the line to Split Rock for the use of the Denver & Transmontane Railroad," Jake Trexler said. "And Occidental Contract, that is to say, Parker, will determine whether the DT line should go as far as Spargill."

"And the railroad'll take Occidental's recommendation on that, no question?" Brandon asked.

"Good chance of it," Trexler said, "as John B. Parker is president of Denver & Transmontane."

Brandon thought this over for a moment, then nodded. "I see. Even if the railroad doesn't make money on operations for a while, or never does, the contract company makes its profit from what the railroad company pays it, and I will bet you one *itzebu* that the railroad's owned by stockholders, who'll have to take any losses, and the contract company's owned privately by the railroad officers."

"You're ahead one *itzebu,* whatever that is," Jake Trexler said. "It's wonderful how defending crafty criminals and such equips you to understand finance, ain't it, Brandon?—sorry, it's Blake, I'll remember that. Anyhow, President Parker told me to shepherd General Manager Parker on this trip, and so I am."

"And that artist fellow came along to do what?" Brandon asked. "And the other one, Ryan?"

"Vanbrugh does paintings railroad companies use for posters to sell the public on traveling in the West," Jake Trexler said. "His stuff's pretty good, makes hills and prairie and what seem really worth looking at. The DT figures that as soon as trains start running they'll get people to take trips down from the main line just to look at the scenery, and Vanbrugh's paintings might just get them to do that. He looks kind of like a fool, but he's dressing the part of an artist so's people'll know to steer clear of him if they don't cotton to artists—which who out here does?—and let him get on with his work. He knows what he's doing, more than he looks. Jack Ryan got drafted from some outfit that's got a deal with the railroad. He's a kind of arranger, sort of fellow who'll get things done somehow, and it's maybe best if you don't look too close at the somehow, kind of like a supply sergeant in the army. He managed to get some lumber his boss needed at the same time some lumber the railroad thought it had wasn't there anymore, and Parker got to know of it and admired his gall enough so that he borrowed him for the trip to see to hiring the horses and arranging lodging and such, act as secretary and general dogsbody. Ryan's the kind of fellow you get to think can do anything . . . or maybe anybody. Just the kind to appeal to John B. Parker."

"What's Parker like?" Brandon asked. "I've read about him in the papers, the corners he's made in different things in the market, calling him the Killer Elephant of Wall Street and so on. 'S he like that?"

"Aside from something about the face that newspaper cartoonists can have fun with, John B. Parker ain't much in the elephant line," Trexler said. "He has been known to emulate the wolverine, that'll rip your throat out and crunch you up, or the vampire bat, that'll drink your blood and leave you alive, and a few other of God's worse ideas, but elephants, no. As a boss Parker's okay, mainly because he has the sense to pick people who know what they're doing and let them do it."

Brandon looked up and saw Jack Ryan had approached their table unobserved and was standing behind Trexler's chair. "I never expected to come in on the end of a conversation about John B. Parker that had something nice to say about him," Ryan said. "I will circle the day in red on my calendar. Trexler, Parker wants you back at the newsroom. Blake, Willson wants you. I'm not sure who wants me, but I'll assume I'm indispensable and go back with you."

The atmosphere in the *Chronicle* office was not happy. In spite of what Jake Trexler had said, John B. Parker did have the look of an elephant—not one in a killing mood, but one confident that no creature in the immediate neighborhood had the power to move it from where it was standing. Judge Gerrish wore the determinedly bland face of a man who is calling upon every minim of judicial temperament to suppress a murderous rage. Abner Willson appeared to have bitten into a lemon—or, Brandon guessed, to have been presented with a major piece of news, all of it bad, that he had no prospect of printing.

"You will understand, sir," Gerrish said stiffly, "that this new . . . requirement on your part changes our situation considerably."

"Bound to," John B. Parker said amiably. "But it is a requirement—make no mistake about that, Judge—and it's up to your folks to work out how to handle it."

"I'll convey that to them," Judge Gerrish said sourly. "And what they'll . . . well, we'll see what happens." He took a deep breath and looked at Parker with determined politeness. "Meanwhile, I have a suggestion to make. There's more than just passenger and freight business down to Spargill and eventually on to Denver to attract the Denver & Transmontane here, and while the situation's changing so much, it might be the time to throw something into the balance on this side. About ten miles from here there's a truly beautiful area, another park, smaller and higher than the one Spargill's in. Run a spur line out there and you've got a steady excursion business, then land development and building a whole new community, with steady traffic to and from Spargill. Most of that would be land grants to the DT, too." Ned Norland's "vacation" retreat, with its "lake like a blue jewel," was doomed for sure, Brandon thought.

"So," Judge Gerrish went on, "I propose we ride out there. You can see for yourself both the attractions of the spot and the character of the terrain the rails would have to go over. I've done an informal survey, and it's difficult but not impossible, and in fact the switchbacks it demands make the route all the more scenic."

"Fair enough," John B. Parker said. "If you show me you can sweeten the deal on your side, there's some chance I can find a way to do the same on mine. No way to cut the basic figure, for I'm looking at nine thousand a mile construction costs over the easy parts, twenty thousand where it turns rough. But there's always side issues to look at, something that'll make it easier for your town council to swallow when it's put to them. We'll have lunch, then ride on out there, take a good look, be back before sundown. Ryan, you arrange for some fresh horses for us. Judge, you need a mount?"

"I have my own," Judge Gerrish said. "Mr. Ryan, tell Soames at the livery stable that you need trail-wise horses, and that Judge Gerrish doesn't want to see that walleyed bay anywhere in the bunch."

"And ask him to charge another one to the *Chronicle's* account," Abner Willson said. "I'll want Blake to go with you, if that's all right. I'd like to have some kind of cheerful news to print in this issue."

Brandon stayed behind when Judge Gerrish led Parker, Trexler, and Ryan off to the Superior Restaurant, which he claimed deserved its name, although being only adequate, as it was clearly superior to the one other eating establishment Spargill enjoyed. "Could have some competition in a while," Brandon heard Ryan say as the party moved up Main Street.

"What's the situation that's changed, and why's it got everybody looking like a mine was exploded?" he asked Abner Willson.

Willson closed the street door and in quiet, venomous tones added several animals to the list Trexler had given of John B. Parker's zoological counterparts. Coyote, skunk, pig, and rat were the main ones, but there were enough in all for a small menagerie of unpleasing beasts, many engaged in uncharacteristic activities. "The deal was set, but the whore-mongering toad reneged," he finally explained to Brandon. "Spargill was going to raise seventy-five thousand dollars with a bond issue for a subsidy to the railroad for the cost of the line, and now the son of a sow says it's got to be a hundred and twenty-five thousand—close to twice as much!"

From what Trexler had told him, Brandon estimated that the subsidy would be to Occidental Contract, not to the Denver & Transmontane, which didn't affect things either way except to assure that it would cushion the risk, such as it was, to Parker and his associates, not to the railroad's stockholders.

"And there's land grants and so on as well," Willson grumbled. "Seems like Parker wants to make everybody else pay for what he wants to do."

"That's how you make a name in Wall Street," Brandon said. "Does this new bite kill the deal?"

Abner Willson shrugged. "The businessmen and merchants in town are mostly hot for it, and a lot of them have been prospering enough so that they could maybe dig a little deeper. It's a close thing, though, and they could get awful sore. It'll take everything Judge Gerrish can muster to keep 'em in the herd."

"Maybe you should send him out for a look at *The Spirit of Spargill*, the way Caldwell wants," Brandon said. "Might soften that flinty heart."

"Unlikely," Abner Willson said, "but Gerrish's notion of showing him the promised land out by Happy Squaw Lake and showing him how much money the DT could make out of it might do that."

"Happy Squaw?" Brandon said.

"Old Indian legend, so they say," Abner Willson said. "Something about three princesses that lived right about here, and every so often one or another of 'em would go off to the lake with the spirit of the goat god and come back after a moon, weak and trembling, but happier than any mortal woman. Damn fool story, but the name stuck."

Brandon wondered what Ned Norland would think if he knew he had been taken into the Indian pantheon as a supernatural goat—flattered, or considering it only reasonable recognition?

The cowbell on the front doorknob clanked as the door opened to admit Nelson Vanbrugh, Parker's artist. "Where's the crowd gone to?" he asked.

"To lunch at the Superior," Willson said, "then for a ride out to look at some property Parker is maybe interested in, or could be. Jack Ryan's hiring some fresh horses for it; maybe you'd best find him and see that he gets one for you."

Vanbrugh shook his head. "I am hoofing it till I have to get back to Split Rock," he said. "Any time I have a chance not to split myself on an animated coatrack with the brains of a carrot and the ethical code of a Congressman, I accept it gratefully. I will go on looking around this burg and seeing what quaint corners and picturesque contrasts of dwelling and pristine scenery it affords. Color isn't all that interesting, but there's a lot of strong lines and angles, and I'd like to work up some studies for etchings."

"Etchings," Abner Willson said thoughtfully. "They're kind of like engravings, ain't they?"

"Some," Nelson Vanbrugh said. "In one the lines are eaten away with acid. In the other they're—well, engraved, with a sharp tool. Either way you're left with a line that gets filled in with ink and printed. I've done both, and etching gives you a lot more variety of tone, for one thing."

"My," Abner Willson said. "Actually done steel engravings, have you? Say, Vanbrugh, I know something you'd admire above somewhat to sketch, and not far from here. Be glad to show you."

" 'Not far' meaning you get there by walking?" Vanbrugh asked.

"Well, sure."

"Suits me. What I'm looking for is something that sort of sums the place up," Nelson Vanbrugh said. "Is this something like that, one thing that has kind of the essence of Spargill?"

"Its very spirit," Abner Willson said. "Come on back here after the ride, Blake, and go over the story with me. I will try to find something snappy to start off with, since it's an almighty dull event. Hey, you got a pistol with you?"

"Yes," Brandon said. "You need one?" He had grown so used to wearing the holstered .38 under his jacket that he had almost patted the gun to see if it was there.

"No, you do. Those rocky trails, all those caves and ledges, there's rattlers all over. You'd be okay, though, if you let 'em bite John B. Parker first—they'd curl up and die, poisoned right through."

Brandon eyed the rock face that walled one side of the trail, checking the irregular crevices that angled across it for the coiled form of a sleeping snake. The early afternoon sun was warm, and the heated rock was ideal for reptilian ease.

His jacket was open, leaving the .38 easy to reach, and he noticed the other men, even John B. Parker, had taken the same precaution.

He looked behind him and saw that they had already climbed some distance above Spargill, which now was displayed like a bird's-eye view in a town promotion brochure. It was, compared to other western towns he had seen, remarkably orderly, laid out in a neat gridiron pattern, the streets intersecting at precise right angles. The intense green of the trees, many of which the town's developers had had the sense to leave in place to shade the streets and houses, combined with the mostly fresh paint on the buildings to give the place the look of a painting that Nelson Vanbrugh might have been proud of. The contrast with the Arizona mining town of Kampen, the last place he had spent any amount of time, could hardly have been greater. Kampen was rock glaring in the sun, dust, sunbleached unpainted buildings scattered over the rocky ground, acrid smoke from the smelters. Spargill was cool, trim, clean.

The course he had chosen, however, made all places mainly the same to him—temporary camps or hunter's blinds to be used as a place to wait for his quarry and, if it came, to bring it down, then move on to the next. All the same, if a man were thinking of stopping someplace, Spargill was the kind of place a man might think of. . . .

The hills at the other side of town rose less steeply than the one the Parker party was now climbing, and on one Brandon saw the dollhouse-sized buildings of Jim Caldwell's sawmill and lumberyard, and the shimmer of water from the stream coursing by it. The cleared area above the sawmill looked larger than it had the day before, perhaps because he was seeing it from a different angle, bare and dusty, like a growing blight. It seemed to him that he caught a glint of red from the long shed that housed the passenger car that Caldwell had crafted with such devotion, and he wondered if Abner Willson and Nelson Vanbrugh were even now inspecting it, with Vanbrugh deciding whether or not to immortalize it in engraved steel. Brandon hoped he would;

it would please Julie Caldwell and maybe make Willson less jumpy.

Brandon found himself suddenly looking at the side of Jake Trexler's horse, a little above him and going in the opposite direction. He saw that the trail had taken another of the switchbacks, zigzagging up the face of the mountain, that had kept the ascent from being impossibly steep.

Parker and Judge Gerrish, in the lead, halted at a level place in the trail. "Hum," Parker said, looking back down the trail. "You seriously think track can be laid on this?"

"There's worse on the Denver & Rio Grande line around Colorado Springs, and even on the DT some above Split Rock," Gerrish said. "Enough switchbacks, this won't be a bad stretch at all, and it'll give the passengers ample time to enjoy the view."

Jack Ryan reined in next to Brandon and muttered, "Parker's used to worse twists than this in how he works, track laying and other things. There's one place on the DT where the joke is that they're saving half the fuel cost, 'cause the loco is both pulling the first car on the train and pushing the last car. It's amazing where those surveyors and track-men can put a line in these mountains that a train'll run on and not fall off, most of the time."

John B. Parker looked over the hills ahead. He did not straighten from his slouched position, but it seemed to Brandon that he was suddenly tenser, more alert. "Interesting country here," he said. "Reminds me of some places I used to know pretty well in Pennsylvania."

"There's a fork in the trail up ahead," Judge Gerrish told Parker. "We'll bear left when we get there, for that goes to the lake. The other fork heads north and west into some rough country that's not been looked through much yet."

Not by the Spargillers, anyway, Brandon thought. It was probably as familiar as waterfront St. Louis was to Brandon to the Indians who had lived there for thousands of years, and to Ned Norland. When it did get "looked through" it would be only a little time until there was another Spargill there.

The fork in the trail was marked by a massive rock, something like the prow of a ship. The trail to Happy Squaw Lake, Brandon was relieved to see, looked broad and passable; the one they were not going to take was not much more than a shadowed, horse-wide gap between the ship-prow rock and a slab almost as massive.

Brandon, last in the loose line, caught a flicker of motion in the gap, then stopped as a harsh call came from ahead: "*Hold* it there, allaya!" He saw that a rider, face concealed with a blue kerchief under a broad-brimmed hat, had appeared from around the trail-splitting rock and held a shotgun, both barrels of which had been shortened to not much more than horse-pistol length, aimed at them. It was an effective weapon for dealing with numbers of people, as the shot would fan out to hit anybody and everybody in its immediate neighborhood. He was also, Brandon saw, pre-pared for detail work, with a large-handled revolver stuck in his belt. Brandon looked behind to gauge his chances of retreating back down the trail but saw that another masked man had emerged from the entrance to the other fork and was covering him and the rest of the party from the rear with a repeating rifle.

"Ever'body outta the saddle an' onta the ground!" the man with the shotgun called. "Fast! Then hands on yer head, *move* it!"

For a couple of heartbeats no one moved; then the man at the rear lifted his rifle and fired four shots rapidly. They snarled between the riders in Parker's party, exploding clouds of dust from the rock dividing the trail and sending rock splinters and tumbling ricochets among them.

The message was clear and urgent enough, and they scrambled down from their horses and clamped their hands to the tops of their hats.

Each was in turn made to step forward and, the shotgun three feet from his head, remove his pistol from its holster with two-fingered care and set it on the ground. Brandon cursed himself for not having tucked the little derringer—like the .38, a sort of legacy from a gambler he had known briefly in Kansas and the Indian Territories—in his vest, though it was not the sort of weapon you'd take along for dealing with rattlesnakes.

The man with the shotgun used it to gesture at John B. Parker. "You! Back on your horse. Now!"

Parker, looking like an elephant determined to remember a face it meant to step on heavily if the opportunity was ever offered, remounted.

The man with the rifle rode at the riderless horses, hitting at them with rifle butt and hat until they had turned around to face down the trail from Spargill. He gave a shrill yell and fired twice at the ground behind them, pelting them with rock splinters, and slapped at the hindquarters of the rearmost horse with his hat. It screamed in anger and fright and bolted down the trail; the others galloped along with it, and in a moment they were out of sight, and a short while after that out of earshot.

"You can catch 'em up when they stops runnin'," the shotgun holder said. "Then you git you on down t' Spargill and get word to the big cheeses at the DT that they c'n start settin' about gettin' t'gether fifty thousand dollars. Word 'll be sent 'em what and when and where to do with, and after they've done it they c'n have John B. Parker back. They try to bargain or play any tricks and they'll get him back also, but not in any shape they'll like."

While he spoke, the man with the rifle dismounted, holding a sack into which he dropped the discarded pistols. He lashed them to his companion's saddle cinches and remounted, taking up station in front of Parker. The man with the shotgun moved behind Parker and said, "Let's go."

They moved toward the narrow gap leading to the trail to the north and west, the kidnapper with the shotgun last in line, half-turned in the saddle to eye the standing men, with his gun loosely aimed toward them. The first rider, and then John B. Parker, disappeared into the shadowed gap. As the last rider approached it he turned to guide his horse through it.

Brandon drew his breath with astonishment as Jack Ryan, silently and swiftly as a snake, seemed to flow along the ground and then leap up to grab at the rider and the gun he carried. The man in the saddle swayed and seemed about to fall; then the gun rose high and the stock smashed into Jack Ryan's head, sending him crumpled to the ground. The rider gave a snorting squeal of rage, like the cry of a wild boar, snatched the pistol from his belt, and triggered off two shots at Ryan's huddled body, then one more at the three men who had not moved—perhaps to encourage them to keep to their state of neutrality, more likely out of general irritation. Then he spurred his horse into the gap and vanished.

Brandon saw two clouds of dust puff up from the rocks near Ryan, so he knew that neither bullet had hit him; then he heard a choked curse from next to him and turned to see Jake Trexler sink to the ground, holding his right thigh with both hands, red seeping over the clenched fingers.

"Flesh wound," Trexler said through compressed lips. "Furrowed the surface, mostly, but it'll be a bitch walking after the horses. Better go see if that fellow brained Ryan, though I think he wouldn't have found much to work with. What possessed the goddamn fool?"

"One of those men who always has to take some action, even in a desperate situation where it'll do more harm than good," Judge Gerrish said. "You saw a lot of that during the war, mainly amongst the Confederates." Ryan stirred and made an attempt to sit up. "Doesn't seem to be badly hurt," Gerrish said, "which I suppose is just as well. But he has messed things up for certain."

"How?" Brandon asked. "We're in a rotten situation, with Parker taken, and while Ryan and Trexler being hurt makes that a little harder, it doesn't really change it."

Judge Gerrish said, "I know this trail, and the trail they took, and I've looked at all the maps there are of this area. The trail those men and Parker are on zigzags considerably and comes back right under this one a couple of hundred feet down, though it's close to half a mile by the trail. Riding it, you wouldn't know that, so I don't expect they have any notion of it, and wouldn't be expecting anything."

"I don't think I would be, either," Brandon said, "not

from four unarmed men I'd left behind. What could we have done?"

"Got down there fast and surprised them," Gerrish said earnestly. "Don't you see, once they have Parker secure, there's no guarantee they'll turn him loose if they get the money. Be easier to cut his throat and drop him in a canyon."

"And you have to consider," Jake Trexler said from where he sat on the ground, tying a once-white but now crimsoning handkerchief over his wound, "that John B. Parker's associates may not figure that John B. Parker's well-being is worth fifty thousand dollars. There are those who have done business with John B. Parker who would probably *pay* fifty thousand dollars to someone who would do away with him. When we tell the DT people that any tricks or stalling will probably get them back John B. Parker in pieces, they could reckon that is the best offer they've had this year."

The surprises and perils of the last few minutes had kept Brandon keyed up, ready to react rather than think, and only now did he take in Parker's situation fully. Nothing he had heard or seen of John B. Parker suggested that he would be any great loss to the world, but he was a more or less innocent man at the mercy of thugs who would probably kill him for safety's, or even convenience's, sake. At the mercy, in fact, of men of the same stamp as those who had slaughtered Brandon's family.

As that realization sank into him Brandon recalled old-country tales his wife's Aunt Trudi—dead with Elise at Mound Farm—used to tell of men who would turn into wolves at the full moon. In spite of the fact that Parker's fate was clearly none of his business, and that in any case the subtraction of Trexler and Ryan from their force made any action foolish, his mind and body were rearranging themselves inexorably, turning him into an organism dedicated to hunting down Parker's captors and even, with some luck, rescuing Parker. It would not undo the horror of Mound Farm, but it would—in a way he could not clearly understand—do a little toward redressing the balance.

These were not Kenneally gang members, but they would do for the moment.

"If I go straight down the hill now, I've got a chance of hitting the trail before they get there?" he asked Judge Gerrish.

"You would," Gerrish said, "but I'm long past anything like that, and Ryan and Trexler are in no shape for it, and you can't tackle them unarmed and alone."

Brandon heard the end of the sentence only faintly as he lunged down the hillside at a run, starting small rockslides with each step, sometimes adding to his speed by kicking off from a rock on which a step had landed him. He slowed a little when he came to a stand of pines, weaving among the stovepipe-straight trunks, bending at the knees like a skater to keep his balance on the slick-surfaced bed of needles; then he was in the open again, half-falling, half-leaping down a short cliff into a shifting pile of scree that almost sent him sprawling. He scrambled ahead, drawing breath to fill his lungs with about twice as much air as he had ever known they held; his heart beat like the drums of an attacking regiment; he felt an intoxication stronger than drink had ever brought him.

He found the trail by skidding onto it from a steep but short slope and managed, by dropping to the ground, to keep from running over the edge of it and into the chasm it bordered at that point.

Brandon saw instantly that this was no place for the confrontation. He ran down the trail, and in a moment it turned away from the cliff edge and into a wide cleft in the rock. Ahead a few yards Brandon found a ledge projecting about ten feet above the trail where some boulders detached from farther up the hillside had lodged. Just the place for rattlesnakes to sun themselves, but also ideal for a human bent on ambush. He threw some rocks up to clack against the boulders, evoked no reptilian response, and scrambled up to the ledge.

The riders coming down the trail would be facing directly into the sun, and its glare on the pale rock surfaces and the deep shadows it cast would, Brandon was confident, conceal him adequately. He searched for a moment, then found a rock about the size and shape of a large sweet potato that fit comfortably in his grasp.

In a few moments he heard the clatter of hoofs on stony ground and eased his head past the edge of the rock that concealed him to peer at where the trail curved into view.

The rider with the rifle came in sight first, still masked. So they were thinking that John B. Parker might yet survive this, and precautions against identification were therefore prudent.

John B. Parker, looking somber but not downcast, rode about ten feet behind the leader. Brandon saw the top of his flat black hat pass his place of concealment almost at eye level. The last man, shotgun laid loosely across the saddle in front of him, rode a few lengths behind Parker.

As he came close enough to the ledge for it to conceal him momentarily from view Brandon tensed. He had only loosely planned what he was going to do, but now he moved as if he had been rehearsing for weeks. When the top of the rider's hat appeared he snaked forward with the speed of a striking rattler, arms and chest over the rim of the ledge. He reached down with his left arm, crooking it about the rider's throat and lifting him from the saddle; his right hand, holding the rock, smashed against the side of the man's head. The rider, who had managed only a choked gasp as Brandon's arm clamped on his windpipe, went limp and fell sprawling to the trail as Brandon released him.

Brandon ran along the ledge a few steps and sprang to the emptied saddle, the horse having continued on its way undisturbed by its rider having been plucked from its back, and he grabbed the shotgun still balanced across the saddle. "Parker! Duck!" he called, and grabbed the gun. Parker promptly flattened himself on his horse's back, sensibly neither hesitating nor asking questions.

The leading kidnapper had already started to respond to the disturbance behind him by turning and bringing his rifle up. Brandon raised the shotgun, aiming high to avoid undue risk to Parker's back, and pulled the left trigger.

The explosion of the gunshot reverberated against the

rock, and dust powdered from the rock face next to the lead rider, mostly at a level above his head. A few pellets must have hit him, for he yelled and clapped both hands to his face, dropping the rifle. Either the noise or some shot got to his horse as well; it screamed and pounded down the trail, its rider cursing and bouncing in the saddle as they vanished from sight.

Brandon ran to John B. Parker, who had straightened up and was looking around him in evident surprise at being alive. "You all right?" Brandon called.

"I would say so," Parker said. "D'you think that fellow will come back at us again?"

"No," Brandon said. "We've got the shotgun and his rifle, and his pal's out of it, so—"

"No, he's not!" Parker shouted. "Quick, Blake!"

Brandon turned and saw the man he had pulled from the saddle scramble to his feet, glare at them, then launch himself over the downhill side of the trail. Brandon ran to the edge and saw him running and stumbling among the boulders, just as he himself had done a short time before. He raised the shotgun to his shoulder, then lowered it. At that distance any shot reaching him would be no more than an irritant; the rifle had enough range, but by the time he got to it the retreating kidnapper would be lost among the trees. He was just as well pleased that the circumstances relieved him from having to decide whether he cared to shoot a running man in the back.

"Trexler's not with you?" Parker said. "I saw that fool Ryan get clubbed and shot, but it's Trexler's duty—"

"He got shot, too," Brandon said. "Or rather, not too, since the kidnapper shot wild at Ryan, missed him, so he only got his head cracked for his efforts to rescue you. Trexler'll be all right, and so will Ryan, if you were wondering."

"Well, that's good," John B. Parker said, ignoring Brandon's irony. "They won't lose by it, you'll see. I'll put in a good word for both of 'em with their employers. You too, of course, Blake. Once Willson learns you've done a favor for John B. Parker he's bound to treat you handsomely."

Brandon picked up the rifle the leading kidnapper had left on the trail and took it and the shotgun to the abandoned horse, which still carried the sack of weapons the bandits had collected. He dropped them in, then mounted the horse. "About ten minutes' ride back to where the others are, I'd say," he called to Parker.

As the horses picked their way back up the trail Brandon considered that Trexler had had the right of it. It would be a bitter thing to have to decide to pay out anything of value for the return of John B. Parker.

Except, the thought came to him, if John B. Parker were the key to a vital deal. . . . In spite of the new demands, Parker was still the only prospect for bringing the railroad into Spargill. He could be negotiated with, but if he were out of the picture, it would take an age for someone new to take over, and the situation could change so drastically that Spargill could be permanently bypassed. Didn't know I was doing it, he thought, but I have pulled Judge Gerrish's chestnuts out of the fire.

"You know," John B. Parker called to him, "we haven't done so badly out of this."

"How come?" Brandon said.

John B. Parker gave a jovial guffaw. "We've got a shotgun, a rifle, and a horse we didn't have when we started out!"

6

"No harm done!" Jake Trexler said. "I'm missing a piece of my ham the size of a thumb, and Mr. Ryan's lying in the hotel with his head stove in—no goddamn *harm?*"

"Not to mention," Judge Gerrish said with asperity, "the assault on and attempted abduction of a figure of national importance in the commercial and financial worlds."

Marshal Tooley looked placidly at them from behind his desk. Jake Trexler had the one other chair in the office, his leg stuck out stiffly in front of him; Brandon and Judge Gerrish stood leaning against the matchboarding of the room's wall. All were now looking at Tooley with a mixture of astonishment and irritation.

"A flesh wound that won't slow you down for more 'n a day or so," he said to Jake Trexler, "and that Ryan with only a headache, and it gettin' better fast, so I hear. And as for John B. Parker, he don't cut any more ice here than anyone else, Wall Street whangdoodle though he be, and what it works out to is that a couple of fellows hoorawed him some, sheddin' none of his blood and breakin' none of his bones, and talkin' big about holdin' him for ransom, likely skunk-drunk. And I don't notice John B. Parker makin' the complaint in person neither."

Parker had in fact made it clear that Trexler, as his employee, and Gerrish, as the man who still hoped to do business with him, would relieve him of the bother of dealing with the law.

Marshal Tooley held up his hand as the three men facing him began to talk quite vehemently, all at once. "Now, gents, I'm not sayin' I'll let it slide. After all, we got a shotgun and a rifle that's about like any other shotgun and rifle, and a horse nobody in town reckernizes, so we got a whole mountain of clues to lead us to these criminals. I will do what I can, but you got to remember I am, like I been for the past two years, day in and day out, marshal of the town and township of Spargill, the municipal limits of which don't extend out to where all this happened by a good couple of miles. I got no jurisdiction."

Brandon had never had a strong expectation that Tooley was one of those who had joined Gren Kenneally in the train robbery and the Mound Farm massacre, though it wouldn't have displeased him to find out that he was. The idea of killing someone, however necessary it was, wasn't pleasant, but it would be less unpleasant with Tooley than with most. But he also was certain at some deep level of awareness that one of the men he sought was in Spargill—it was as if some animal coiled inside him had awakened, lifted its nose and sniffed, and caught the scent of prey. It wasn't much to go on, but it was what he had.

"You're the only law officer around here!" Judge Gerrish said.

"Not countin' Nason, which most don't," Marshal Tooley said. "A deputy bein' a kind of third leg, as much in the way as useful. Nason or not, you bein' a judge, you'll appreciate how my hands is tied. I'm willin' to stretch things some, like chasin' men that pulls a job in Spargill, town or township, but escapes acrost the town line. Them I'll foller till they drop, but there's no evidence anything about this stuff happened in Spargill. Not the crime itself—not the plannin' of it, even. So I can't go scourin' them hills after them fellows—job for the county, if anybody. And since Split Rock's the county seat, when you get you back there, Mr. Trexler, you could dump the whole business on Sheriff Yamilton, which it's his job t' deal with it, not mine."

He threw a glance of dislike at Brandon, who had found himself speculating on how somebody as unprepossessing as Tooley could be cutting such a swath among the more undemanding Spargill wives. The marshal did radiate a kind of power and implacability that could impress some women, he had just decided, and he wondered fleetingly if Tooley had read the topic of his thoughts in his expression. "Since there ain't any owner for that horse you took from those fellows," he said, "I guess it falls to you. You better find something that'll show you have title to it; they don't take kindly here to men with horses they can't prove they own."

"As a bill of sale is out of the question, I'll draw up a valid document, Marshal," Judge Gerrish said. "It'll have a gold seal and everything. Thank you for your time."

Brandon thought they were not quite out of earshot of the marshal's office when Jake Trexler, limping next to him, said savagely, "What an excuse for a marshal! With him in charge I expect crooks have about a free hand in Spargill, Judge."

"As a matter of fact," Judge Gerrish said, "Tooley does a pretty good job; we don't have much crime or disorder, and what we get is usually handled fast and capably. Only thing against him is that he seems to live a little better than his salary allows, but that's standard with town marshals and chiefs of police—skimming a little graft off the saloon keepers, gamblers, and whores is one of the perquisites of office, and it hardly counts as corruption, I suppose. I have to say he's right on the matter of jurisdiction, though he's interpreting it more strictly than most law officers out here do."

As the only crime and disorder Brandon had encountered in Spargill proper had occasioned neither swiftness nor capability from Tooley, he considered the judge's characterization over-kind. He also wondered if the judge considered Tooley's tomcatting worthy of reprobation . . . if, of course, he knew of it at all.

Brandon was not asked to attend the final conference with John B. Parker the next morning, but as it was held in the front room of the *Chronicle* office and he was working on the story of John B. Parker's near-abduction in the composing room, he heard most of the proceedings.

Abner Willson spoke little, seeming to be there mainly to give Judge Gerrish the feeling that someone in the room was on his side. Jack Ryan, his hat perched on a substantial turban of bandage, seemed to have recovered his health, and kept a record on behalf of Parker.

Gerrish did not even try to argue against Parker's demand for a fifty-thousand-dollar increase in the subsidy on grounds of fairness, but he did emphasize the difficulty of getting the town council to agree to a bond issue so much larger than the one agreed on.

"It'll pay off handsomely, once the railroad's in," John B. Parker said. "They ought to be able to see that."

"That may be so," Judge Gerrish said, "but they got used to the first figure, and now they'll dig their heels in."

"They'll be digging their graves with their heels, then," John B. Parker said placidly. "If the line comes here, Spargill's made. If it don't, why, another town's likely to spring up in a while, and the track'll go there, and Spargill withers on the vine."

At a turn in the trail, events took a strange turn when two masked men accosted the travelers. Brandon contemplated this sentence with impatience. It wasn't only the idiot repetition of "turn"—the whole thing seemed lame. The problem was, he couldn't stomach writing himself up as a daring rescuer, but if there wasn't a daring rescue, there wasn't a story.

"Keep in mind," Parker said, "the telegraph line'll come in about the same time as the tracks, and that's something you're getting for free, connection to the whole outside world. Willson here can put out a paper with real news in it.

And with regular trains and telegraphic service, remember, your bank can be run professionally, not just serve as a storehouse for cash and gold that you don't want to trust to the freighters."

Stoically the magnate? financier? executive? submitted to his fate, accompanying his masked captors on a journey which—Get it down any which way, Brandon thought, and Willson can edit it so it doesn't look too foolish.

"That is important, of course," Judge Gerrish said. "But the council's already taken that into account, Parker. We've worked up the figures, and there's no way that the town can pay off more than the seventy-five thousand in bonds, and that's all it can issue."

"Well, now," Parker said, "there's a point to consider. You're paying off the bonds with tax revenues, right? And you've got a figure of, what, ten thousand dollars for each mile of track in the township, as a tax assessment?"

"That's it," Judge Gerrish said.

"All right," Parker said. "I will recommend to the Denver & Transmontane that an assessment of eighteen thousand five hundred per mile be agreed on. You work out the arithmetic on that, and I believe it'll go a long way toward meeting the council's objections."

Brandon squinted thoughtfully at his pencil. Parker's proposal had the sound of reasonableness, but its introduction at this stage in the negotiations, and the calmness with which he laid it out, made Brandon uneasy. He could not count the times an opposing attorney had come up with something in just that same way that later turned out to be an attractive piece of bait concealing a hook. Come to that, he had threaded a few such morsels on hooks himself.

"It helps, but I don't know if it'll turn the trick," Judge Gerrish said.

"Let me know in, say, two weeks if it does," John B. Parker said. "After that, don't bother. The Denver & Transmontane will make Split Rock its terminus, at least for this year."

* * *

"Two weeks, remember," John B. Parker said an hour later, leaning down from his horse. "At the least, clear word how things are going by then, so I'll be able to tell Denver & Transmontane they'd do well to hold off committing themselves to stopping track at Split Rock."

Brandon wondered if Occidental General Manager Parker would be able to swing DT President Parker around to his way of thinking when the time came. A fair chance, he decided. He, Abner Willson, and Judge Gerrish stood next to Parker's party, now mounted and ready to leave the livery stableyard. A day and two nights of rest seemed to have restored Jack Ryan to full health, and indeed he looked readier for the journey than Nelson Vanbrugh, who shifted constantly in the saddle as if in the forlorn hope of at last finding a comfortable position, even though one had never yet appeared.

Brandon looked past them to the stalls and saw the white-marked brown face of the horse he had taken from the kidnapper. He had no special wish to own a horse, but it seemed worthwhile to stable it there until he had decided what to do with it.

"If that marshal ever gets his elbow out of his ear and catches those fellows that grabbed me, I'd admire to know of it," John B. Parker said. "He could ship them up to me, and I could see that they enjoyed a fitting accident. You wouldn't believe what being between two cars when the coupling slips does to a man." Brandon saw Tooley looking at them from about fifty yards down the street, standing impassively on the shaded plankwalk, making sure that the visitors departed safely, or anyhow departed.

Farewells were exchanged, Judge Gerrish's to Parker a model of manufactured cordiality. Nelson Vanbrugh bent to address Abner Willson, nearly toppling from his perch as he did so. "I will get at that—whoops, damn!—maybe next week and freight it on down to you, okay?"

"Thanks," Willson said. "It's . . . mighty good of you."

"A positive pleasure," Vanbrugh said cheerfully.

Brandon walked with Abner Willson back to the *Chroni-*

cle office after the cloud of dust the Parker horses kicked up on Main Street subsided. "What's Vanbrugh doing for you?" he asked.

"Did a sketch of *The Spirit of Spargill* yesterday," Abner Willson said, "and he'll do an engraving of it up in Split Rock, send the plate on down so's I can use it. Real elegant drawing, a lot better than Caldwell's that Julie wanted me to have done up."

"You don't sound all that elevated about it," Brandon said. "I thought you were set on seeing that Miss Caldwell got what she wanted."

"From me," Abner Willson said gloomily. "Not from some blond ox of a matinee idol with a soft hat and a line of gab that'd gag a buzzard! Told her that if time permitted, he'd have admired to do a portrait of her that'd do her justice and make his reputation in the artistic circles of Philadelphia and the world in general. Ain't that awful?"

"I wonder she didn't slap his face," Brandon said. "But he won't get any more chance to buzz around her, Split Rock being a tough trip from here."

"Not after the trains come in," Abner Willson said.

The Mountain Goat was the nearest thing to a dive that Spargill afforded, though in some places Brandon had been—particularly Kampen, over in Arizona—it would have been considered on a level with a tea shop. Brandon had been there for half an hour, and there had been no shootings, stabbings, or fights, and only one or two shouted arguments. It had struck him as the kind of place where interesting trifles of news might be found, or made; and, Willson having no assignments for him, he had decided to try some prospecting for reportable material. So far he had not hit a vein worth mining and was reduced to talking to the bartender.

"Place like this," Brandon said, "imagine it's pretty profitable."

"I stay in business," the bartender, a broad-faced man called Cromie, said. "I own it, along with being bar dick."

"The side stuff, gambling and so, that brings in something, too?" Brandon said. He felt in his side jacket pocket to make sure of the folded sheets of copy paper, in case anything was said that was worth noting.

"Don't get much in the way of gamblers here," Cromie said. "They prefer a town on the railroad, where they can get out fast if they have to. Also, though there's good money here, it don't come in like a freshet, the way it does in mining camps and cow towns, but slow enough so's them that gets it aren't in such a hurry to turn loose of it. Some fellow wants to run a game here, I'll let him, if it's straight, and he'll hand over a percentage of the pots, but that don't amount to any more 'n I get by selling Sazerac cocktails, the which there ain't hardly any call for here." He fixed Brandon with a sharp look and said, "As for any other amusements, the ladies don't work the bars here, there's a few places back off Pike Street where they entertain, and those that want 'em know where to go. In Spargill we pay attention to business and keep things simple—a bar's a bar, a cathouse is a cathouse, and so on. Keep your eye on the grindstone and the money'll follow, as the saying goes."

Brandon blinked. If Cromie was telling the truth—and the near-Presbyterian atmosphere of the Mountain Goat bore him out—the idea of Marshal Tooley augmenting his income by ladling up graft from the profitably tawdry activities of Spargill's saloons didn't hold up.

"Judge Gerrish been in lately?" he asked.

Cromie shook his head. "Not one of our patrons, don't believe he's ever rested his foot on the rail here. Exercises his bump of sociability at the Businessmen's Club, don't rub elbows with the rabble. Which it makes sense, him being a judge. It is hard to hoist a few with a fellow one night and then decide whether to jail or fine him the next day."

"True enough," Brandon said. But that judicial aloofness meant that Gerrish had at least one blind spot about what went on in Spargill. And that apparently he had the wrong explanation for Marshal Tooley's extrasalarial prosperity.

He looked at the glassy-eyed head with massive coiled horns that surveyed the patrons from above the bar. "You shoot that? Named the place for your trophy?"

Cromie shook his head. "Fellow gave me that a month or so ago to settle his bar bill, and I took it because of the name. Called it after some Injun tales about a magic goat that got up to shameful tricks with their women, figurin' it'd give the place a lively kind of tone."

One way and another, Ned Norland's left his mark on the West, Brandon reflected. Blue-eyed señoritas in Santa Fe, a lake and a saloon in Colorado, who knows what else where else, since the old man seems to have fornicated his way across half the continent. There's famous statesmen and philanthropists who won't leave as much behind to be remembered by, he thought, and what's that say about statesmanship and philanthropy?

"Hey." The growled monosyllable came to him on a gust of beer-rich air. He turned and saw Sut Liebwohl, the freighter who had attacked him on his first day in Spargill, standing alongside him. Liebwohl's face was twisted in a grimace that appeared to be ingratiating.

"I shouldn'ta beat you up that time," Liebwohl said.

"You didn't," Brandon said.

"Well, I shouldn'ta tried. Listen, I didn't take it in you was the press, see? Just some nosy bastard jerkin' some pore freighter around about the morphodyke railroad, 's what I thought, and I seen red."

And then, if I'm not mistaken, yellow, brown, and green, Brandon thought, recalling Liebwohl's involuntary decoration of Main Street after the belly punch.

"But I seen it's the press, nothin' personal," Liebwohl said. "I mean, the press, it's gotta go pawin' around garbage heaps, turnin' over rocks to see what comes out, snuffin' through filth, that's what it's s'posed t' do, so I done wrong in goin' for you, and I stands ready to make up for it by drinkin' yer health."

"Thanks," Brandon said. When Liebwohl made no move to attract Cromie's attention, Brandon realized that the amend offered was the drinking of the health, not the purchase of the drink, and he ordered beers for himself and Liebwohl.

"Yer health," Liebwohl said, carrying out his part of the

bargain, and lifted his mug and drank. He set it on the bar and said, "Now, you may think the railroad's got it all its own way."

"Not completely," Brandon said. "There's still—"

"Well, it ain't," Liebwohl said. "There is powerful forps." He swallowed, effectively stifling the next hiccup, and went on. "Forces. Powerful forces that will defend the freighters and keep all them loyal mules and oxen at the work they loves so well. Forces as will make the iron horse crap outta pure fear. Why, already—"

"Sut." Marshal Tooley was standing next to Liebwohl, somehow seeming larger than the freighter who towered over him by a head. "Believe you've taken enough on board for the evening."

"But I was . . ." Liebwohl looked at Tooley and seemed to shrink a size. "Sure, Marshal, I'll be gettin' on back t' the wagons. Glad to talk to you, Blake." He gulped the remainder of his drink, turned and left.

"Thanks, Marshal," Brandon said. "He was talking kind of crazy."

"Then you shouldn'ta bought him that last drink," Tooley said, looking at Brandon with dislike. "Or were you lookin' to start another fight and get wrote up in the paper about it? I seen that piece of crap Willson wrote about that stuff with Parker on the trail, makin' you look like some Fred Fearnot in a Beadle's novel, boy hero of the Far West, enough to make a goat puke."

"Hey, Marshal, I didn't write it," Brandon said. "That stuff about me, I didn't like it any more than you did. Willson laid it on way too thick." Brandon's own account had wound up being stiff and strictly factual, and Willson had used it as a framework for some lurid flights that Brandon had cringed to read. Only the fact that the heroic Calvin Blake would fade into thin air in not too long a time had eased the feeling of bone-deep embarrassment.

"It wasn't anything like that," Brandon went on, determined to underplay the facts as some kind of redress of the balance. "Like you said in your office, it wasn't that big a thing. Likely those fellows would have lost Parker without me—the whole thing was such a bungle, no planning. It couldn't have been planned by anybody but a halfwit. No credit to me in spiking it." That was putting it a bit strong, he thought, but it might ease the marshal's irritation.

It did not seem to do so. Tooley gave Brandon another glower and strode out of the Mountain Goat. Given Tooley's reputation among the matrons of the town, Brandon thought, it ought to be his spiritual home, though he suspected the marshal approached his amours in colder spirit than Ned Norland had done—or, in spite of his age, might well be doing right now. Brandon frowned. Tooley's tomcatting also suggested that he was not, in the time-dishonored tradition of some Western lawmen, imposing on the "soiled dove" community for unpaid-for satisfaction of his urges.

Ben Stoddard shrugged. Brandon had asked him for his reaction to the town's vacillation on the railroad bond issue and its effect on his freight business; Abner Willson had pointed out that freighters and investors in the freight company read the *Chronicle,* too, so might as well have the pleasure of seeing their names and opinions in print. "If the railroad comes in, it'll just about kill our runs to the north, but we'll still be the only way to get goods up from Denver for some time; getting a track down there's a tougher proposition than from Split Rock. So don't count us out either way. This company's got roots in Spargill, Blake. Some of 'em you may not know about."

"We are damned if we do and screwed if we don't," the man in the barber chair said, bent forward as the barber snipped industriously at the back of his head. "It puts us on the horns of a lemon, which I suppose is the two pointy ends of it, that's sour when you bite into them."

This, Brandon knew from the barber's introduction when he had entered, was Charley Pratt, dry-goods merchant and unknowing wearer of his own horns, owing to Marshal Tooley's attentions to Mrs. Pratt. Brandon was the only waiting customer, and leafed through a tattered copy of

Scientific American that he had picked from the "literature" table in preference to the *Police Gazette*s and some well-thumbed publications printed on pink paper. There was a nicely illustrated story on the beginning of construction of the Eads Bridge at St. Louis, which, since he had seen the dedication of the completed bridge two years ago, sent him to the cover to check the date of publication. The issue, it seemed, was rather older than Spargill itself, and he wondered how barbershops managed to acquire only the oldest of magazines for their customers' perusal.

"Spargill purely needs the railroad if it's to grow," Pratt said. "There is everything around here, good land for crops and stock, minerals in the hills, timber. We can build, manufacture, grow just about anything as we want, if the railroad's here to bring us supplies and take out our products. And the bank can be a real bank, not just a storehouse for our cash, once the train's in—you see, Blake," he called, making it clear that Brandon was included in the conversation, which until now he hoped he hadn't been, "we aren't happy sending cash or gold or silver out to banks in Denver or Omaha by freighter, so it accumulates here, which ain't businesslike or in the long run all that safe, so regular trains with express cars and guards, and telegraphic transfers—why, that'd make all the difference."

"Some tar soap 'd make all the difference to your hair," the barber observed, massaging Pratt's scalp with stiffened fingers. "Want some?"

"No," Pratt said. "But be sure you slop some bay rum onto me at the finish. Mrs. Pratt takes to it about like to catnip. It is a crying shame, Blake, that this Parker is gouging us on the bond issue, for if that was out of the way, there's nothing we couldn't do with this country. Every bit of land, every tree, every blade of grass, every rock, we could take and turn it into money, and in only a little time you'd never recognize it. Spargill could become another Omaha, St. Louis even. Where there is wilderness now there'll be an unending vista of civilization, streets thronged with carriages stretching to the horizon, factories rising like castles, choice homesites replacing worthless woodland, chimneys pouring out the incense of prosperity! There it is, but can we beggar ourselves to make it happen? If we raise the money Parker wants, we'll be near broke and in no position to take advantage. I'm torn this way and that, twisting in the winds of change and circumstance. Have to come down on one side or the other pretty soon. I don't require my ears to be clipped, just the hair, thanks."

Brandon fingered the folded paper in his jacket pocket and decided against taking notes. For a howling bore, Pratt had a few interesting things to say, but only worth filing in memory, not taking down. Later a pretty good story might come out of it; he could sense it taking shape in his mind: the saga of progress thwarted or threatened, and at the same time the destruction such progress would bring. That, he supposed, was what journalism did—take boring facts and circumstances and turn them into something people would be avid to read. A lot of the law, as he had seen it in practice, went the other way, desiccating the juicy dramas of crime and family conflict to dusty spiderwebs of litigation.

"It is like being bled same time you're taking in rich broths and powerful tonics," Pratt said mournfully. "Can you get enough down you to keep alive till you get the benefits? Don't be stingy with the bay rum."

Abner Willson's lame joke about sending Brandon to cover a class in meat cookery had had no impact: Browning Societies were enough of a phenomenon in the East for Brandon to be well aware of their existence, if not of their sense. What he had read of Robert Browning's verse struck him as energetic and sometimes breezily melodramatic— good enough, but not worth forming groups to study and discuss. He suspected that the poet's soulful photograph and the novelistic circumstances of his courtship had as much to do with his popularity as did his work.

Whatever the reason, the ladies of Spargill had their own Browning Society, and Brandon was now in the parlor of Mrs. Samuel Hardy, the society's madam chairman, taking down particulars of the week's meeting.

"That is Hardy with a Y, not I E," Mrs. Hardy said, "and

Mrs. Pratt has two Ts. Mr. Willson made a mistake about that once, and the poor soul was mortified, so be sure about it this time. I don't think there's any problem with Mrs. Conklin and Mrs. Parsons."

Mrs. Hardy was a strong-faced, sturdy woman in her forties, and Brandon found it hard to imagine her in clandestine transports with Marshal Tooley, though a certain restlessness in the way she sat, shifting in her chair and lacing and unlacing her fingers, suggested an inherent vigor that was afforded few outlets. Mrs. Pratt, seated with the two other women on a settee to his left, was taller and a few years younger than Mrs. Hardy, but no more of an apparent adulteress; her companions were cut from the same cloth. Recalling the barbershop gossip about the scope of Tooley's conquests, Brandon wondered if Mrs. Parsons and Mrs. Conklin were among them—and if, it suddenly occurred to him, some or all of them knew about some or all of the others.

"You can put it down that we are going to be discussing 'The Last Ride Together' at today's meeting," Mrs. Hardy said. "Do you know it? 'To be together, breathe and ride, so one more day am I deified: who knows but the world may end tonight?'"

"An elevating thought," Brandon said, scribbling. "I'm not familiar with the work, but you can't go wrong with Browning." He speculated on whether she was recalling her last ride with Tooley, probably neither deifying nor edifying.

Mrs. Hardy frowned. "Maybe," she said, "but sometimes it seems as if he's jumped the tracks and gone bumping along the ties. A couple of poems, you wonder if you're crazy or he is, but most of it's grand, of course."

Brandon, contemplating a story that would have rather less interest for the *Chronicle*'s readers than the latest information on shooting cannonballs at the sun, seized the chance to drag in something relevant to Spargill's concerns. "What you said reminds me that the railroad is a pressing concern to all of us. Do you think you and the other ladies of the society could give the *Chronicle* your views on this great question?"

Mrs. Hardy gave three women on the settee a swift look and, after a moment, said, "Of course, the railroad coming to Spargill would be a great thing. But there're a lot of questions about whether it'll be possible, as you know. As it happens, all our husbands are on the town council, and they're making up their minds about the bond issue now. It wouldn't do for us ladies to let on how they're inclined until they're ready for it to be known. You'll understand that, Mr. Blake."

When Brandon concluded that he had enough for the story he had been sent for, including taking particulars of the decorated morocco binding on the society's volume of the Works, he took his leave, declining an invitation to attend the actual meeting on the grounds that other events of almost equal newsworthiness demanded coverage.

Mrs. Hardy saw him to the door. "I have written some short pieces myself—musings on nature, sort of—that I wonder mightn't go in the paper," she said.

"Send them along. Mr. Willson'll be glad to consider them," Brandon said, pretty sure that he was lying outright.

"They might not be . . . I'd be embarrassed to have him see them if they weren't good enough," Mrs. Hardy said. "I thought that maybe before I sent them in I could show them to you and you could tell me . . ."

"Ah . . ."

"If you come here tomorrow afternoon, four or so, I could show them to you," Mrs. Hardy said, looking steadily into Brandon's eyes. "I believe you would be sympathetic with the . . . emotions I express. You may think I might do better to ask Mr. Hardy's opinion, but he, like so many other men in town, is preoccupied with matters of business, and . . ." Her hand gave a forlorn flutter of resignation.

It was clear by this time that the emotions Mrs. Hardy proposed to express, should Brandon visit her, would not be confined to paper, though sheets might well come into the picture. "Ma'am, I have to confess I'm not qualified for the kind of criticism you're looking for," he said firmly. "Much as I am honored by the request."

He was also, he was surprised to find as he walked away

from the house, rather excited by it. Seeing Mrs. Hardy—
and, for that matter, Mrs. Pratt, and probably the other
two—as women who respected their right to have their
needs fulfilled, and who set about fulfilling them with
efficiency if not fastidiousness, evoked in him a sort of
respect, and also an awareness of sexual power that stirred
him to a not unpleasant unease. What they were up to was
wicked and foolish, of course, but . . .

In any case, leaving aside any number of reasons to do
with Cole Brandon, Elise Brandon, Gren Kenneally and his
gang, Abner Willson, and so on, he had no intention of
putting himself on a footing with Marshal Tooley. Isn't the
way it sounded at first—Tooley as Don Juan, he reflected.
Face it, the ladies are using him, and one of 'em just had a
try at seeing if Cal Blake was usable.

He walked on a little further and slowed his pace,
frowning. Yeah, Counselor, but Marshal Tooley isn't the
kind that gets used, is he? A user, that's Tooley, Brandon
mused. There's got to be a way he's using them, too, even
while they're using him, and it's not the obvious way—
that'd be too much an even exchange. There's something
else he's getting that I don't see, and something tells me I'd
best try to find out what it is.

By now, after a fortnight in Spargill, Brandon had developed the habit of a late-morning patrol up Main Street in
search of morsels of local news and, at Abner Willson's
insistence, to remind merchants of the benefits of advertising sales and new merchandise in the *Chronicle*. This
morning provided two surprises.

The first was a cordial greeting from Marshal Tooley,
walking briskly away from the freight office. "Fine day, ain't
it, Blake?" he said. "Sunshine, fresh air, folks all law-
abiding, peaceable, and prospering. Kind of day you
'preciate bein' alive and well, you agree?"

Brandon was interested to see that Tooley did not always
speak in a kind of grating snarl, that his mouth did not at all
times turn down at the corners, and that his forehead was
not perpetually furrowed like that of a careworn bulldog;

there had been up to this point no clear evidence of any of these.

He returned the greeting and went on his way, speculating. Maybe Tooley had picked up at the freight office a package he had been waiting for, containing something that had mellowed him. It would have to be something small, as he had not been carrying a package. The only object of appropriate size that came to Brandon's mind was a locket containing the portrait of a long-lost love, and possibly a lock of her hair, and he dismissed the fancy the instant it intruded into his awareness.

A more likely possibility was that he had just completed another tryst, though this was not an unusual enough occurrence to warrant such a revolution in mood and manner. Brandon forced himself not to speculate just who might have done just what to produce this remarkable effect.

The second surprise was also a matter of reversal of mood. Judge Gerrish, habitually courteous and cordial, returned Brandon's greeting with a kind of grunted snarl that sounded like "Bah!" or "Tchah!" when they encountered not far from the Superior, where Brandon was considering taking lunch. The process of consideration was not a taxing one, as there were no reasonable alternatives for someone who wanted a clean, reasonably well-cooked noon meal.

The judge was standing on the steps of one of Spargill's few brick buildings, which housed, Brandon knew from report, not experience, the Businessmen's Club and, occupying a couple of rooms on the second floor, Gerrish's office.

Brandon stopped and studied the judge's expression of savage gloom. Unlike the marshal, he seemed of the opinion that this was a day without sunshine or any redeeming qualities whatever.

Judge Gerrish looked at him, blinked, and drew a deep breath. "Thanks for not saying 'Anything wrong?' or 'Had bad news?' Saved me from having to kill you on the spot, which I'd have regretted. Yes, there is lots wrong, and bad news, too, and I am going to deal with it in a rational and civilized manner by having a stiff drink and another stiff drink and trying out all the filthy words I know. Care to join me?"

Brandon decided that a look at the relatively inaccessible club premises was worth delaying lunch for, let alone his obligation to see what news the judge was talking of.

The main room looked something like the library of a medium-size metropolitan law firm, though bookshelves occupied only a small area of the dark paneled walls. There were several overstuffed chairs and small tables, and a few card tables. The tenuous resemblance to a law library ended at one long wall of the room, which was taken up with a mahogany bar behind which stood an open cupboard with an array of bottles. The air was bitter with stale cigar smoke, and Brandon could detect the tang of whiskey fumes as well.

Judge Gerrish flung open a window and flapped the dark curtain in front of it vigorously. "The herd or flock or pack or whatever you want to call them just left, as you can deduce," he said. "The best business and financial brains of Spargill, which God help, and He'd better, since if the aforesaid brains were butter they wouldn't grease a skillet enough to fry a hummingbird's egg."

"Some disagreement with the town council, Judge?" Brandon said.

Judge Gerrish laughed bitterly. "Sure," he said. "I'm convinced it'd be better for Spargill to stay alive and not become a desert of dead business and rotting houses, and they don't seem to see it that way. Have a drink, Blake. Have lots of drinks, and maybe you'll be able to think as clearly as the town council does sober." He splashed two glasses nearly full of whiskey and handed one to Brandon.

"They wouldn't approve the bigger bond issue Parker wants?" Brandon asked.

"They would not. I showed them that the higher tax base would increase revenue enough to pay for it in a reasonable time, but they wouldn't go for it. The damned ribbon clerks pushed themselves to go for the seventy-five thousand at the start, but that wore out their nerve, and they're stuck there, no matter how the deal gets sweetened other ways. Drink that and have another, Blake. I likc my company to keep up with me, and I am burning this stuff up like coal oil, I'm that mad."

Brandon accepted a refilling of his glass, sipped, and felt a mixture of interest in what Gerrish was expounding and a kind of impatience with his morose anger. What the judge needed was some gloriously preposterous suggested solution to his problem, as there didn't seem to be a rational one; a good laugh would at least put him in a better frame of mind, and then his keen intelligence could usefully be brought to bear. It was an old Missouri tradition to spin a tall tale with a straight face, and right now would be a good time to do that, if he could find the basic fiber to start with. The whiskey was a good fuel for that kind of work, too, no denying it. Back in St. Louis, Lunsford, Ahrens & Brandon had defended an entrepreneur operating with more imagination than ethics, and Brandon had been impressed by the reckless resourcefulness the man had displayed in many of his enterprises. It seemed to him that something of what he recalled was trying to announce its appropriateness for this situation; and something more nearby and recent seemed to have teamed up with that tenuous memory to demand his attention. The shape of something sublimely ridiculous began to be dimly visible, though not identifiable.

"The thing is," Gerrish said, "the fools won't believe that Spargill's doomed without the railroad, and without the railroad *now*, at that. Any time, like Parker said, a new town could spring up that'd do as well as us for a terminus on the DT, and if that happens, *ave atque vale,* Spargill."

Brandon found he was beginning his third drink, and at the same time the ripely zany notion the judge needed to cheer him up came full-blown into his mind. It was tall-tale time, and he had a regular beanstalk ready to go. "Leapfrog 'em," he said.

Gerrish looked sharply at Brandon's glass, then at his face. "Leapfrog, Blake?"

Brandon gestured with the glass, recalling vaguely that he

had skipped breakfast, and that this was therefore about his sixth ounce of whiskey on an empty stomach, then dismissing the point as unimportant. "Out where we didn't go with Parker, Tired Squaw Lake or what, that's all open land. What you do, you get title from the county or what, plan out a town on it, sell lots, sweet-talk Parker and the DT, and you've got your own fresh new town, railroad coming into it, and Spargill and its myopic town council can bleach in the sun like old buffalo bones."

"You're suggesting I do something so . . . so . . ." Judge Gerrish seemed unable to decide on whether to denounce the lunacy of the plan or the wholesale betrayal it involved.

"Of course not," Brandon said. "Not *do* it, *say* you're going to do it. Or say somebody is. Like the South Sea Bubble or what. Talk a scheme up, folks'll persuade themselves it's true and act according. The council'll fall all over itself issuing those bonds, and the townspeople'll dig into their mattresses to buy them, and it'll all be done so fast it'll make John B. Parker's tusks ache."

Judge Gerrish gave Brandon a sharp look, then pondered for a moment on what he had just said. "It would seem," he said, "both a precarious plan and one that would constitute a total betrayal of the interests of the people of Spargill, and in particular those who have come to trust me."

"That's why they'd never expect if of you, Judge," Brandon said cheerfully, pleased that Gerrish was still dealing with the yarn seriously, or anyhow going along with the jape. "Do the unexpected and you carry the day. Start up Whooping Squaw Lake City and you'll be a rich man in no time—and so will I if you do the right thing by me."

He sat back, waiting for Gerrish's slow realization that he'd been strung along by a masterly piece of improvisational nonsense, and belatedly hoped the judge didn't set so much store by his dignity that he would be offended.

As it turned out, he was not, but played along to the end, assuring Brandon with grave courtesy as he saw him to the door, "You've given me much to think about, Blake. You're an original thinker, I'll say that for you."

81

"Thanks, Judge," Brandon said, pleased. It was nice that Gerrish had turned out to be a good sport, a man who appreciated a good joke as well as good whiskey.

He turned up the street toward the Superior. After the booze on an empty stomach he felt that a substantial lunch would be a good idea before getting at the afternoon's work; just what that was, he found at the moment, was not entirely clear.

7

By the time he finished lunch Brandon had come to see that his attempt to cheer up Judge Gerrish with a Missouri-style tall tale had been feeble. The judge's whiskey had made it seem a lot funnier, the kind of straight-faced preposterousness Petroleum V. Nasby amused his readers with; but without the genial fumes of the spirits to buoy it up, the joke seemed as earthbound as a hot-air balloon with a split seam.

And if the joke failed, what was left was a crude suggestion that the judge embark on a course the stupidity of which neatly matched its treachery. Brandon supposed that the judge was man of the world enough to assume that such an act of crassness had to be caused by one pre-lunch drink too many, but he felt compelled to set matters right and tender Gerrish an apology. He wasn't sure that Calvin Blake would have been as punctilious, but here was one point on which Cole Brandon's standards would have to govern.

He walked briskly down Main, absently noting with an eye that two weeks on the *Chronicle* had trained that a number of freight wagons had arrived, and they were being unloaded at the general store; he would come back later and see if the shipment contained anything he could persuade the storekeeper should be advertised. At the building that housed the Businessmen's Club and the judge's office he found the club premises downstairs empty. On the second floor he knocked on the door, and opened it when he got no reply.

Dust motes glinted in the early-afternoon sun that slanted through the windows facing Main Street and fell in burnished patches on the dark wood surface of the desk. Brandon felt a pang of something that was not quite homesickness—more a sharp recognition at the sight of the shelved bound volumes of law reports and statutes, the array of deed and file boxes, and the inkwell and pen stand with its collection of penholders and nibs, and a neatly folded penwiper next to it. The very smell of the place, with furniture polish and leather predominating, took him back to the chambers of Lunsford, Ahrens & Brandon in St. Louis, a thousand miles and a whole universe away from here.

There was no suggestion of where Gerrish had gone or when he would be back. Brandon determined to make his amends when the chance offered itself and tried to dismiss his lapse from his mind for the moment.

The few assignments Willson had given him for the afternoon were undemanding but tedious, taking up time without providing anything that would be even moderately interesting to write or to read. Brandon, walking up Main Street, was mentally going over his recollection of the contents of *The National Encyclopedia of Business Forms* for something livelier to occupy the *Chronicle*'s columns— the table of time differences among cities, say, showing that when it was noon in New York it was 9:28 in Salt Lake City—when he was accosted by Marshal Tooley.

"Blake," the marshal said heavily.

"Marshal."

Tooley's expression was by no means as jovial as it had been in the morning, but was not as hostile as at his office during the exposition of the kidnapping attempt on John B. Parker. Left to himself, it seemed to say, he would not have created Calvin Blake or set him down in Spargill, but since the Almighty had seen fit to do both, Tooley could live with it.

"Understand you been visiting some of the ladies," Tooley said.

Brandon was puzzled. "On Pike Street? I haven't been—"

"*Respectable* ladies, damn it!" The marshal glared at him. "At Miz Hardy's last week."

"Oh." Brandon thought for a moment. "Yeah, the Browning Society. We ran a piece on it, last issue."

"Never you mind Brownings and what," the marshal said. "What we are talking about is you giving the eye to a married lady and suggesting private get-togethers whereat you could instruct her in writing love poems. Pore woman was 'shamed to bring it up to her husband but confided in me as a officer of the law and a man used to handling depravities of disposition without making a scandal of it."

"Ah," Brandon said. He would have felt safe in wagering a whole Bavarian ducat ($2.27, according to *The National Encyclopedia of Business Forms)* that Mrs. Hardy had inflated and embroidered their brief exchange at her door to pique Tooley's interest by suggesting that there was a rival for her favors. It would be ungallant, tactless, and plain foolish to indicate that it had been she who had made the advance, and that he had reversed away from the proffered berth with full steam up. "There was some discussion of Mrs. Hardy's literary efforts, and I am sorry if she mistook a possibly encouraging comment as something of an improper nature. In any case, the pressure of work forbids me from offering her any counsel or arranging any meetings."

"Best so," the marshal said. "This is as upright a town as you'll find out here, and we set store by proper and respectable conductings. Maybe it's as you say, and there's no harm intended. But write it down on your cuff, whereas you can consult it frequent, that it don't do to mess with married ladies in Spargill. A woman's got only one reputation, and she loses that, she's lost it all, and it's my duty to see that our good ladies keep their reputations clean and unspotted—particular that some outsider don't come in here and smirch and stain 'em."

"I take your point, Marshal," Brandon said. "I will be at pains to avoid the very appearance of impropriety— though, as I assured you, there was never any substance of it. Good day to you."

He went on his way up Main, wondering if Tooley could possibly be ignorant that the reputations of the very matrons of Spargill he expressed such concern for were about as spotless as the Mountain Goat's bar rags, the result of Tooley's energetic endeavors. What was apparent was that Tooley, for whatever reason, wanted Calvin Blake to stay away from his part-time harem. Jealousy might be the motive; then again, it might not.

"Mr. Blake?"

Brandon recognized the man who stopped him, with a deference and courtesy Tooley had not shown, as a regular customer at the barber's. "Hello, how are you . . ."

"Jake Stevens," the man said. "Mr. Blake, there was somethin' in the *Chronicle* some of us hoped you c'd explain."

"I'll try," Brandon said, rapidly reviewing recent news stories and wondering if, after writing them, he retained enough recollection of them to talk on them intelligently, or to pretend to.

"Why is F like a cow's tail?"

"It isn't," Brandon said firmly, wondering if Stevens was drunk or manifesting an idiocy that had not been apparent in the relaxed atmosphere of the barbershop.

"That's what I said," Stevens said earnestly. "Cow's tail is like a I, mostly, or C if she's whippin' it up, or L if it maybe got broke when she was a heifer. But no Fs atall into it as I c'n see, nor any of the fellows at the barbershop. But there she was in the paper amongst the riddles."

"Oh," Brandon said. He remembered that Willson had made up for the brevity of his account of the Browning Society's proceedings by slapping in an inch or so of choice tidbits from the "Conundrums" section of the *Encyclopedia*. At the last minute the answers had been squeezed out by an advertisement for a new shipment of oysters the grocer was anxious to sell quickly, and would not run until the next issue. "I'm afraid I don't know. I'll ask Willson and tell you next time I see you."

"Be grateful, Mr. Blake," Stevens said. "I keep seein' as it might be a cow with a kinder forked tail, or some other ways to make it come out a F, and it sits in my mind like the screwworm, a-itchin' so's I can't stand it."

As he approached the newspaper office Brandon reflected on the awesome responsibility of a free press in bringing enlightenment to the public, and on the obvious and maddening fact that there was no resemblance whatever between a cow's tail and the letter F.

To his surprise, Abner Willson was standing by the press next to a couple of knee-high piles of freshly printed newspapers, what looked like at least a full edition, perhaps more; yet his normal practice was to close the paper late at night and print it early in the morning, distributing it in bundles to the tobacco store, barbershop, and a few other places of sale by around eight.

"Brother Blake, what d'you think of this?" Willson called as Brandon entered the pressroom. He picked a paper from the pile nearest him and handed it to Brandon. "Won't it just knock their eyes out!"

Brandon had to agree that it would.

NEIGHBOR OR RIVAL?

the headline proclaimed, in bigger, blacker letters than Brandon had seen the paper use.

"Fetched out the wood type," Abner Willson said proudly. "Not a chance they'll miss it at twenty paces."

New Town Planned on Wilderness Lake; Growth and Fortune Said to Be Guaranteed by Rail Link—Spargill Spurned

With a mounting sensation he thought might be either consternation or simple nausea, Brandon read Willson's fevered account of the purchase by outside financial interests of the tract surrounding Happy Squaw Lake, of said interests' proposal to sell lots to all comers, of their secret negotiations with the Denver & Transmontane Railroad and Occidental Contract—in pursuit of which, it was noted, Occidental's general manager, John B. Parker, had lately ridden to inspect the site—to bring the tracks into their town once Spargill had refused to meet DT's terms.

"We cannot be unmoved by the spectacle of men of vigor and vision planting a focus of civilization in the wilderness," the story continued, "and, if our hearts be generous, must wish the new venture well. And if it is Spargill's fate to be, not a central sun of civic life and commerce in this area, but a satellite merely, let us accept our pallid reflection of another's radiance as our due for our prudence in refraining from undertaking the hazard that they have dared."

"That last is some scrambled in the syntax," Abner Willson observed as Brandon looked up at him, "but it gets across a pretty good kick in the wind under the guise of faint praise, which is the point of it."

"The point," Brandon said blankly. "The point . . . the point I want some enlightenment on, Willson, is where the hell did this cartload of horseshit come from?"

"Why, Judge Gerrish," Abner Willson said. "Came in here a touch before noon, said he'd just got in some confidential information of immense import to the town, and we'd best trumpet it around expeditiously. Worked with me much of the afternoon composing the story, feeding me facts, suggesting wording. I have to admit that some of the best turns of phrase are his, the man's got the touch. Comes of swaying juries, I expect. I don't know why you say horseshit, Blake—I'll allow that we're pulling out all stops and giving it a lot of vibrato, but the judge feels that if the responsible businessmen of Spargill see the danger that threatens, they'll do what has to be done to avert it. It is kind of like the Ghost of Christmas Yet to Come in that story, if they'll wake up and buy the turkey, Spargill won't be buried in a lonely grave."

"God help us, every one," Brandon muttered, looking with horrified fascination at the typeset materialization of the fantasy he had spun to elevate Judge Gerrish's sagging spirits, and which, it now appeared, had addled the judge's wits entirely.

"*Chronicle*'ll have an evening extra," Abner Willson said, "first in its illustrious history. Have the news out and around in a few hours, then we'll see the balloon go up."

8

When, a little short of sunset, the special edition of the *Chronicle & Advertiser* went on sale, rushed to its outlets by its publisher and reluctantly drafted reporter, the effect was not so much that of a balloon ascension as of a kettle of boiling water poured into an anthill. Within minutes the streets were swarming with men rushing agitatedly until they encountered others, all holding copies of the paper, then frenziedly talking and gesturing, then rushing on to another encounter and another round of talking and waving.

Brandon moved among them, avoiding contact and showing no inclination to stop, thankful that nobody grabbed him and demanded information. He decided against going back to the *Chronicle* office, considering that the crowd was mercurial enough so that it might strike it as a good idea to burn the place out and lynch anyone present.

The crowd eddied confusedly, then began to flow down Main Street, leaving Brandon less and less surrounded. Abner Willson hurried up to him and said, "Come on!"

"Where?"

"Businessmen's Club—the judge's called an emergency

meeting of the town council, and you'd best be there to write it up. I'm on the council, so it's best if I don't do the story, though I'll go over it and make sure it comes out right, and if you miss something I'll fill it in. Any questions?"

The chief question Brandon had was how he had come to be caught up, as he appeared to have been, in some opium-eater's fantasy; but he settled for something perhaps more readily answerable. "Sure," he said sourly. "Why is the letter F like a cow's tail?"

"Comes at the end of beef," Abner Willson said absently. "Come on!"

The eight members of the town council were seated at one side of the long table, facing Judge Gerrish, though frequently turning to eye the crowd that had forced its way in and was occupying much of the rest of the main room of the Businessmen's Club. Marshal Tooley had tried to keep all members of the public out, since council meetings were closed, but had to content himself with restricting admission to the twenty or so most vehement and prominent citizens, and he now stood glowering at the doorway. Nason, the deputy marshal, was outside with the crowd, demonstrating by his presence that even official status was not enough to guarantee admission, so why should the general run of taxpayers complain?

Brandon leaned against a wall to one side of the crowd, taking notes on the folded copy paper, which he held against the paneled wall. He had half expected to see Gerrish sticking straws in his hair or gibbering, but the judge seemed as much in possession of his faculties as ever as he began addressing the council.

"This is a grave day in the history of Spargill," Gerrish told them. "But when have the people of Spargill failed to rise to any occasion, to meet any challenge?"

From what Brandon had heard of the history of Spargill, the only occasion presenting any challenge had been the bond issue for the railroad, which it had clearly failed to rise to or meet, but he supposed that the judge was not looking for a factual answer.

And it came to him—a good deal later, he considered, than it ought to have—just what in fact the judge *was* looking for, and the kind of opportunity he had seen in Brandon's tall tale.

His suspicion was confirmed when Gerrish began going over the details of the revised particulars of the bond issue, the scheme that the council had finally rejected, pitching his voice so that it carried clearly beyond his ostensible audience to the crowd.

"As I reminded you gentlemen last night," he said, "I have John B. Parker's undertaking that the tax assessment base will be eight thousand five hundred dollars per mile more than the original figure, which will assure revenues ample to cover the increased amount of the bond issue, though over a longer period of time. In your wisdom you found that insufficient, and I do not quarrel with your decision—the decision you made in light of the facts as you knew them at the time. But"—he raised the newspaper with its black banner headline, and shook it like a club at the council and at the crowd beyond them—"that situation no longer holds. Those facts are changed beyond recognition. Ruin stares us in the face, gentlemen, ruin in the shape of a scheme hatched by predatory but preeminently practical men, men who can bend John B. Parker to their will and have him bring the railroad to their door."

He shook the paper again until it rattled in his hand. "You have read this story, gentlemen, as have I, with the greatest interest." You should be interested, Brandon muttered subvocally. You wrote the damn thing, practically. "You will see from it, indeed, you need nothing more than common sense to see, that the rejection of the bond issue does not mean today what it meant yesterday. Yesterday an argument could be made that Spargill could do well, as it has done, being served by the industrious freighters"—a group of men in the crowd, among whom Brandon recognized Sut Liebwohl, cheered and clapped—"and pursuing its own interests, in adequate if intermittent and delayed contact with Denver to the south and Omaha and other centers to the north, in the absence of a railroad. But it is now no longer a question of *no* railroad, but of a railroad that bypasses Spargill, a railroad that carries the lifeblood of commerce steadily *past* but never *to* Spargill, till we grow anemic and perish."

The council, still twisting quite often to survey the crowd, seemed to be impressed, or perhaps dismayed, by Gerrish's argument. They appeared considerably relieved when, after repeating the provisions of the bond-issue terms that they had rejected, Gerrish did not urge them to reconsider.

"And that offer, gentlemen, though I recommended you accept it, is not, I will say, a satisfactory one . . ."

The crowd, which, like Brandon, had by now a pretty clear opinion on where the judge was heading—though definitely lacking his knowledge of the bizarre route Gerrish had followed to get to this point in his approach—stirred in surprise.

". . . as it stands," the judge said slowly, after an impressive pause. "Spargill is asked to make a serious commitment, to take a serious risk. Very well, then, so should the railroad, so should John B. Parker, take a risk. Gentlemen of the council, I formally propose that the new bond issue in the amount of one hundred twenty-five thousand dollars, as presented to you yesterday, be approved—with the proviso that if the Denver & Transmontane track is not laid past the Spargill town line by August first, the entire subsidy to the railroad be forfeit—that not one penny of taxpayers' and bondholders' money be paid to the Denver & Transmontane! Spargill's policy is, they don't do the work, they don't get the pay! Are you with me? They don't do the work, they don't get the pay!"

What the council might have been replying to this could not be heard, since the crowd—except for the freighters, who looked sullen but defeated—had taken up Gerrish's repeated slogan and was chanting it enthusiastically: "They *don't* do the *work,* they *don't* get the *pay!*"

Brandon could see a brief debate, conducted almost in dumb show, then eight raised hands, and a nod of acknowledgment from Judge Gerrish, who then raised his hands in a wide V, gradually bringing the crowd to quiet.

"Thank you, gentlemen of the Town Council," he said. "Men of Spargill, I am proud to tell you that your town fathers have had the vision and the courage to bring Spargill into the modern world and have authorized the bond issue, with the forfeiture clause which will protect us and guarantee that we receive what we are spending so much to achieve. Three cheers for the Town Council!"

Brandon, writing a squiggle he hoped he would remember later to read as "unanimously," shook his head in silent admiration for Gerrish. Give that man a tall tale, he thought, and he uses the damn thing to pole-vault out of the swamp and into the clover. Brandon recalled Savvy Sanger, the legendary confidence man who had made himself mayor of the Arizona mining town Brandon had spent some time in a few months back, and decided that, judge though he was, Gerrish could hold his own with Sanger. He caught the judge's eye and gave him an admiring grin.

To his alarm, the judge again raised his arms to still the noisy crowd and pointed at him. "I would be remiss and ungrateful," he called out, "if I did not mention the part played in this historic turn of events by one of Spargill's newer citizens, Mr. Calvin Blake, news reporter for our esteemed journal. Mr. Blake it was whose investigations brought to light the complex machinations that might have resulted in the extinction of Spargill as a living community but for his disclosures."

Brandon was thankful that Judge Gerrish did not call for him to be cheered by the crowd. He could tell that two elements of it would not have joined in. The freighters were glaring at him with frank dislike—fair enough, he thought; as they see it, my meddling's helped get the railroad in and them out. He was a little surprised to see that Marshal Tooley's expression was close to murderous, then realized that even a fleeting and falsely based fame might, in the marshal's view, inflame the passions of the ladies he considered his property and incline them to yearn after Calvin Blake.

The spectators poured out of the meeting room, eager to

spread the news among the larger crowd outside. Brandon leaned against the wall, unwilling to move, and eyed the approaching Judge Gerrish with rancor.

"Almost forgot to acknowledge your part," the judge said. "Good thing you tipped me the wink."

"Thanks," Brandon said bitterly. "Judge, damn it, you know . . . ah, what's the use."

Gerrish glanced around and saw that there was no one within earshot. "The bond business is set, Blake, that's the great thing, and the railroad's coming in, and the threat is averted. If it's ever discovered that there wasn't really a threat—and I don't see anybody digging through records and interviewing financiers to check that out, why, then it won't matter. The railroad'll be in and the money flowing into Spargill's coffers, and nobody'll be interested in ancient history. That yarn of yours wasn't much of a joke, you know, but it was the kernel of a humdinger of a hoax, wasn't it?"

Brandon considered that, while a couple or three morning drinks had been the foundation of this waking nightmare of a day, a couple or three evening drinks might be just the thing to mitigate its impact, and he made his way to the Mountain Goat. By sitting at a table in a shadowed corner of the room, hunched over his glass, he managed to avoid, if not recognition, at least the effusive attention of the bar's patrons.

"Newspapermen, a big story like that, it takes it out of 'em," he heard a customer say. "All that poking and prying, and his life not worth a moment's purchase if them as he's investigating find out beforetimes. It's like a man that's run twenty miles from a Injun war party. He's tuckered out, and it don't do to pester him with handshaking and offering of drinks."

"That Blake is somethin'," another man said. "You see him walkin' up and down and about, takin' notes of funerals and ladies' socials and persuadin' merchants to advertise, and you put him down as pretty much of a poodle-dog kind of a man, and all the while he's up to somethin' deep and consequenceful like this. Goes to show you cain't ever tell what a feller's like just by lookin' at him."

"If that's so, *you're* one might lucky man," one of his companions said, and, to Brandon's relief, the conversation turned away from the exploits of Calvin Blake to an exchange of more or less amiable acrimonies. The comment about his reporter persona masking a deeper purpose reminded him that it was, in another way, true, and he considered what progress he had made in finding the Kenneally gang member he had come to Spargill to encounter. None so far, evidently; but he was prepared to wait.

He left the barroom after half an hour and made for his boardinghouse. Main Street was still thronged with Spargillers exchanging pretty nearly identical views on what had happened at the council meeting, and he turned into a side street to avoid admiring recognition. As he picked his way along the lightless street he heard steps—those of two men, it sounded like, behind him—and he grinned. His route, he realized, was also the way to Pike Street, where the light ladies plied their trade discreetly, and the men were likely bound that way.

It was only when the footsteps suddenly increased their pace and he sensed the displaced air that indicated a rapidly moving body far too close to him that Brandon realized his mistake, and he started to turn to face his followers.

He managed to complete half the turn before something hard and heavy took him in the side of the head, and the evening dimness turned to absolute dark.

A ferocious headache dragged him back to unwilling consciousness, and his first thought was that he had somehow drunk himself into the grandmother of all hangovers, including the standard axe buried in his skull and the stone in the pit of the stomach. The curious feeling of something like a rag stuffed in his mouth, a deadening constriction about his wrists, and the constant severe tremor that jolted his body were alarming novelties. He opened his eyes and saw that on a few points at least his troubles were not caused by a hangover. Above him the feeble light of a coal-oil lantern showed the quivering hoop-supported canvas roof of a wagon, and his eye, rolling downward, picked up the edge of a wad of cloth tied to cover his mouth.

Memory seeped back, reminding him that the headache, and presumably the nausea, were the predictable result of the blow on the head he had received in the side street. He flexed his hands and verified that they were in fact lashed together.

The lantern's light also revealed Sut Liebwohl seated on a crate and holding a shotgun pointed at his head.

9

In the dim light of the lantern the wagon seemed room-high, swaying like a ship as it jolted along at a bone-shaking clip. Brandon could hear the clatter of the mules' hoofs on what sounded like scattered rock, the creak and jingle of their harness, the almost constant snap of the driver's whip, and the bawled obscenities with which he encouraged them to their best speed.

Crates were piled almost to the roof, and Brandon saw that Sut Liebwohl was in effect nested in a space among them, crouched and cramped, but for all that holding the shotgun steadily on Brandon. It was not sawed off, as the one the kidnappers had brandished had been, but at that range it didn't matter. Brandon's single-shot .30, uselessly tucked into his vest pocket unless Liebwohl had relieved him of it, would have been an equal deterrent to hasty action.

"Woke up, have you, Blake?" Liebwohl said in a shrill whisper. "Might's well have saved yerself the trouble, fer I'll only have t' douse yer lights ag'in 'fore as I frees you up and arranges you as you'd best be found if the search parties ever stumble on you."

Brandon rolled his eyes, grunted, and drummed his heels on the wagon bed, suggesting, he hoped, an inquiry about just what was going on and why.

"Goddamn snooper," Liebwohl said in the same quietly venomous tones. "I should have stopped yer clock for you that first time 'stead of lettin' you go." Only thing you let go was your lunch, Brandon thought, but the gag kept him from objecting to Liebwohl's distortion of history; even without it, the shotgun would have discouraged forceful disagreement. "Damn town was gonna drop the whole railroad business, go on givin' the freighters the business, till as you come up with that stuff about that other town, which I think there's somethin' fishy about it anyhow, as nobody never heard nothin' of it afore it was in print."

Brandon wished that the town council had possessed Liebwohl's skepticism, then thought that a town whose leaders could be outthought by someone like Liebwohl was in bad trouble.

"No more of that," Liebwohl said with satisfaction. "Couple minutes, we taps you square on the bump o' curios'ty, unwraps you for display, and tips you over inter No Chance Gorge. You c'n see what stories there is to scare up in Hell, if there's anything to print 'em on that won't burn up."

Brandon raised his eyebrows to their fullest stretch, reawakening the headache he had forgotten in the shock of comprehending his situation and probable future. He hoped by this to convey the idea that the harm had been done, so what would retaliation accomplish?

"Maybe the railroad'll come, and maybe it won't," Sut Liebwohl said. "There's still a couple hands t' be played, though you won't be sittin' in on 'em, Blake, snoopin' 'round and turnin' up what's meant t' be unturned."

Though what Liebwohl was saying was all too clear, Brandon had to strain a little to catch his actual words, still harshly whispered and sometimes blurred by the noise of the wagon and its mule team. He cursed himself for not earlier putting together the facts that Liebwohl was whispering and that he himself was gagged and realizing that the freighter driving the wagon was not part of this abduction and projected murder. There was some hope, then, if he could attract the driver's attention . . . which amounted, he bitterly concluded, to no hope. If he kicked hard on the floor, that might do it, but Liebwohl would brain or shoot him at the first move to do that.

Brandon's body was pressed against the latched tailgate as the wagon tilted upward and the pitching motion increased. "Climbin' the trail t' the gorge, not long now." Liebwohl chuckled. "Johnny Hedges gets a turn o' speed outer a mule team you wouldn't credit. Count on Johnny t' git this rig inter Denver in record time, and when he does, maybe them fat merchants in Spargill'll see whatas they owes to the freighters. What they needs delivered when they needs it, and at a fair price, and mules don't set no forest fires with sparks outer their stacks."

Another thought occurred to Brandon that he saw no prospect of surviving long enough to investigate: He was certain two men had rushed him in the dark street, and if the driver wasn't one of them, who was and where was he?

The wagon leveled off, and its swaying increased as it picked up speed; Brandon could hear the driver condemning his animals to lurid fates and treating them to a fusillade of whip cracks. He both heard and felt the wheels skid as the wagon made a sharp left turn and heeled drastically to the right. "Dead Man's Curve, and five minutes ahead of time," Liebwohl said, fishing a watch out of his pocket and consulting it. "Johnny Hedges is doin' hisself proud this night; likely he'll do better when he's a hundredweight and a half lighter, which that happens whenas we gits to the Devil's Hairpin in hardly any time atall."

Without perceptible slackening of speed the wagon seemed almost to revolve, like a locomotive on a roundhouse turntable, and tilted further than at any time during the trip. Liebwohl started to rise from his niche, and Brandon was sickly certain that here was the Devil's Hairpin and his unwilling descent into No Chance Gorge. He flexed his legs, ready to try a kick at Liebwohl that at the worst would get him killed a few seconds sooner.

The wagon failed to right itself and continued to tilt. The crates piled behind Liebwohl shifted and leaned outward over him.

"She's a-goin' over, Sut!" the driver called. "I'm cuttin' the mules loose and jumpin'—save yerself!"

Two crates slid together, pinching Liebwohl's foot firmly between them. He shot a horrified look at Brandon, still clutching the gun, and tried to wrench loose.

Brandon arched his body like a hooked fish and did a back flip over the tailboard. He landed partly on a jagged slab of rock, partly on empty air, and realized he was half over the edge of a precipice. He twisted and rolled frantically, seeing at the corner of his vision the white bulk of the wagon almost completely on its side before it vanished as if through a stage trapdoor, trailing a long, diminishing yell of rage and fear. A horrifyingly long time later, and surprisingly faintly, there came the sound of something hard and heavy destroying itself on jagged rocks.

Breathing heavily, almost choking on the gag, Brandon scrabbled his way to his feet and stood, breathing deeply as best he could through his nose.

Ahead of him in the dimness a point of yellow bloomed, and then a larger glow as the struck match illuminated the lantern the driver held. Brandon could see him now, and the shadowy forms of the mule team behind him, long straps of leather trailing on the rocky ground.

"Jesus, Sut, so you got out. You give a almighty yell, though, but no wonder. How . . ."

The driver stopped speaking and held the lantern higher as he approached Brandon. "You ain't Sut." Brandon nodded. The driver looked at the gag and said, "*And* you didn't do no yellin'. What's goin' on?"

Brandon rotated his head wildly and twisted half around, moving his bound hands as vigorously as he could. "Oh, yah," the driver said. He slipped the gag from around Brandon's mouth and cut the cords around his wrists.

"Thanks," Brandon said. "Sut went over with the wagon. He was set to dump me into that gorge, which is why the gag

101

and so. I expect you didn't know anything about that, Hedges."

"Fer certain, no," Hedges said. "Sut ast me fer a lift down t' Denver, and I took him on, though I could have done without the extry weight, seein' 's I was tryin' to make record time. Didn't tell me he was bringin' along another feller, though, the which if I'd knowed I had aboard, I'd likely have took that last curve a hair slower, and we'd still be haulin' freight towards Denver."

He looked toward the sharp edge of rock over which the wagon and its cargo, and its freeloading passenger, had vanished. "I ain't got the heart to go back t' Spargill," he said. "Told everybody in earshot as I'd get the goods to Denver 'bout as fast as a train could, if there was one, and they'd be jist as well off with the freighters and the mules as they would with the trains, and no bond issues t' worry about. But thisyer ain't no advertisement for that proposition, so it ain't. I don't see that I got anything left t' say to anyone in Spargill now, particularly as the freight company don't pervide cargo insurance. You're that newspaper feller, ain't you?"

Brandon said that he was, and Hedges nodded. "Sut was in an almighty taking ag'inst you after that meetin'," he said. "Talkin' with this one and that one, and alla them workin' theirselfs up to how as it was your fault that the railroad was gonna come back. I think the marshal tried to talk some sense into him, fer I saw them two a-talkin' earnest and serious together one time, but I guess he kept his mad. I don't see that myself; if somethin's happenin' and it's your trade to find it and tell it, I don't see there's any else you c'n do. Findin' out and not tellin', that'd be as bad as just plain makin' stuff up and printin' it, wouldn't you say?"

"Every bit as bad," Brandon said. He looked past Hedges at the mules, who stood stolidly looking into the night. "Where'll you go from here?"

Hedges sighed. "The mules'll make good time to Denver, not pullin' the wagon, and I'll sell 'em there as a team or throw 'em in with my services to another freighter that's bound in about any direction but up this way."

He looked again at the edge of the precipice. "Or maybe it's time I went into another line of work entirely. Six mules, I could get into farmin' pretty easy, and farmers don't as a rule have to worry about goin' over cliffs and bein' smashed to stew meat."

10

The sky was paling in the east as Brandon turned onto Aspen Street and let himself into Mrs. Deckle's boarding-house. He could have used even the dim pre-dawn light to advantage a couple of hours ago when what had seemed like the fork in the road that would lead to Spargill revealed itself when embarked on as a dry riverbed leading to what was, during the rains, a precipitous waterfall. He was thankful that he had managed to retrace his steps to the main wagon road, more thankful that he was finally back in Spargill and less than a minute from bed.

He was also, it turned out, less then two and a half hours from Mrs. Deckle's clarion summons to breakfast, which dragged him from a profound sleep, into which he dropped again gratefully after persuading the landlady that he would not perish if he forwent the oatmeal, steak, eggs, grits, pancakes, and muffins that she considered the necessary foundation for a day's work.

Brandon slept till noon; then he woke, feeling more or less normal, though there was a distinct lump on the side of his head where Liebwohl—or his companion, and who would

104

that have been?—had hit him with what the police reports called a "blunt instrument," a term which had always prompted Brandon to visualize a heavy flute. What had hit him had at least one sharp edge or corner, since the skin over the bump was split for an inch or so and had bled down his face. He sponged the dried blood away with the water from the washstand pitcher and decided to shave himself today rather than giving the barber cause for questions and comments about his injury.

A little later, walking down Main Street, he considered what he should do about what had happened to him and was still unsure when he entered the Businessmen's Club building and climbed to Judge Gerrish's office. This time the judge was in, and he listened with interest to Brandon's account of his adventures.

"Thing is," Brandon concluded, "I don't see that there's much use in telling Tooley about this. He doesn't like me much, and I don't get the idea that he stirs himself to investigate anything—he just keeps walking around, looking dangerous, which I suppose gives people the idea that it'd be bad to start something, and that's as good a way of keeping the peace as any."

"But not much good when it gets breached," Judge Gerrish said. "What he might well do, mainly since Sut Liebwohl was better known around here than you are, is raise all sorts of questions about your story, for which there's no physical evidence except a man dead in a wrecked freight wagon, and only you to say how he got that way. I've seen men tried and condemned to hang on less grounds, including one case in which the victim turned up alive after the murder conviction."

"A relief for the condemned man," Brandon said.

"His family was to some extent grateful for the posthumous vindication," Judge Gerrish said. "As for the loss of the cargo, I can't see that you have any real responsibility to pass the news along. The Denver office that was to have received the shipment will notify Stoddard in due course, and there's no kindness in hurrying bad news when there's nothing to be done about it." He consulted his watch and said, "As it's now past noon, I suggest a drink to sluice away the dust of the day. We still have some matters to discuss."

"Discussion is fine, Judge," Brandon said, "but I will pass on the drinks, as I haven't yet lunched. Yesterday when I did that the upshot was something I'll always remember and wish I didn't."

"It's true that the elevation of your spirits was probably responsible for the broadly original tenor of your thinking," the judge said amiably, "but the upshot, as you call it, has on the whole been beneficial. Spargill has at last decided to act responsibly to see to its future. The bonds are even now being prepared, with Mr. Willson promising his most elegant typefaces and stock engravings of mountains and locomotives suitably juxtaposed for their embellishment. Word has been sent by fast messenger to John B. Parker in Split Rock, and I would suppose that even now the track crews are beginning their strenuous but useful work." Judge Gerrish squinted thoughtfully at Brandon. "And I myself am spared from even the contemplation of a course that, aside from being highly illegal and unethical, would probably have misfired and landed me in perpetual disgrace and, for a shorter but sufficient time, in jail as well."

Having seen the judge flimflam the entire town into approving the bond issue, Brandon was not as surprised at this as he would have been twenty-four hours ago, and wondered mainly what it was that he had found too outrageous to want to get involved in.

"Because of our isolated situation here," the judge said, "our banking practices are idiosyncratic. Cash and precious metals enter and leave Spargill only at some risk, as the fate of the wagon you rode in last night emphasizes, and we have tended to keep it here, especially as currency is much in demand for our very lively commercial life. So we have in the bank vaults quite a lot of bills, coins, and bar gold and silver. As John B. Parker pointed out, once we're linked to the rest of the world by fast trains and the telegraph, we can bank as others do, with documents of transfer and so on, but for now we're sitting on a substantial hoard, much like the dragons in old legends."

Brandon considered this a moment and said, "Enough, in fact, to give Parker the subsidy he wants for the railroad."

Judge Gerrish nodded. "Just so. As a trustee of the bank, I could have in effect looted it and pressed the proceeds on John B. Parker, assuring that the railroad would enter Spargill and assure its future."

"It would also pretty certainly have carried you off to prison not long after it got here," Brandon said.

"Of course," Judge Gerrish said. "The bond issue's the way to do it, however it happened to have come about. But if the bonds hadn't been possible, it would have been a temptation. This country out here, it's got to grow, and railroads are the arteries that bring the blood that feeds growth. Everything worthwhile comes from civilization, and that's a word that means 'making cities,' Blake—settlements growing to villages to towns to cities, like seeds that sprout into crops and flowers. Letting a town like Spargill wither, that'd be like cutting down a plant before it had grown to what it was supposed to be. Not worth breaking the law for, of course, certainly not worth going to jail for . . . but I'd have given the idea house room for a while before evicting it, all the same. So even if you didn't intend it, Blake, you've done me a service and made a real contribution to Spargill."

Brandon looked at the judge with curiosity. Growing up in St. Louis, he had thought of cities as the norm, the way people naturally lived, places that had somehow always been there. But when you came to look at it, a hundred years ago St. Louis had been considerably less than Spargill was right now, and turning a settlement into a city was by no means an easy and inevitable process. The passion for civilizing a wilderness was not one he shared, but he appreciated its force in the judge. And it somehow had a grander feel to it than Charley Pratt's frank hymn to greed in the barbershop. As for himself, he was a creature of the wilderness now, a tracker and hunter and, when the tracking was successful, a killer; and forest, settlement, and city were important to him only as hunting grounds.

Spargill was, in fact, a pleasant place to live in, even for someone not concerned with pleasantness; and however irrelevant it was to his purposes, it was in some way gratifying to have had what could be a deciding hand in the development of the town. And it was undeniable that the work for the *Chronicle* had its interest. A man could . . .

He slid out of his chair and rose. "Thanks for the talk, Judge. I'd best be getting on to the office to see what Willson wants of me this afternoon. He'll be wondering where I was this morning."

"I expect he'll be more concerned with where you are tomorrow," Judge Gerrish said. "Now that they're starting to lay track to Spargill, that's where the real news is, and Willson's bound to send you up there to do a piece, maybe a whole issue."

"Four, five stories anyways," Abner Willson said glumly. "Hardy laborers at the railhead. How same unbutton and relax come nighttime—you make it clear what kind of time they're having, but put it so's the ladies can claim they don't understand what's being written of—descriptions of the mighty engines waiting to pull their loads on to Spargill, not that narrow-gauge locos are all that mighty. Discomfiture of the proud Split Rockers or Rockians or whatever the hell they are."

Brandon wondered at the publisher's apathetic manner, which had not altered much at the account of his reporter's abduction and near-death; he had not even seemed to regret that what could have been a pulse-pounding narrative calling for wood-type headlines could not prudently be printed.

"That Ryan fellow can probably steer you to what you need," Abner Willson said. "And you'll have to look up . . . Vanbrugh." The artist's name might have been a large and bitter pill, to judge by Willson's expression. "He'll provide you with some engravings of track laying, scenery, and other

such, God rot his fingers and choke him with that fool hat."
He stared savagely at the floor.

"Oh," Brandon said. "What'd he send her?"

"These." Willson handed over a sheaf of stiff, thick sheets
of paper. "Sent 'em down by freighter as a 'memento of a
delightful visit,' the damned affected popinjay! Julie set
such store by 'em she had to fetch 'em to show me, would
you believe such heartlessness? Bastardly Vanbrugh sent me
a note by the same freight, said he'd engraved a few plates of
typical scenes of railroad work and routes and I was
welcome to use 'em in the *Chronicle & Advertiser*. Wrote the
name out in full in the note, as if he was mocking it
somehow. Just like him. Of course, now he's offered, I'll
have to use the damn engravings, for they'll dress up the
paper something wonderful, even if they're as stiff and dull
as I expect they are."

Brandon was looking at the papers Abner Willson had
handed him. They were a series of ink sketches, and
Brandon thought it unlikely that the hand that had produced them would impart dullness even to the side view of a
standing steam engine. "A woman who gets a gift from a
man she's fond of," he observed, "will keep tight hold of it,
stick it in an album or under her pillow or in a bureau
drawer. If Miss Caldwell showed these to you, left them with
you, all it means is that she thought they were good and that
you'd appreciate them, having the kind of taste she admires."

Abner Willson straightened from his morose, drooping
stance as if someone had just watered him, sending needed
moisture surging into his stem and leaves. "You think so?"
he said happily. "Damn! I think you're right. She does kind
of value my opinion on writing and art stuff, asks me about
that a lot. And you know, those aren't bad after all. If
Vanbrugh engraves as well as he sketches, I expect it'll be a
feather in the *Chronicle & Advertiser*'s cap."

The sketches were good. They were portraits—some
heads, some full-length, some with a suggestion of
background—done with a sure, energetic line, and bizarrely

amusing in that almost every subject, though recognizable, had somehow taken on the aspect of an animal. The eyes of Julie Caldwell, with the boxy, stacked shape of the sawmill behind her, had been given a slight slant, and her high cheekbones had been emphasized just enough to suggest an immensely appealing cat. Abner Willson stood thoughtfully on one leg, looking downward at a newspaper-reading frog, making Brandon see that in spite of his coarse black hair, the bird he resembled was far more the stork than the crow. A street scene held a wandering pig at the far end, even at a distance clearly Tooley. Judge Gerrish's image had the dogged strength and latent menace of a badger; Jack Ryan emerged as sharp-eyed, sharp-nosed, sharp-eared—foxy; John B. Parker not as the obvious elephant, killer or circus attraction, but a snarling, dangerous-looking creature that Brandon was able after some effort of recall to identify as a wolverine. One drawing puzzled him, a man in a suit and hat, standing loosely but alertly, but with a face that somehow eluded notice. All the features were there, but they were hard to fit together in a memorizable total. It seemed to be Vanbrugh's only failure.

"Don't make much out of this one," he said, showing it to Abner Willson.

Willson looked at it closely and then at Brandon. "One of his best, I'd say. That's you to the life, Blake."

Even though he had risen late, Brandon was tired enough after his ordeal of the night before to want to turn in shortly after dinner, especially as he would want to get an early start in the morning for the long ride to Split Rock.

As he walked toward Mrs. Deckle's the light was about as dim as it had been on his approach at the beginning of the day, only now it was getting dimmer, not brighter. Ahead of him he saw a bulky figure, and he grinned as he realized how accurately Vanbrugh's pen had rendered that disordered massiveness. "Marshal," he called.

Tooley stopped dead and spun around. "Who—*Blake*? What're you doing here?"

"On my way home, Marshal," Brandon said. "Ma Deckle's is just down the way, corner of Aspen." Even in the dimness he could see the glare of intense dislike, even, perhaps, consternation, that the marshal threw at him, and refrained from returning Tooley's question. Natural that the man would be embarrassed to be encountered as he made his way from, or perhaps to, one of his habitual rendezvous, particularly by one whose profession it was to gather and spread about any items of interest.

It would do no good, he decided, to show any awareness of the situation by somehow indicating that whatever the marshal was up to, Calvin Blake had no intention of taking any notice of it, and he contented himself with saying, "'Night. I'll be getting on back; had a tiring day."

The irritated grunt the marshal gave in reply brought Vanbrugh's drawing to mind once again.

Brandon did not fall asleep as rapidly as he had expected. The easeful darkness was held off by a flickering vision of Tooley embracing a woman, or perhaps several women, faceless but somehow known to Brandon as the ladies of the Browning Society. It was a repulsive image, but disturbingly compelling. At the very last the man seemed to be someone slimmer than Tooley, whose face he either could not see or could not recognize, and the woman had the look of someone he should recognize but did not. She had a squarish alert face, not conventionally pretty but powerfully attractive. The image vanished like a pinched-out candle, and as he slid into sleep the name to fit the face came to him: Jess Marvell.

The sun struck gold fire from the aspens that glowed among the evergreens on the hilltop to Brandon's left, but shadow and some of the chill of night lingered on the riverside path he traveled. The track was fairly wide, and the loose surface of crushed stone and hardened dirt was grooved by the wheels of the last freight wagons to pass through, and embellished at intervals by the droppings of the mules that hauled them. It seemed to Brandon that if the roadway was this good all the way to Split Rock, there would be no trouble getting the track laid within the time limit Spargill had set.

The DT's passengers would certainly be treated to some spectacular views. As his horse plodded around a bend Brandon saw, across the river, swift but shallow, shimmering over a pebbly bottom, a stand of aspens, yellow leaves trembling in a breeze he could not feel, above them a steep slope covered with red and purple flowers, then reddish-brown cliffs heavily striped with lighter and darker horizontal layers; and he tilted his head back to see, higher still, a blunted peak covered with dark evergreens against a cloudless expanse of vivid blue.

If he kept his eyes away from the obviously traveled roadway, Brandon could believe that he was here thirty years or so ago, in Ned Norland's Eden, or a hundred, or a thousand.

But in five weeks or so that would be finished. Steel rails would catch the sun in a way that water, leaves, blossoms, and rocks did not; smoke-spewing machines would haul clacking cars through these hills, and the bird calls he only now realized he had been hearing would be overborne by new sounds.

From Gerrish's point of view, of course, that was what had to happen, and it was all for the best. From Ned Norland's it was simply a matter of paradise turned to hell. Brandon found that he had no strong opinion about it. Advancing civilization or maintained wilderness could both harbor Gren Kenneally and his gang—three fewer of them than there had been at the beginning of the hunt—so either would do for Cole Brandon's purposes.

He wondered if Ned Norland had trapped in this river. He remembered the old mountain man's account of the bone-chilling ordeal of choosing and setting the trap in water where the beaver would eventually come, sometimes smearing it with a little of the scent they exuded as a sexual lure. And when the trap closed the panicked beaver would dive, be held under, and drown. Brandon realized that without his planning it, that was what had happened over in

Arizona—the man he had sought had gone after the potent lure of the rumor of gold and had, in a way, drowned in his own horror at being trapped underground. If Brandon could ever be that sure of where some of the rest of them could be found, he might try something along those lines. . . .

The sun was almost overhead now, reaching down to him and warming him. He recalled last night's pre-sleep vision and stirred uneasily in the saddle. He had not dreamed, or anyhow had not recalled any dreams, and he felt somehow that that was a good thing. He admired Jess Marvell's enterprise and good sense; he had found a few nuggets of helpful information in the reports that she and Rush Dailey had managed to get to him; but he strongly wished not to think about her more clearly, more personally than that. The last time he had seen her, in Kansas, more than a year ago, it was at a distance. He could have walked the block or so to the lunch wagon she and Rush Dailey were manning, but he had decided not to, and he took the coach out of town without that final farewell. Their earlier parting an hour or so before had left him disturbed; he knew she could easily divert him from his mission and lead to any number of sorts of disaster. Since then he had been attracted to a couple of women, not particularly urgently, but enough to show that the potential was still there, yet had not experienced that surge of sure desire that Jess Marvell had aroused. He wasn't sure why; she was in a lot of ways ordinary, except that she was supremely . . . supremely Jess. That was as clearly a he could put it. He did not think loyalty to his murdered wife came into it; that was what kept him on the track of her killers, but feeling for her didn't seem to touch the rest of his life anymore. He wondered if Elise had been supremely *Elise* in that same way.

Now that the train and telegraph would link Spargill to the civilized, bustling world Judge Gerrish doted on, it would be an easier matter to be in touch with Jess Marvell and Rush Dailey—for the expeditious receipt of their reports, Brandon assured himself. He should probably send word to them, care of the Bright Kentucky Hotel in Inskip, Kansas, their last fixed address. Rush Dailey, chance-encountered in Arizona, had been full of the wonders of Jess Marvell's new scheme, a series of restaurants planned for the quick but luxurious feeding of train passengers during the brief scheduled stops. Dailey had told him that, improbably, Jess Marvell had got some backing from the U.P. management in Chicago and was starting up an experimental restaurant in Inskip.

In the early afternoon he found that the roadway to Split Rock was indeed not as hospitable as it had started out. The cart track, which had turned away from the river and climbed to a rocky plateau, seemed to end at a cliff, but on examination proved to take a right-angle turn down its face at a grade that must have placed a strain on the brakes going down and on the hearts of the mules going up. He had not seen Dead Man's Curve or the Devil's Hairpin in daylight, but he suspected that this descent was as alarming as either.

The gorge seemed about a hundred fifty feet deep, and perhaps four hundred across. He looked down on a silver thread of river fringed by pines, immensely tall yet with their tops far below him. As he watched one quivered, leaned, and fell across the river, the sound if its impact coming after an instant's delay. He looked along the river and saw a party of men busily stripping branches and bark from other felled trees lying like piled straws along a stump-strewn clearing.

Brandon set his horse to picking its way down the cliffside path and, after what seemed like nearly a mile of switchbacks and appallingly steep grades, was among the working party.

"You ought to stay here and write this up," the engineer in charge, a cheerful, burly man, said after Brandon had introduced Calvin Blake of the *Chronicle*. "We got the word yesterday that it was ho! for Spargill, and trains to roll in five weeks, so we got at this right away. You wouldn't credit how fast this trestle will go up, Blake, but once you know how, it's just a matter of getting the right kind of timbers and lashing 'em right, and there you are. Looks like a heap of jackstraws when it's done, but it'll take track and trains and bear 'em safe across the void."

Brandon recalled a stretch of track on the way to California, at which a curve in the line had revealed that the train was about to cross just such a trestle, which, seen at the distance of a quarter-mile, looked more like a dense spiderweb than something so substantial as jackstraws. The woman passenger in the window seat had a better view than he, and at first sight of the trestle she set up a low, whining moan, which increased to a sobbing shriek as the train clattered onto the bridge and, with a revolting swaying motion, across, and subsided into snuffles only after they were safely on the other side. Brandon appreciated keenly how she felt but had become accustomed to safe passage across these flimsy-looking feats of engineering.

Three hours after climbing the far side of the gorge and resuming his journey, Brandon heard a rhythmic medley of metallic impacts and an ordered series of shouts. He came from a pine grove into the open and saw a seething swarm of men, those in advance leveling the surface with picks while others with wheelbarrows of crushed stone and gravel darted in to dump their loads where more fill was needed; behind them pairs of men carrying heavy, squared lengths of timber rushed to lay them at even intervals along the roadbed; then teams of men carried gleaming lengths of rail, set them down, and rushed away for the next load. At the outside of each rail pairs of men, one crouched and inserting spikes, one standing and driving them in with a massive hammer, performed their automaton's ballet, then moved on and repeated it, while a man with a doubly grooved measuring instrument moved ahead of them, laying it on the tracks to keep the gauge accurate. As Brandon watched, the track seemed to move toward him like a slow but inexorable snake.

He rode beyond the frenetically working track layers to where a locomotive, smaller than those he was used to, stood with a wisp of steam coming from its diamond-shaped stack. Workmen unloaded supplies from flatcars behind it and laid out piles of rails and mountains of spikes on the bare ground. Behind the flatcar was a passenger car, a good deal boxier and plainer than *The Spirit of Spargill,* with three men standing outside, lounging and talking. They were better-dressed than the workmen, and Brandon supposed they were railroad executives or local businessmen or some such, out for a look at how the work was progressing.

They looked up as he approached, and he saw they were not in fact railroad executives.

"Hey, Blake," Jack Ryan said. "Didn't expect you, but you're not unexpected, if you take my meaning. It figured Willson'd send you up to get some stuff for the *Chronicle,* and this is the way you'd have to come. Our good luck we're here to meet you. Trexler wanted to come out to check on precautions against pilferage, though what the market is for stolen steel rails I don't know, and Nelson here's wanted to get some heroic studies of the labor force taming the wild."

Brandon nodded, returning the two men's greetings, and started to dismount. "And," Ryan continued, "I thought my boss might as well have an excursion, a little break from the cares of business, so I exercised my powers of persuasion to that effect, as you see." He waved toward the passenger car, the steps of which the last passenger was descending.

Brandon's toe caught in the stirrup, and he nearly pitched face-forward to the ground, but saved himself with a grab at the cinches, extricated his shoe, stepped away from the horse, and raised his hat to Jess Marvell.

11

"Boss," Jack Ryan said cheerfully, "this is Calvin Blake, fearless and fluent correspondent for the Spargill *Chronicle & Advertiser,* up here to see what's worth advertising and chronicling. Blake, meet Miss Jess Marvell, deviser of and driving force behind Marvel Halls, the latest wheeze in fine feeding for the frantic and famished traveler, and fortunate employer of yours truly."

"Ma'am," Brandon said, settling his hat back on his head.

"Mr. Blake," Jess Marvell said, looking at him with the polite interest of someone meeting a total stranger. Brandon was grateful that, like Jake Trexler, she had the ability to avoid registering recognition when it might create awkwardness to do so. He also wondered why people considered the West as an unpeopled wilderness; it seemed to him that in half the places he came to, someone he knew from somewhere else—and who knew him under another name—turned up. In only a few weeks Ned Norland, Jake Trexler, and now Jess Marvell; it wasn't quite strolling through downtown St. Louis, but getting close to it.

"I have heard something about the Marvel Halls,

ma'am," Brandon said, "and I'd appreciate getting the full story from their originator."

"That's usually Mr. Ryan's job," Jess Marvell said, "but I'm glad of the chance to toot my own horn now and then. Let's sit down in the car, and I'll tell you the whole thing."

She turned, climbed the car steps, and vanished through the door. Brandon looped his horse's reins over a post and followed her. Jake Trexler was looking at him with his usual appraising stare, a professional trait, Brandon supposed; and Nelson Vanbrugh exercised his own profession by peering down the track and sketching busily. Brandon noticed that Jack Ryan's face had gone a little tight and doubted that it was because he was not getting the chance to publicize Marvell Halls. It was a fair bet in *itzebus,* marbles, or chalk that Jack Ryan had at least a moderate case on Jess Marvell.

As, Brandon thought, any man might who spent much time at all close to her.

It was cool in the car, and Brandon sank gratefully onto the seat beside Jess Marvell. It was narrower than the ones he was used to, meant for two passengers rather than three, but the planned-for passengers were of broad enough beam so that there were a few inches of space between them. On the opposite side of the aisle, he noticed, the seats were single, so if they were there, she would have to sit on his lap. . . . He forced the thought away from him with surprised irritation.

It was a year and some since he had seen Jess Marvell, and then only for a few hours on a few days, but she was somehow as familiar to him as if she had been a daily part of his life for the whole interval: fair-haired, complexion as pale as a wide-peaked sunbonnet could keep it in this sunwashed land, animation playing on her face like glimmers of sunlight on the surface of a stream, eyes that always seemed to be fixed thoughtfully on something, as if learning the essence of whatever she saw. Only in her early twenties, but clearly grown up. Not a woman you would call pretty right out, but . . . He stopped short of finding a word to describe her.

"I'd better keep to calling you Mr. Blake," Jess Marvell said. She had known him as Charles Brooks and had report of him from Rush Dailey as Beaufort Callison, and evidently accepted the need for serial aliases as an occupational necessity of the detective she supposed him to be.

"That's who I am," Brandon said. "For now."

"Have you found any of those train robbers?" Jess Marvell asked. Back in Kansas last year she had drawn her own conclusions about Brandon's—or Charles Brooks's—trade and intentions, and Brandon had let them stand, indicating that he was on the track of an unspecified group of men wanted for robbing a train. She and Rush Dailey had offered to provide him with reports of anyone passing through the cow town of Inskip who might have something to do with the crime, and they had devised ways of getting batches of them to places where he might some day be able to pick them up. Brandon had been careful to keep the Kenneally name out of it, both because it would be an unwanted link to Cole Brandon, Esq., supposed to be traveling in Europe, and because expressing any kind of direct interest in the Kenneallys would expose Jess Marvell and Rush Dailey to dangers no fee would cover. As far as Brandon could see, the main result so far had been that what he had paid them had financed their Inskip lunch wagon, which in turn apparently had led to the Marvel Halls enterprise.

"Haven't been able to make any arrests yet," Brandon said, truthful literally though not in spirit. Arrests were not on his agenda. Two were dead so far, and the rest were slated for bullet or blade, not handcuffs. "The reports you've sent, they've been useful, though," he went on. "Eliminated some possibilities, led me to some that were worth following up." He gave a wave of his hand and a slight smile, as if indicating that there were intricacies in the detective business that she would not understand. Fair enough, since he certainly didn't.

"I'm glad you think so," Jess Marvell said. "Rush Dailey and I were wondering if it wasn't time to stop sending them and let you stop paying for them. The money's still useful, for it'll be a time before there's any coming in from the Marvel Halls, but I wouldn't want to be taking it for something that's not worth it. And it's interesting to keep an eye out for what might be helpful to you—I have to say that it's given me a sharp eye for men who might be troublesome to deal with, so it's been helpful to me, too."

"Where is Rush Dailey?" Brandon asked. "When we met up over in Arizona he told me about your scheme, and I'd have expected to see him with you. He's still . . ."

"A full partner, yes," Jess Marvell said. "Junior, of course." Rush Dailey would be half past eighteen or so by now, Brandon reckoned. "He's up in Omaha right now, settling some things with the DT management. I expect him back 'most any time. He works with me on planning and some details, but it's Jack Ryan who's laying the track, as you might say—Rush and I figure things out, and Jack sees that they get done."

"His background in railroading or restaurants?" Brandon asked.

Jess Marvell grinned. "Half the men out here, you never know what their background is. I haven't any notion of what you were before you took up the detective line, and I don't expect to. Jack turned up one day in Inskip, got fascinated by the lunch wagon, which he'd never seen the like of, and how could he, seeing as it was Rush and I had the idea of it? He was the first customer ever to ask intelligent questions about it, and even gave us a couple of good ideas for it that we used. That was just after I got the go-ahead for Marvel Halls from the railroad people in Chicago, and we saw right away that we needed someone to handle practical things like buying materials and bossing work gangs, and Jack sort of got to hear of it and said we ought to try him. And so we did, and he's been a wonder at it. Got two halls built along the U.P. line in half the time I expected, and materials bought at prices I'd hardly believe. Whatever Jack Ryan did back where he came from, he was probably a dab hand at it, and he's certainly making a difference to us. And it didn't do us any harm for me to lend him out to John B. Parker for that trip to Spargill. Parker appreciated it considerably and told me so."

Brandon considered that if Jack Ryan heard his boss's glowing praise of his value, he would likely cut his throat. Jess Marvell's pleasure and pride in Jack Ryan sounded uncannily like that of the owner of a first-class horse or a champion hunting dog. That was a little cold for Jess Marvell, as Brandon thought he knew her, and he was puzzled for a moment. Then he let a trace of a grin twitch his lips. She would have seen Ryan's attraction to her from the beginning and instantly armored herself against it, inaccessible as the mountain of glass in the old fairy story Elise's Aunt Trudi had been fond of telling. Kinder to the poor fellow to make it clear from the start that there was no chance, of course.

Brandon did not ask himself why he found the certainty of Ryan's dismal prospects with Jess Marvell satisfying.

"I'll ride on ahead to Split Rock," he said. "I'll want to find a room, start looking around town, and find things to write about for the paper."

"Be sure to take a look at the Marvel Hall just across from the station," Jess Marvell said. "It's halfway done now, and it'll be finished next week, I'd think. We worked out plans with Montgomery, Ward in Chicago, and they've made up buildings to our specifications, ship them in sections, and we can build them in hardly any time. Any Marvel Hall anywhere'll look like the others, so people will know what to expect. I'll have Jack Ryan show you over it, and he can give you a tour of the town and the . . . well, where the track gangs go for fun. You remember the other side of Front Street in Inskip? Well, this is like that, boiled down thick and seasoned with sulphur and brimstone, plenty to write about if your boss is brave enough to print it."

Brandon was about an hour on the way to Split Rock, following the track, when he heard a scolding scream from behind him and a rhythmic huffing. He steadied his horse as the train with its single car overtook them and steamed by.

He had a glimpse of Jess Marvell waving at him from a window, and Jack Ryan's flourished hat, before an eye-stinging cloud of woodsmoke from the stack rolled down on him.

When it drifted away he looked ahead at the vanishing train, then behind him at the straight line of track to the south. In the afternoon sun it gleamed like a fresh scar dividing the brushy, rolling land that stretched away on either side.

Brandon squinted at the sketch on Vanbrugh's easel, then looked up at the scene beyond it. The drawing was recognizably a depiction of what lay in front of the artist, but startlingly different. For one thing, the drawing, though merely black lines on white paper, was somehow more real than the actual scene.

A little to the south the two upthrust slabs of stone that gave Split Rock its name jutted into the air, twenty or so feet apart, with the railroad track running between them. Less than half a mile away was the former end of the line, and the town itself: the high-pitched roof of the train station; a nearly-completed two-story building nearby, fresh lumber gleaming in the sun, the incipient Marvell Hall. A little away from it stood the town's tallest building, the Nickerson House Hotel, four stories, the top one mostly false front, where Brandon had taken a room, stabled his horse, and left his gear. The Main Street stores looked well-kept, even at this distance, and there was a stir of pedestrians and wagons that spoke of brisk commerce.

Across the tracks to the east some sturdy sheds, an array of neatly aligned passenger and freight cars, and a small locomotive marked the railroad yard. At the moment the yard was inactive except for the movement of one passenger car being pushed into place by a crew of workmen; the one that Jess Marvell and the others had ridden in being returned to its stable. Two cars rose above the others much as the Nickerson House dominated the town, and served the same function; behind three rows of windows lay the narrow bunks the track-laying crews slept in. Beyond the yards was what looked to Brandon like a combination of a municipal rubbish heap and a Gypsy encampment: a straggle of tents, shacks, lean-tos, battered-looking wagons, and heaps of what might have been trash or improvised dwellings.

This was the disordered nest of those who battened on the work crews, therapeutically draining them of whatever money might have festered in their pockets, creating greed for more and ambition for more rewarding work. At nightfall the tents and shacks would become saloons and gambling dives, and many of the wagons would jounce with the paid-for passions of the railroad workers and their briefly rented companions. When the railhead moved on the whole assembly would follow it and set up in business again, so the sacrifice of comfort for portability was highly practical.

To Brandon Split Rock looked like a pretty ordinary place, like many he had seen in the last year, but Vanbrugh's sketch gave it a disturbing vitality and portentousness.

The town, with its hotel and stores and houses, seemed to be drawing back from the station and what lay beyond; the two large windows on the top floor of the Nickerson House seemed almost to stare in horror at the station, which squatted stolidly at the apex of an intricate web of tracks and ties that entrapped the marshaled cars. The dwellings from which the gamblers, saloonkeepers, and whores would emerge at the descent of darkness lay on the drawing paper like sucked-dry carcasses of insects. The two slabs of jutting stone had the look of huge jaws that might at any moment close upon the scene and obliterate it. Brandon was unpleasantly reminded of the petrified giant lizards Ned Norland's charges were probably chipping out of the desert sandstone even now; it was as though one of those, long buried, was emerging to the surface now, ready to feed after millions of years of fasting.

"Not for the tourist booklets, I guess," Brandon said.

"Nope," Nelson Vanbrugh said happily. "For that stuff you have to mix plenty of cream and honey in with the pigments, so to speak, depict Possum Gulch and Stinking Creek so's the customers'll line up to buy tickets to see such wonders of natural beauty. This is for me, and I do it the way I see it." He squinted at the drawing. "Pretty strong, ain't it? Sometimes I don't know how I saw it till I draw it."

Brandon looked at the town and back at the easel. The drawing seemed faithful in every detail, nothing in it that wasn't there to see, but the picture had an atmosphere, almost a story, that the mundane actual view did not. "Like those pictures you sent down to Miss Caldwell."

"Some," Vanbrugh said. "When Parker came out a wolverine, that put the notion of animal resemblances in my mind, and I pretty much stuck with that . . . where it made sense, of course," he added, with a thoughtful look at Brandon.

Brandon, recalling the nearly featureless sketch that Abner Willson had hailed as a speaking likeness, decided not to try to find out what it was Vanbrugh had seen in drawing him. "Thanks for the engravings you gave me for Willson. I've got 'em packed to take back with me. How's the one you're doing for Miss Caldwell coming? Any chance it'll be ready for when I go back, day after tomorrow?"

"Almost done," Vanbrugh said. "Sharpen up a few lines around the roof, make the lettering clear, and there she is. Probably finish it before dinner, and I'll give it to you later on."

"Where?"

Vanbrugh tapped the left side of the sketch with his pencil. "Across the tracks, in the dwellings of the unrighteous. I'll be there because that's where I go at night, and you'll be there because Ryan'll insist on giving you the tour, and anyhow there's no place else to go in Split Rock once the sun's down."

12

John B. Parker wouldn't appreciate that kind of talk," Jack Ryan said. "Prides himself on offering heat and all modern conveniences to the traveler that wants to pay for them."

"It's that there very convenience that makes 'em pay with their lives," the drunk said. Brandon had caught his name as Hammammam when he proclaimed it during a moment of diminished coherence, and supposed it could be Henderson or Kimberly or even, distorted as it was by a resonant belch, Jones. A dark man a little older than Brandon, he seemed to know a lot more than Brandon had ever wanted to know about railroad disasters and was eager to impart that knowledge to any nearby ears, especially those connected to a hand willing to pay for his drinks.

"It's the stoves and the lanterns as does it," Hammammam (perhaps Ampersand) went on solemnly. "The car is stove in, as it might be by a derailing, or telescoped by the next train going half through it, or dropped into a gorge when a bridge goes, and it ain't the mangling and crushing as does for the poor souls mostly, though that'll take its grisly toll—no denying, for being in a coach that's smashed to flinders is no picnic. And d'you know, the only way out of it looks sure suicide? If a bridge is swaying like a sidewinder, anybody in 's right mind'd slow down, but the only hope is the crazy way, pull down the throttle and let 'er rip, and you might make the far side. Slow and safe, and you're amongst the rocks and tore to tatters. But it's the fire that turns a disaster into a horror. Stoves spill out their coals, busted lanterns pour oil out, and next as you know there's a scene of hell and the torments of the damned right before you."

The scene in which Brandon, Jack Ryan and the drunk were both spectators and participants seemed to Brandon to be a fair representation of hell in a somewhat less extreme mode. They were seated at a flimsy table—like everything else in sight, capable of being knocked down fast for easy portability—in a sagging tent about thirty feet square, which seemed to serve as a kind of convenient anthology of most of the diversions offered in the quarter. Along the back wall long planks on waist-high trestles formed a bar behind which three men scurried constantly to fill orders; a lower, shorter plank counter against another wall provided a community gaming table, on which Brandon could see a faro bank in action, two poker games being played, and the flicker of a spinning chuck-a-luck cage. Half the rest of the floor space was filled with tables like theirs at which men sat and drank and for the most part yelled hilariously or angrily. The central area, harshly lit by a huge lantern that appeared to have been salvaged from a locomotive, was cleared enough to allow room for a frantic fiddler in a chair to ply his bow and for a succession of women, up to three at a time, to dance around the thick pole that supported the tent with an abandon that reminded Brandon of the market woman in Santa Fe during the tarantula's exploration of her bosom. The nearer spectators greeted these performances with appreciative hoots and yelps, and occasionally one would rise, whirl a girl around a few times, then stagger with her out of the tent.

The central lantern was abetted by stubs of candles in thick mugs made from the bottoms of bottles and set on the tables, and a few kerosene lanterns that looked as if they had once been railroad property and, in the eyes of the law, might still be so, hung from ropes strung across the tent. The light had an eerie, flickering quality brought about by the clouds of smoke from cigars, pipes and cigarettes that eddied through the air, rising to form a cloud into which the tent pole disappeared as if everything above were without form and void. Through the tent's entrance opening Brandon could see a line of men waiting in front of a closed wagon, which shook on its wheels like someone afflicted with a mild but persistent palsy. Every two minutes or so a man would descend from the rear of the wagon and another leap up its front steps. Brandon tried to guess if there were two women at work inside, or one extremely effective one.

All in all, it was a pretty fair representation of what an evening out in hell might be like, a good variety of vices being grimly enjoyed by the denizens. Any kind of accident at all, like one of the ropes supporting the lanterns breaking, could bring it more into line with the kind of thing the drunk had been dwelling on, a sudden barbecue of everyone in the tent. The Split Rock Horror, the papers might call it, if they considered this class of victim worth writing up.

Hammammam had been seated at a table with two vacant chairs when Ryan and Brandon had come in, and they had joined him before wondering much why he had no companions. Brandon thought he knew now but felt disinclined to move away. Ryan had fetched a bottle and glasses from the bar, and this was as comfortable a place as any in the tent—or, presumably, in the area—to sit and drink. Brandon felt uneasy and found he was relishing the drinking more than he was accustomed to. The uneasiness seemed to crystallize around the flushed, sweat-shiny women gyrating around the pole and the rhythmically rocking wagon outside the tent.

"Like as elephants having carnal knowledge of each other," Hammammam said, and Brandon realized that he must have missed something of interest while brooding on his surroundings.

"What's like that?" he asked.

"The two locos I saw up on the U.P. line, like I just said." Hammammam gave a sharp look at the bottle in front of Brandon, the sternly disapproving glance of a drunk who has had the luck to find someone who might be even more fuddled than he. "The one rammed t'other from behind and clumb up on it, with its nose in the air and its drivers cuddling t'other's cab. Fellers in the yards said as they'd keep an eye on her to see if she birthed a donkey engine in nine months or so."

Brandon looked around the tent, wondering if it would be a good idea to thank Ryan for this glimpse, brief as it was, of Split Rock's night life and go back to the Nickerson House. But that would leave a lot of night to get through, and the disquiet the dancers and the quivering of the wheeled brothel had raised in him would, he feared, persist while he was awake. And Jess Marvell was staying at the Nickerson House, too—not surprising, and not significant in any way, except that any strong awareness of her seemed to make the disquiet even stronger. Sitting here and drinking seemed like not a bad way to pass the time until he could be sure of sleep. If, that was, he didn't have to hear more about train wrecks.

"Know a lot about railroads, don't you, Mr., uh . . ." he said.

"Hammammam, like I said. My daddy was a Syrian man. Got in trouble with the pasha there—that's a kind of governor that works for the sultan—and shipped out with a load of figs bound for Baltimore. Set up a store in Ohio, and raised me into buying and selling, so as when I got my growth I took to the road as a drummer, traveling right now in notions, though I've handled ironmongery, harmoniums and compendiums of universal knowledge by subscription, traveling to the remotest corners of the Union. So railroads is a thing I know up from sideways and through to the bone."

"More to train travel than wrecks, though?" said Jack Ryan, who appeared to share Brandon's wish for a change of subject.

"Why, accourse," Hammammam said. "Drama and interesting incidents at every turn, about everything you can imagine, one time or another. The man that is tired of train travel is tired of life, is how I sees it."

He tapped the bottle with an inquiring look at Jack Ryan and at Ryan's nod poured himself a drink and gulped at it. "Now, for a newspaperman like yourself, Mr. Blake, here is a item that you might want to give some space to, free and for gratis, you being the openhanded gentleman you are. The experiences of a man that has seen the countenances of Frank and Jesse James over the barrel of a pistol. That was a wreck, too, but 'twas the James boys that wrecked the train—pulled a rail loose and sent the engine over on its side. That was their first robbery, two years back, over in Iowa, on the Rock Island Line, and I thought I'd been preserved out of the perils when the jolting stopped and I was whole, but then the gang come through and took what they would. Businesslike about it, but not harsh, you might say. Folks talk of the James boys as being kind of Robin Hoods now—"

Jack Ryan cut in abruptly: "The Jameses are stupid bastards, glory-hunters, as soon have plays written about 'em as rob. Train robbery's not a melodrama or a dime novel."

Hammammam bridled at the interruption. "It ain't me as paints 'em in bright colors but common report. As a man in business, I got no soft feelings for thieves and robbers of any kind. Not only did I suffer loss at the hands of the James boys but not long after, my ma's cousin Sam Walters got shot by some fellows that ain't got even no fake glory about 'em. Express messenger, Sam was, and killed over in Missouri by a bunch that cleaned out the train and then went on to murder a St. Louis family to cover their escape."

Brandon was pervaded with a vast chill which, though it came on him suddenly, seemed also to have been there for a long time. He had become used to the patient, purpose-hidden life of the hunter, playing the role he had chosen, waiting until some scent would drift to him or some print in the grass would show the presence of his prey. Leading that life, he could for long stretches not forget why he led it but put the reason aside, in some little-visited region of his mind. Hammammam's reminiscence brought that reason back forcefully, and Brandon seemed once again to be standing outside the smoldering ruins of Mound Farm watching the sheeted bodies of his family being carried out.

He felt a surge of impatience, of near-rage. There had to be something more he could do than wait. This whole newspaperman masquerade seemed a silly sham, a time-wasting game. *Something* had brought him to Spargill to encounter a Kenneally, and if that something were anything more than a delusion born of need, there had to be a Kenneally to find and face and kill.

Brandon took a deep breath, forcing himself to remember something Ned Norland had told him: "Whenas you give up an' move away from whar you been hid 'cause the critter you been jist cain't nohow be thar no more, that's when he's goin' t' saunter out an' take his ease. Be right about him bein' thar in the fust place, then stick with it." Maybe he was right about his quarry "bein' thar," maybe not, but there was nothing for the moment but to go on with it.

This inner conflict and its resolution had taken only seconds, and he looked up to see that Jack Ryan seemed to like Hammammam's anecdote of the Kenneallys' venture into train robbery even less than the salesman's experience with the James brothers. "I think Mr. Blake and I can do without the blood-and-thunder stuff, Hammammam," Ryan said with a scowl. "If you want to soak yourself in horrors, you're welcome to the rest of the bottle."

Ryan stood up abruptly, and Brandon did the same. He fleetingly wondered if something useful might be extracted from Hammammam, some news or hint of news of the Kenneallys, but decided not. In any case, Jack Ryan seemed determined to have nothing more to do with Hammammam, and there seemed no ready pretext for prolonging the conversation.

Brandon followed Ryan toward the entrance, but stopped

when a man lounging at a table stuck a leg in his path. He saw Nelson Vanbrugh tilted back in a chair, hat down almost over his eyes, smoking a thin cigar and sketching on a tablet of creamy paper.

"Hey," Vanbrugh said. "Told you I'd be here, and so would you. Here." He lifted a paper-wrapped flat oblong from the table and handed it to Brandon. It was heavier than it looked and bore a carefully executed picture of a passenger car. Brandon recognized *The Spirit of Spargill,* though in the picture it was somehow more imposing than he remembered in reality.

"Finished the engraving, ran off a proof, and wrapped the plate in it," Vanbrugh said. "One time you can tell a book by its cover, only it's not a book nor a cover neither, but what the hell. Seven and a third inches across, which'll just fit three of Willson's columns, four inches high. He's getting damn good work, so he'd better feature it strong. You can tell him I liked doing it. It's nice to do something that detailed, get it as close to a photograph as you can. Makes a change from the advertising paintings, I'll tell you."

"What about the other stuff you do, the sketching like I saw this afternoon?" Brandon said.

"Like I said, that's for me, I do it 'cause I have to. Don't know if it's any good or not, and don't care, really. That's what I do privately—the paintings, engravings, that's the professional stuff."

Brandon tried to stuff the wrapped steel plate into his trousers pocket, but it bumped against the handle of the .38 he was carrying—setting out for an evening's fun across the tracks had seemed to call for going armed. The plate fit, with a little easing, into his jacket breast pocket, and he nodded to Vanbrugh and walked toward the entrance, through which Jack Ryan had disappeared. As he passed behind the artist he saw that he had been sketching the dancing women and the drinkers at the tables nearest them. The drawing had an almost ferocious liveliness and energy of line . . . although Vanbrugh had depicted dancers, fiddler, and spectators as animated, gesturing, grinning skeletons.

Outside the tent he found Jack Ryan looking around impatiently. "That's the liveliest place around," he said, looking back at the tent, from whose entrance noise and smoke billowed out, "but that damn fellow's spoiled it for tonight, gassing about the Jameses and . . . stuff he doesn't know crap about. Nothing worse than a gabby Arab, no doubt about it."

"How many Arabs have you met?" Brandon asked.

Ryan grinned. "He's the first. Now, next best place for drinking is Brogan's shack. Quieter, serious crowd that mostly don't talk to anybody but themselves, though sometimes one or another'll get to quarreling pretty fierce with himself, particularly toward morning. Or do you feel like calling it quits and getting a whole lot of sleep?"

A few feet from Brandon the line of men outside the wagon moved up one place as a new customer replaced an old, and the wagon kept up its steady shudder. The frenzied screeches of the fiddle brought the whirling dancers to his mind's eye, which seemed to blink, presenting sometimes quivering expanses of moist flesh, sometimes swiftly moving frameworks of ivory-colored bones, then an irrelevant and upsetting magic-lantern flash of Jess Marvell's face.

"Let's get a whole lot of drink," Brandon said.

He had no idea how much later it was, in terms of drinks or time, when he and Jack Ryan made their way with extreme care out of Brogan's. The moon was a crescent, low on the horizon, but since Brandon did not know where it had been earlier, it was no use as a guide. The thought of not being able to tell time by the moon struck him as enormously funny, though he did not think it would be much use to try to explain the joke to Jack Ryan, who seemed to have had more to drink than was good for him and was flickering unpleasantly in the dim light.

The tents and shacks immediately around them were dark, and nobody was visible nearby. The tent where they had started the evening still glowed in the distance, and the faint sound of the fiddle could still be heard, but the rest of the quarter seemed to have ceased activity. Brandon did not feel sick or tired, but as if sickness and fatigue were lying in wait for him behind some flimsy screening; it seemed to him that he would have to keep moving to fend them off.

"Hooh," Jack Ryan said. "Brother Blake, you can drink like a, drink like a drink liker. Liquor liker."

Ryan lurched, even though he was standing, not walking, and Brandon grasped his arm to keep him from falling. He found that they were somehow in motion, and kept walking, picking their way through the night. After some time it seemed to him that they should be near the Nickerson House, and he attempted to focus on his surroundings. Against the sky, which seemed to be decorated with tiny whirling pinwheels of light, he made out flat-topped shapes jutting up around them, and almost immediately hit his foot with a metallic clank against something unyielding.

A rail, likely. And the silhouettes against the sky would be freight cars. "What're we doing in the yards?" he asked Jack Ryan. "Whyju bring us here?"

"Didn't," Ryan said. "You did."

"I didn't," Brandon said.

"Nobody did, then," Jack Ryan said cheerfully. "Bess guide in Wess, ole Nobdobby. Nobody. Damn, 's right where we need t' be. Nobody never lets you down. *Come* on."

He stumbled away, and Brandon followed. "Here we are," Ryan said a moment or so later. "Hop up."

Brandon squinted and saw that Ryan was looking down on him from a platform with a kind of seesaw structure in its center. Ryan leaned down, grabbed Brandon's hand, and hauled him up. He now saw that they were standing on a handcar, one of those used by small parties of track workers, that worked by rocking the long bar up and down, presumably transferring the motion by a gear train to the car's axles.

"Juss what the doctor'd order," Jack Ryan said. "Half hour healthy exercise, blow fumes away, leave us fid as a fittle. Putcher back into it, Blake."

He bent over one end of the bar and pushed down. The other end rose and nudged Brandon sharply; he felt the car shudder under him and saw the boxy silhouettes against the sky shift position.

Brandon edged around to the other end of the pivoted bar, grasped the handles that protruded from it, and pushed down, then let Jack Ryan's answering push, and the momentum transmitted from the wheels' forward motion, raise it. The effort required grew less with each push as the car picked up speed. The last of the cars and sheds in the yards fell away behind them, and the handcar rolled north. Brandon moved faster, enjoying the diminishing resistance, until he and Ryan were bobbing up and down like jointed wooden figures on a child's toy, keeping the handcar at a constant momentum with almost no effort. Except for times he'd gone fishing in a rowboat upriver from St. Louis, or riding a horse over grass, it was the most silent traveling he'd ever experienced: the click and rumble of the wheels as they passed over the rail ends, the creaking of the machinery, and his and Jack Ryan's gusty breathing were the loudest sounds.

Brandon was facing backwards, watching the faint shape of Split Rock's low and darkened skyline, indistinct against the star-strewn sky, recede behind Jack Ryan's bobbing form. Two massive blocks of darkness loomed beside him and then grew smaller behind the car, the jaws of rock Vanbrugh had been sketching that afternoon. He had no way of judging how fast they were moving, but it seemed a good clip, and the wind pressed his jacket against his back. To his right the moon was moving down toward the invisible horizon, washing the western half of the sky with a light that paled the stars and picked out features of the landscape, trees and low hills, showing that they were there but not giving any clear details. There was enough light to see that Ryan was grinning broadly as he dipped and rose at his handle, and Brandon felt a bubbling exhilaration that had nothing to do with the liquor he had had, except as it resulted from the vigorous muscular work that seemed to be driving the whiskey fumes from his brain and body as if they were being boiled off.

The moon seemed to sink almost as he watched it, and he realized that his sense of time had become detached from his moment-by-moment experience. He might have been working the handcar, speeding through the night, for a couple of minutes, a couple of hours, or a century, like a modern version of the Flying Dutchman. The rush of the wind past him, his steady, rhythmic motion, the flickering retreat of telegraph poles and bushes all seemed to be divorced from time, to be something that just was. Here and now, he wasn't Cole Brandon or Calvin Blake or any of the others whose names and masks he had assumed, just a living piece of machinery, experiencing the pleasure of motion.

"Up ahead, that's got to be the section shack," Jack Ryan said. "We've come farther than I thought." He sounded a lot clearer than the last time he had spoken, and Brandon realized that he himself was hearing a lot more clearly. He wondered if they were still drunk at all and decided that they probably were, just enough to be enjoying this.

"Section gang'll be sleeping there," Ryan said. "Let's give 'em a war whoop as we go by—that'll ruin their sheets for them, there's been Indians seen up this way, and talk of trouble."

"We do that," Brandon said, "and they'll be awake and shooting-jumpy when we come back by them later."

"True enough," Ryan said. "Maybe we better . . . oh, God, we are dipped in shit now, for sure!"

Brandon turned to look behind him. He could see the blocky shape of what had to be the section shack some distance up the track—could see it more clearly each second as a nimbus of light grew behind it, and a noise, muted by distance to something like the snuffling of a sleeping bull-dog, came to him, faint, then steadily louder.

"No train scheduled now," Jack Ryan said, "but there the sonofabitch is. They won't see us in time to stop. Track curves around above the shack, and the train won't turn so's the light hits this stretch until it's too late."

"Then we . . ." Brandon began, and stopped before saying "jump off right now." If the locomotive hit the empty handcar at forty miles an hour there would be a lot of damage, almost certainly a wreck, for Jack Ryan and Calvin Blake to bear responsibility for.

"We pump like hell," Jack Ryan said. "There is a switch to a spur line just this side of the section shack, and I think we can just make it. *Push!*"

Brandon jackknifed, driving his end of the bar nearly to the platform, and unbent, his arms almost at full stretch, as Ryan did the same. He could feel the handcar pick up speed, and he and Ryan increased the pace of their movements. He was not sure whether it was better to be driving them toward the horrifying impact with his back to the oncoming train or, as Ryan was, facing it and seeing the engine's light growing larger by the second. Its illumination was enough to show Ryan's strained face as he peered past Brandon. The noise of the locomotive grew inexorably louder, and it seemed to Brandon that he could feel the tracks quivering under its weight and force. Several tons of steel were about to hit him in the back at a speed in excess of forty miles an hour, and it went against every instinct to propel himself toward it as hard as he could.

He was surprised to find that what he felt most was an intense aliveness, a sharpening of all his senses, so that he could even, it seemed to him, smell the friction-heated oil lubricating the pumping mechanism, gears, and wheel bearings, hear the rushing of the wind under the swelling noise of the train, feel how the wind stirred each hair on the back of his neck. He knew that he and Jack Ryan were moving with utmost speed, but it seemed to him that everything was happening slowly, as if there was plenty of time for them to reach the switch. Look at it one way, he thought, we have the rest of our lives to get there, which right now looks like about two minutes.

Brandon saw Jack Ryan drop his end of the handle and leap from the handcar, then sprint ahead. "Lemme get ahead a bit," he called back.

Brandon slowed his pumping, turned, and saw Ryan twenty feet ahead, grappling with an angular shape projecting above the tracks. "Damn the damn switch, sonofabitch doesn't want to . . . *move,* there you go, you bastard, *pump* her, Blake!"

Brandon pushed and pulled at the handle with a force that seemed to threaten to pull his arms from their sockets; the handcar leaped ahead, shuddered and bumped, swerved to the left and rolled over the opened switch, and was still moving forward as a blast of displaced air and furious sound seemed to push it on, and a red glow from the engine's firebox washed over it for an instant. Then the train, trailing red sparks into the sky that whirled among the pallid stars for some seconds before dying, was past them and puffing away south toward Split Rock.

"Only one passenger car," Jack Ryan said thoughtfully. He climbed back onto the handcar. "A special, I guess. Like I said, not on the schedule."

"It's nice to know we wouldn't have been disrupting the timetable if we'd got ourselves killed wrecking it, then," Brandon said. "Anyhow, we missed giving Hammammam more to talk about, which is nice to think of. What now? We take a breather, then pump this thing back to Split Rock?"

Jack Ryan shook his head. "I vote no, Blake. We have just been preserved from phenomenal perils, and fate has placed us on this spur, which as I recollect runs on a mile or so to a pleasant grove of trees by a babbling brook or a chuckling creek or some such, a pleasanter spot than anything short of the Nickerson House for a night's rest, and a lot nearer. Also, who's to say that train isn't going to Split Rock to pick someone up? Could just as well be that as taking 'em down, and if so, it could be heading north again while we're pumping south. A long chance, I admit, but I don't know as I feel like taking it. Let's light out for the shady grove—it'll be fun."

Brandon considered that Jack Ryan's ideas of fun so far had been more stirring than he cared for, but he had to agree that a short haul to a pleasant sleeping spot was more attractive than a long one to town, especially with even the remotest prospect of another encounter with a train.

In the cool night air, they bent to the pivoted handle again, and sent it trundling over the track into the setting moon.

13

Brandon came awake as a nearly horizontal spike of sunlight eased its way under one eyelid and pried it open. Seeing the deep green of leaves against a brilliant blue sky above him, he knew immediately where he was: the grove at the end of the spur line where Jack Ryan had insisted they sleep.

The turf under him was soft, and the night had been warm and dry enough so that he was not chilled or soaked. Brandon could recall very clearly what had happened the night before, from drinking with Hammammam to drinking at Brogan's to the crazed ride on the handcar and the narrow escape from being minced by the unscheduled southbound train. Right now he felt all right, or at least felt nothing wrong, just the nothing-much feeling that comes with waking up. Experience—of course, he had never had a night quite like this one, but there had been a few that shared some common features—told him that the first move he made would start up the horrible vaudeville of the hangover: the whips and jingles, the clog dancers in the stomach, the rail-splitters' competition in the skull, the deep brown fog in throat, mouth, and nostrils. Back in St. Louis, the Germans called it the *katzenjammer,* cat yells, and why not?

He gave a resigned sigh and pushed himself up to a sitting position, bracing for the wave of pain, nausea, hammering, whatever his abused body chose to make its complaint.

In fact, he felt fine. Gingerly, warily, he stood up. Still fine. No headache, no nausea, no throbbing, no pervading horror. His arms and back buzzed with a reminder that they had had an extraordinary workout, but no more than they often had after an afternoon's row on the river. He blinked. It seemed as if pumping a handcar for who knew how many miles across the prairie, then missing dismemberment by instants, was a good way to avoid a hangover. Effective as it was, he doubted it would catch on as a remedy.

He ran a hand across his chin, rasping it. He might feel in top form, but he was also unshaven, dressed in trousers wrinkled like twin concertinas, and, his nose told him, smelling like a whaler's sock worn for a year's voyage, then dipped in whiskey. Not much to be done about the shaving just now, but he recalled Jack Ryan's mention of a stream of some kind nearby, so a sketchy wash-up might be possible.

Brandon looked around the small grove, now glowing where the beams of the early sun struck the tree trunks and bounced along the grass. At one end it opened on the end of the spur line, a massive chunk of a log rolled against the last tracks to act as buffer; the handcar rested against it. A few rough-hewn ties lay scattered around next to the tracks— some extras that hadn't been needed, Brandon supposed. Pretty close figuring at that, or maybe if there'd been too few ties they would just not have laid the last length of track. He wondered why the line had been built; probably to promote a town at its end, land sales for the railroad, and steady business if it ever prospered. A pretty enough place for one, gentler than most of what he had seen of Colorado, the land covered with patches of trees set out on a tapestry shot through with vivid wildflowers. Early birds darted through the trees and above the rolling meadows. The track stretching toward the east lay quietly on the land, but in time it would bring the material and the people that would change it out of all recognition. All his life Brandon had been used to railroads and thought them nothing remarkable, but where they were new, they were like giant syringes, pouring new substances—maybe nourishing, maybe toxic—into what had been there forever.

He walked to the far end of the grove and found the stream running clear over a pebbly bottom. Jack Ryan, shirtless, knelt next to it, splashing water over his face and chest. "Cold, but it wakes you up!" he called. "Sluice yourself off some, and we'll trundle on down to the main line and beg some breakfast from the fellows at the section shack. There's good hunting up this way, and antelope steak and eggs isn't out of the question. Come on down."

Brandon looked past Jack Ryan and spoke in a low voice, pitched to carry to him but no further. "Ah . . . you said something about trouble with Indians last night. Did you mean real trouble?"

Ryan looked at him with a puzzled frown. "Well, yeah, they don't take kindly to the trains coming through, and . . . oh." He turned and looked in the same direction Brandon was and saw the same thing: glittering eyes in a beaky, bronzed face peering at them around the edge of a flowering shrub.

Waving or calling out a greeting somehow did not seem like a good idea. Ryan said briskly, *"Well.* Believe I've finished washing, and I guess it's time to move off and leave this very fine place completely alone and just as we found it, just like we'd never been here."

He scrambled up the bank, pulling on his shirt, and stood beside Brandon. "We saunter back to the car as if we hadn't a care in the world and then pump the sonofabitch twice as fast as we did last night when the train was coming at us, right?"

"My sentiments exactly," Brandon said.

Their pace back to the handcar was a good bit faster than a saunter, but short of outright panic. "Maybe there's only the one," Brandon said.

From behind them a wild turkey gobbled and was answered from the right and the left; an improbably wakeful owl made a few comments, and a couple of coyotes gave interested yaps. "Half a dozen anyhow," Jack Ryan said. "But they probably won't . . ."

Another set of wildlife vocalizations came to them, this time from ahead as well as behind. "They seem to be," Brandon said. He looked at the pile of redundant ties at the end of the tracks. "Hey, help me heave a few of these on the car."

Ryan trotted to help him, saying, "Why? They'll slow us, and what good'll they do?"

"Come in handy, I think. Along the sides, one on top of another, that's the way."

Brandon and Ryan hopped onto the car and began pumping the pivoted handle. The car moved off smoothly, and Brandon felt a surge of relief, which drained out abruptly as four dark figures trotted out from the woods and began running after the car. They were bare-chested, wearing skin trousers and a single upright feather in the hair. Three carried bows and one a short rifle, which he now raised to his shoulder and fired. He was still running, and the shot came nowhere near, but it made clear what the game now was.

The running Indians seemed to be able to increase their pace so the car, gathering speed, did not pull ahead of them, but Brandon saw that they would not be able to stop and take aim with either bow or gun without losing ground.

Then, above the clatter of the car wheels over the rails and the grinding squeak of the handle, he heard a heavy drumming. A mounted Indian, herding three riderless horses, pounded out of the receding woods, calling shrilly to his colleagues as he caught up with them. They scrambled up onto the horses' backs as the man who had brought them raced ahead, slowing as he approached the handcar and raising a short bow, and firing an arrow from it.

Brandon saw a black line darting between him and Jack Ryan and thought he heard a wasplike whining buzz. He let go of the right-side handle of the pivoting lever, grabbed his .38 from his trousers pocket, snapped off a shot at the

Indian, then slid to the floor of the car. Ryan goggled at him but kept pumping. Brandon jammed the soles of his boots onto the handles at the bottom of the downstroke and pushed upward as hard as he could.

"Hot damn, what a notion!" Jack Ryan called. He eeled into the same position as Brandon and caught the handles with his feet in time to assist the upstroke.

Brandon found that he could exert more force with his leg muscles than he had with his arms and back, and he had the sense that the handcar was moving more swiftly than it had the night before. The two ties laid on each side of the car formed a missile-proof wall high enough to protect their heads and bodies, and he doubted that their pistoning legs would provide an easy target.

"You wrote up a story about some track hands saving themselves like this?" Ryan called. "That how you know about it?"

"No," Brandon said. "Sort of came to me all at once, saw that it'd be a poor idea to stand there pumping away while those fellows shot at us, then that we'd need some protection down here, only thing to do."

"You are wasted on newspapering, Blake," Jack Ryan said.

A couple of gunshots were paired with thumps on the ties next to Brandon, and the clear morning sky against which the oscillating lever and their rhythmically pumping feet and legs moved was streaked with black lines that vanished as quickly as lighting bolts. Once an arrow slammed into the post that supported the pivot and stuck there, quivering. Brandon saw its guide feathers, vivid blue in the sunlight. Probably a bluejay, he thought, if they had them out here.

He darted his head up over the ties for a snap look at their pursuers, then dropped it back as the rider with the rifle triggered off two rapid shots. They were bunched up, riding almost level with the handcar, about fifty feet from the track. Fortunately the track layers had been thorough, or just disorderly, in preparing the track bed, and the ground to either side of it was dug up, rutted, and strewn with debris so that there was no good horse terrain close to. If the Indians wanted to get next to the track, they could, but they would lose speed and be left behind.

It was a damned strange business, he reflected. Here he was, a modern man, city man, attorney, using the most advanced of nineteenth-century machinery, and in danger of losing his life and scalp to a bunch of Stone Age nomads. On the other hand, what he was out here for was Stone Age stuff; if the pursuing Indians knew his objectives, they would acknowledge them as more sensible than drawing a writ or driving an engine and would probably value his scalp all the more for it.

"I think it's only a mile and some to the main line now," Jack Ryan called. "If the section crew's at the shack, they'll likely turn out and drive these fellows back."

Brandon poked his head up again and saw that the Indians were approaching a mounded hillock that rose about six feet above the general level of the ground and veered to within ten feet of the track. If the riders reached it as the handcar passed, they could pour arrows and bullets down into it at will.

"Keep pumping!" he yelled to Jack Ryan, and disengaged his feet from the handles. He took a careful grip on the .38, visualized where in the group the rifleman had been riding —last but one, if he had it right—inhaled deeply, and sprang up and sideways into a crouch, facing the riders.

He took a second that every instinct in him protested against to steady the pistol as if he were shooting game, leading his target just enough, the front sight aimed at sky just ahead of the man who was already bringing the rifle to bear on him. The Indian's horse would be an easier target but might not respond to a hit fast enough. He squeezed the trigger, the gun bucked in his hand, and the noise of the report seemed to drive the Indian off the horse's back, one leg flourished briefly in the air as he vanished on the far side of his mount and the rifle turned end over end in the bright air.

At the same instant, Brandon felt a blow in his chest and saw a feathered shaft protruding from his jacket; a yell of triumph came from the remaining Indians and a protesting groan from Jack Ryan.

Brandon rose to his knees, pulled the arrow out, waved it contemptuously, snapped it between his hands, and threw the pieces away. The Indians pulled up their horses, calling to one another in what seemed to be confusion and consternation. The handcar, propelled as fast as ever by Jack Ryan's efforts, sped past the hillock and out of imminent danger.

Brandon leaned on the ties and sent two more shots back at the suddenly indecisive Indians. One horse gave a shrill, complaining neigh and rose on its hind feet with a corkscrewing motion. His rider managed to keep his place, but he and his remaining companions seemed to feel that this last setback, following the shooting of the rifleman and the demonstration of Brandon's supernatural immunity to their arrows, was enough of an indication that the spirits did not want this enterprise to prosper. They turned away, and one dismounted, presumably to aid, or if necessary bury, the man Brandon had shot, and in any case retrieve his rifle for use on a less star-crossed occasion.

"Safe now," Brandon said. He rose, grasped the handles of the lever, and began pumping. Pumping with the feet might be more efficient, he thought, but it was nice to be able to see where you were going.

"My," Jack Ryan said, getting to his feet and taking up his station at the other end of the lever. "Just a neat little hole in your coat and no blood at all. There is more to newspaper training than I would have thought, Blake."

"You're not far off," Brandon said. He reached into his jacket pocket and took out the flat, paper-wrapped package Nelson Vanbrugh had given him the night before. It was deeply dented in one corner, but not pierced. "An elegant three-column engraving rendered on a quarter-inch steel plate."

"I hear the Chinese say a picture is worth a thousand words," Jack Ryan said after a minute. "True enough this time, especially if the words are in the obituary column."

* * *

By Brandon's estimate, three quarters of an hour had passed between the time an Indian arrow punched him squarely over the heart and that at which he and Jack Ryan were sitting on a plumply upholstered seat watching their cigar smoke drift out the car windows to mingle with the locomotive's darker cloud, pushed westward by a light wind.

They were on the regular morning train to Split Rock, due to arrive at eight-thirty, half an hour from now. The section gang, at Jack Ryan's urging, had flagged it down, and by invoking John B. Parker's name with the totally unjustified implication of a mission too confidential to be discussed, Ryan had been able to turn aside the engineer's wrath at the delay and even persuade him to have the handcar coupled to the caboose and towed behind the train.

"Now," Ryan said, "if the Split Rock Marvel Hall was open and running, the conductor'd have wired our breakfast orders ahead, and they'd be waiting for us when we got there." The section gang's breakfast had been temptingly substantial, as Jack Ryan had predicted, but they had had to choose between sharing it and catching the train. "We'd eat off of linen tablecloths, with clean silver and china, perfectly cooked food and good coffee, and be fed and happy and back on the train in twenty-five minutes. And we'd know we'd have the same treatment at any Marvel Hall on any line in the West, no surprises."

"How many are there?" Brandon asked.

"Four so far, counting the Split Rock one," Jack Ryan said. "The first one, back in Kansas, and a couple others on the U.P. line. But Miss Marvell's got plans for more, never stops working out how to grow. She's a wonder, for fair."

The conviction Brandon had formed yesterday, that Jack Ryan felt more than an employee's loyalty to Jess Marvell, was conclusively confirmed by the tone of the last sentence.

"I guess she'd have to be," Jack Ryan said ruefully. "I could be working for John B. Parker and on the road to riches, but I can't help wanting to do what I can to push Marvel Halls along. When Parker saw how I went about getting the one in Split Rock built he was impressed, even though I was kind of borrowing some stuff from the railroad construction materials. Maybe because of that—John B. Parker admires a man that gets things done and doesn't pay overmuch mind to the legalities of it. I expect I am by bent and bringing-up suited to John B. Parker and his ways and could make my fortune doing what he needs done, which I'd be good at, but I hooked up with Miss Marvell first, and I don't seem able to cut loose, or want to."

He looked out the window for a moment, then said, "Onliest thing wrong with her is that addled kid she's made a kind of partner. It don't make sense to cut an idiot boy like what's-his-name in on a deal like this."

"Rush Dailey," Brandon said.

"She talked about him to you? Damn," Jack Ryan said morosely. "I think he's soft on her, too, and that's another reason she shouldn't have him around, and it's a good thing he's out of town for a while. It don't do to have sentiments going on in a business relationship."

Except if they involve you, in which case you wouldn't mind a bit, Brandon thought. I'd say you're right about Rush Dailey, too, though it's more worship than romance at the moment. Looks as if Jess Marvell is something out of the ordinary, to have two men so impressed by her.

Well, three men.

"Hey," Jack Ryan said over his shoulder, which, with his head, was extended from the car window as the train slowed, puffing fiercely, for the Split Rock station. "We are in luck. John B. Parker's on the platform talking to somebody. We can go on down to him and greet him warmly and publicly, and the damned engineer and conductor'll see us and know enough to back off from asking any questions about why we and the handcar were all the way up the line."

Brandon, when he stepped down from the car, saw Parker at the far end of the platform. He also saw, as Ryan apparently had not, a lean, nattily suited figure debarking from the car ahead and hurrying down the platform. The brief glimpse he had of the profile told him that Rush Dailey had also been a passenger on the train.

John B. Parker, when they came up to him, was not

effusive but greeted them politely enough, Brandon a touch more so than Ryan. He was standing with a tall man with a long face, round glasses, and a long brownish beard that hung down his shirtfront like a hank of Spanish moss. His face was lined and, though pale, somehow weatherbeaten, and it bore a studious expression. He was dressed in outdoor clothing, with a broad-brimmed hat that looked faintly incongruous. He was, in fact, quite close to the way Brandon had imagined the dinosaur-hunting professors Ned Norland was now guiding. Who or what he was John B. Parker evidently had no intention of imparting to Brandon and Jack Ryan, ignoring him as he spoke to them.

Jack Ryan, after a brief glance at the locomotive's cab to make sure that the engineer was getting the benefit of the scene, spoke animatedly to Parker about the progress of the newest Marvel Hall, eliciting a nod of approval or at least acknowledgment. "Could need you for something in a while," he said. "I'll let Miss Marvell know if I do." He seemed confident that his needs would supersede any that Jess Marvell might have for Jack Ryan's services, and Brandon supposed he was right. Jess Marvell needed Parker's approval for her project's existence and was experienced enough to know that thwarting him in any way would curdle that approval instantly.

"Well, even though the Marvel Hall's not ready, the Nickerson House does a good breakfast," Jack Ryan said. "Join me, Blake?"

"I've something to say to Mr. Blake," John B. Parker said. "You go on, Ryan." Jack Ryan hesitated for a second, then walked away.

Brandon contemplated following Ryan, since he had nothing to fear or hope from John B. Parker and disliked obeying the implied order, but he was curious about what he had to say.

"Good thing Gerrish made those fellows in Spargill see the light," Parker said. "That stuff with the bonds and what it all costs, that's nothing to the difference the railroad'll make. Once the tracks are in, that town's connected to the whole world, Omaha, Chicago—China and Austria-Hungary, for that matter. Since I saw you, Blake, I've been across more than half the country, Pennsylvania and back, fast as the wind, and it could've been anyplace on the continent where the rails run. I'm doing them a favor, even though they may not see it that way." He gave a wintry smile. "Spargill's more fortunate than it knows, some ways."

John B. Parker jabbed a finger at Brandon's chest. "Something I want you to tell Judge Gerrish, Blake. It was mighty clever of him to get in that business about the tracks getting in to Spargill by August or no subsidy. You tell him that what John B. Parker likes best is dealing with clever men. It's always highly rewarding."

He dropped the finger and turned to talk to the bearded man. The message had been delivered, and Calvin Blake was no longer, in John B. Parker's view, present, any more than a letter that had been stamped and deposited in the mailbox.

14

Brandon walked down the platform, wondering just what it was he had been asked to transmit. It had the form of a compliment, but, John B. Parker being John B. Parker, that was not likely. And what John B. Parker found "rewarding" might well assume a different aspect for anybody else. . . .

"'Morning, Blake." Jake Trexler waved to him from where he sat on a bench along the station wall, his feet elevated on a battered suitcase.

"On your way again?" Brandon asked.

Trexler nodded and jerked a thumb toward where Parker continued his conversation with the bearded man. "John B. Parker came down in the middle of the night on a special train with that fellow and three others, bounced around town like a bullet ricocheting in a stone cistern talking to this one and that one, now he's heading back out on the regular morning train in about half an hour. Brought me orders to go see to some machinery that's walking away from the yards up in Omaha, which if it was hereabouts and timber and such, I expect I'd solve it with a little talk with Jack Ryan. But Ryan's been neat about it, I'll say that, and

150

taken no more than's needed to keep Miss Marvell's eating house a-building, so no great harm done, and John B. Parker don't seem to mind it overmuch. But this stuff in Omaha, it can hinder operations on the whole division, and I better stop it soon. Parker's set on me traveling with him, so's he can give me all the instructions and information, he says, but I'll bet you one of them itchywhats you spoke of that someone to keep him safe from garroters is what he has in mind."

"Garroters?" Brandon said.

Trexler nodded. "Since the crash in 'seventy-three, lots of men that worked on the railroad are on the bum, and some of 'em go to the bad, and there's been a fashion for slipping up behind men that look as if they might be worth plucking, sliding a cord around the neck, and pulling it tight. Victim folds up like a boiled noodle, and the garroter goes through the pockets unhurried. Victim may wake up in a while, or never. A lot of the out-of-workers are that way because of what John B. Parker did with the companies he and his pals ran, and Parker suspects that about any of them, given the chance, would garrote him, and I can't argue with his thinking. I think he stood up to those fellows that kidnapped him so well because he could tell they weren't out to strangle him."

"Not many garroters taking the morning northbound, I'd suppose," Brandon said, taking a seat on the bench next to Trexler.

"No," Jake Trexler said. "Though there are times when it seems to me that any normal man that had a spare length of twine in his pocket when he came upon John B. Parker would just naturally want to put it to good use. But with me along he'll feel he doesn't have to worry about them. And he'll also have someone to open the window when it's stuffy, and lower it when the smoke and soot come in, and give messages to the conductor to have the train go faster or slower, according as John B. Parker thinks it should do to use the least fuel. I came with him first to do the bodyguarding. Then, when it suited him he cut loose on his own for his trip East, left me to look at pilferage here. Now it's back to bodyguarding again. There's a man that feels poorhouse-bound if he don't get at least three benefits out of anything he does or anyone that works for him."

Brandon started to speak but was drowned out by a shrill whistle blast from the locomotive. Now detached from the passenger cars, it pulled its tender over a series of switches and arcs of track and made its way toward the back of the train, which would become the front for the outbound journey. It seemed a clumsy way of doing things, but he supposed that Split Rock's strictly temporary status as the end of the line made it uneconomic to build a roundhouse and turntable. "Makes it hard for you to get along with him?" he said when the noise died down.

Jake Trexler shrugged. "Easier than you might think. John B. Parker knows everyone thinks he's a brass-bound, triple-riveted bastard, so you don't feel the urge to let him know that or to pretend he ain't. But I'll be glad to be shut of him and doing the kind of work I'm best at. I could go to two places in Omaha soon's I get there, and it's close to a certainty a bunch of the stuff that's missing'll be there, and I'll wrap up the business fast. I know the railroads, and I know the kind of crimes that get committed against rail-roads, and I am at home in working with them. It's what I do best and like most, and that's the thing I really know, what makes me Jake Trexler and not somebody else."

He looked at Brandon closely. "What you told me down in Spargill, that's something you don't know, what it is you're meant to do, even who you are. Well, out here's where a lot of men find that out, and it's a good place for it. There's men that's tried different kinds of work, different kinds of lives, finally settled on one and made a go of it, so it makes sense. But, no offense meant"—he flicked a sideways glance that revealed no one within earshot—"Mr. Brandon, I have to say you don't smell like you look, you know what I mean? You look like a man that's trying to put his life together, make sense of it after the worst kind of blow, and you talk like that man. But there's a whiff of something else, the kind of scent you might get on a tree that some animal's rubbed against. I don't know what it means, but if something sudden and direful happened in a place where you were, you're the first man I'd look into the whereabouts of."

"I guess if you're a detective, it makes sense to be over-suspicious instead of under," Brandon said mildly.

Jake Trexler grinned. "I really don't take any interest in the doings of Mr. Calvin Blake or whoever you want to be," he said. "And the past's the past and best left there, no doubt. You've got to get on with your life without looking back at what happened. And from the time that man Casmire disappeared after you shot at him in court I haven't had word of any of the men that rode with Gren Kenneally. But it might come about that I did, and it might come about that what word I got wouldn't be enough to get that man arrested, and that'd leave me feeling uneasy and out of balance."

"Not a good thing to be unbalanced," Brandon said.

"No, it isn't. But I have a crazy kind of feeling that if I was to let you know of such word of such a man, it'd balance things again, the two of us knowing it, see, instead of just one."

Jake Trexler had chosen his words with evident care, and it was clear to Brandon that he was walking a tightrope, getting his meaning across as plainly as he could but determinedly avoiding admitting, or even knowing, what he suspected Brandon's mission to be. "I can see that," Brandon said. "Kind of laying off half a heavy load somebody's put on you. I don't mind your doing that, Trexler, even if it brings up the past. Anything like that you heard, you could send it to someplace I might be in touch with now and then, and in time I'd get it. Say the Marvel Hall in Inskip, over in Kansas."

"The one in Inskip was the first, of course," Jess Marvell said. "Finished a few months ago, and doing nicely, but we learned a few things about how to do it better already." She pointed toward the unfinished wall they were facing. "Two

153

doors from the counter to the kitchen, on the left and right, instead of one in the center. That's sped things up wonderfully and cut down on collisions and breakage."

She and Brandon were surveying the almost-completed Marvel Hall just before sunset. The window and door openings were framed out but empty, and the lengthening shadows made irregular bars of black across the floor of what would be the dining room, cluttered with tools and lumber.

"Jack Ryan was telling me that you've got it worked out to a science," Brandon said. "Wiring ahead from the train so anything the customer wants'll be ready when it pulls in. That's pretty original thinking."

"Not so much," Jess Marvell said. "You figure you want to give the people a meal they want, ready so they can eat it and get back on the train when it moves on. So you ask yourself how, and first thing is that you can't ask them what it is they want when they get here, for anything that's worth eating takes time to prepare. So you ask yourself how do you find out ahead of time, and if you can't work your way from that to the telegraph, you don't have much attic space. It's been my experience that if you work out the right questions to ask, the answers are pretty usually right there in front of you."

"That's about true of . . . the detective line, too," Brandon said. It was also true of the law, which he had barely stopped himself from saying. It was for some reason difficult to keep up his now-ingrained barrier of caution with Jess Marvell.

"I suppose Mr. Trexler knows you're a detective," Jess Marvell said. "Or is it like men working for different companies, they don't let on to each other what they're doing?"

"Trexler and I, we're kind of cooperating," Brandon said. "He hears a lot of things to do with the railroad, and it may be he'd get a line on the robbers I'm tracking. In fact, I asked him to send anything he came across to your place in Inskip, so you can put it in with your reports."

"The reports," Jess Marvell said thoughtfully. She leaned against a beam supporting the rafters overhead and looked at Brandon. In the deepening shadow he could not clearly see her expression. "We've been collecting bits and pieces of information for a year and some now, Rush and me, and sending them on to places you might be, and no idea if they're doing you any good."

"Oh," Brandon said. "Sure, they've . . . I've made lots of use of them."

"But you haven't caught any of the robbers you were after."

"No," Brandon said firmly. Killed one, found the other dead of horror, but caught them, no.

"Mr. . . . Brooks," Jess Marvell said. "Say, I had to reach back for that. I'd best use Blake, as you're doing. Mr. Blake, what you told Rush and me last year about wanting any information on any Missouri train robberies, that made sense for about a minute and a half. It just seems that you'd want to be more particular about it if you wanted to get information that was useful to you. But that was how you wanted it, and you paid for it, and Heaven knows we're grateful for what you paid, since that got the lunch wagon going, and the wagon led to the Marvell Halls, which are my true dream."

Brandon could see that Jess Marvell had shifted her position against the beam, and the glint of white at the eyes in her shadowed face showed that she was gazing at him intently. "I am not going to ask you to tell me anything you don't want to," she said, "but I think it'd make it easier to find out the things you really want to know if Rush and I had a better idea of what to look for. Whatever you want to tell us, you can, and I guess you know it'll be safe with us."

"I know it would," Brandon said. "It's just . . . well, it's best it keep on this way."

"Fair enough," Jess Marvell said.

Brandon thought for a moment and said, "I wonder . . . this is a lot of work for you and Rush Dailey. What I send you isn't all that much, not a patch on what you're making or will be making on the Marvel Halls, and if it's taking time away from the more important work, what you call your true dream, then . . ."

He left the sentence unfinished, and a palpable silence seemed to swell until it filled the room and flowed over both of them. It seemed to Brandon that he or Jess Marvell might at any instant say something very important, something that probably should not be said here and now. Such as the reason why Charles Brooks, whom she did not yet know as Cole Brandon, could not relinquish contact with her; such as the reason why she had persisted in communicating with him, convinced that the work was valueless. If anything like that were said, anything could happen. Here or later in the night, in the seclusion of a hotel room. . . . For the first time in a long while he felt the pulse beats of anticipatory lust in his throat and temples, and, the dimness of the room masking her face, he had the sudden conviction that Jess Marvell felt the same thing.

"It's best it keep on this way," Jess Marvell said lightly.

Brandon relaxed. He wondered if he had slipped some kind of mental gearing, to have entertained such a preposterous set of fancies both about himself and about Jess Marvell.

The early twilight was bright enough so that the street lamps had not been lit when they stepped outside the unfinished building. They walked slowly toward the Nickerson House.

"I saw Rush Dailey getting off the early train this morning," Brandon said, not mentioning that he had been a passenger on it as well. There was probably an appropriate audience for the story of his exploits with Jack Ryan, but he had not been able to think of one yet, beyond Ned Norland the next time they encountered.

"Good to have him back," Jess Marvell said. "Jack Ryan's a wonder at getting things done, and fun to talk to, but Rush, young as he is, has got the kind of mind that comes up with new ideas that push Marvel Halls ahead a big jump at a time. Was Rush that saw that once we had the pattern we liked for the buildings it'd pay to have 'em built in sections and shipped to where they're going to go up."

"Did Jack Ryan work for the railroads or restaurants before you took him on?" Brandon asked.

Jess Marvell shook her head. "Turned up when we were putting up the second hall, up in Wyoming, and having trouble with carpenters and such. Saw what was needed, sort of took over and got it done, and said if I was satisfied, I could hire him on, and I did. I don't expect I know what half the men I've met out here were doing two years ago, and certainly not Jack. He came along when he was needed, so I suppose his track and mine were set to run together then, no matter where he'd been before."

"Tracks?" Brandon said, remembering Ned Norland's comments in Santa Fe. "I know someone who thinks some lives run on tracks, like a railroad, and they'll meet when they're meant to."

"I think he's right," Jess Marvell said. "Most things you do, most people you meet, there's a choice. Sometimes there isn't. The tracks run where they run, and sometimes they run alongside, sometimes they come to a switch and the two tracks turn into one. Or they can cross, and there's a chance of an almighty wreck."

Brandon put the memory of Nelson Vanbrugh's drawing of the dancers and fiddler as skeletons firmly out of his mind. Without Jack Ryan, for whom he had made only a perfunctory search, and with two satisfying belts of bourbon already warming his stomach and loosening the tight feeling in his head, he was determined to relish the rowdy pleasures of the huge tent they had been in the night before.

With the bottle he had brought from the bar in front of him, a cigar fuming between his teeth, and his hat pushed back on his head, Brandon felt ready for whatever the evening might bring. Three women were dancing around the central tent pole, kicking up their heels, two of them revealing a froth of petticoats like giant, if somewhat grimy, carnations; the third seemed to have dispensed with at least those undergarments—perhaps, Brandon speculated, all, as there was no evidence of corsetry under her spectacularly undulant shirtwaist. She was a tall redhead who looked both vigorous and stupid and seemed clearly to be presenting a floor sample of the services she had on offer: Yes, gents, for a small fee you get the full treatment, the power and drive of a reciprocating engine executed in hot, vibrant flesh; step up and strike the bargain and get your boiler well and truly scaled.

Last night the fascination the dancers had exerted on him had driven him away to dissolve his awakened desires in drink. Right now he could not think why he'd felt he had to do that. That moment in the darkening building with Jess Marvell had unlocked something in him that—if it was not to be, as of course it could not be, satisfied with Jess Marvell—would have to find other avenues. The vibrating wagon outside the tent was not a conceivable one, but the dancing women had a smoky fire to them that was kindling one in him.

The fiddler sped up his sawing to a finishing flourish and fell back in his seat, grinning and gasping. The dancers stopped, and the redhead took the pole in one hand, moving her grip up and down gently as she breathed deeply and looked around the room. She caught Brandon's stare and gave him a loose-lipped grin. In about five minutes, he realized, he was going to be working off a physical drought of very long standing, and he proposed to enjoy it to the hilt. He started to raise his head to beckon her.

"Hey, Mr. Blake! Now, that's a surprise and a half, running into you again, not that I ain't pleased as a horse to do that. You got to let me tell you all the great things that's been going on since we gave ourselves the pleasure of a conversation. You'll reckleck over in Arizona when I hired that cook . . ."

Raising his creased, wide-brimmed hat with one hand, flourishing a tall mug of beer with the other, beaming over his stiff collar, Rush Dailey was in the seat at Brandon's table and launched into an unstemmable spate of conversation before Brandon could complete his intended gesture.

Experience told him that a tête-à-tête with Rush Dailey could be abbreviated only by drastic measures, somewhat but not much short of shooting him. He answered the redhead's inviting grimace with a sideways shake of his head and a frown and saw her, without a change of expression, shift her aim to a man a couple of tables away who was on his feet and lurching toward her within seconds.

Brandon listened to Rush Dailey's accounts of deeds undertaken on behalf of Marvel Halls, the great prospects for the Halls, the continued progress of railroad construction and what it would mean for the Halls, and the intricacies of financing the Halls. For someone just about eighteen, as near as Brandon could figure it, Rush Dailey had an immense fund of knowledge and a deplorable willingness to share it. Brandon decided that he might as well listen, since no matter if Rush Dailey dried up right now, he had effectively deflated Brandon's urgency.

He wondered idly what uncharacteristic whim had drawn the clean-cut young entrepreneur to this sleazy place, a singular piece of bad luck for Brandon's plans for some satisfyingly depraved relaxation. Then he wondered less idly, and only for an instant, how it was that Rush Dailey came to call him by his present name, never having met him under it.

If she'd been at all sensitive to the atmosphere in the darkened building where they had spoken, Jess Marvell would have had a good notion where and how Brandon planned to spend his evening. And just what, given her absolute control over Rush Dailey, she could do to stop that. Whatever was ahead down their tracks, it seemed she didn't want that particular whistle stop behind him.

Brandon grinned and set himself to pay cordial attention to Rush Dailey. Whatever he was, Rush Dailey had carried a message he hadn't been aware of, a message that warmed Brandon more than the whiskey. Tonight wasn't the time to act on it, and he'd be out of Split Rock and on his way to Spargill in the morning, but somewhere down the line the Cole Brandon track and the Jess Marvell track had some territory to go through together, he was sure of that.

15

"No, Marshal, nobody's been killed, you're right about that. But the harassment's slowing the track-laying, and that could be a worse thing for the town than a few sudden deaths." Judge Gerrish did not say who of Spargill's citizens might be dispensed with, but Brandon was pretty sure, going by the judge's expression and tone, that Marshal Tooley would figure prominently on the list.

"Shots fired into the workers' camp at night, materials stolen, rails prised up so that the supply train could have been wrecked," Judge Gerrish said. "And one of the night guards knocked out, left to lie unconscious all through his watch. The men are spooked, and that makes them work slower, and then there's missing tools and such, and they work slower still. They're not making the progress they need to, and that's something that should worry all of us."

Marshal Tooley tilted his chair back and squinted at the judge over his boots, the heels of which were solidly planted on his desk. "Main progress the railroad's makin' seems to be t' make trouble," he said. "Six weeks or what back, before the thing was even settled, that Parker man that's such a big cheese in railroadin' come down here and got choused

160

around by some drifters, and you fellows got into such a takin' about it."

" 'Choused around' is not how I would describe a brutal armed assault and kidnapping," Judge Gerrish said.

Marshal Tooley shrugged, for an instant imperiling the balance of the back-tilted chair. "There's fights the bartender settles, with everybody friends again and no need to call me in, that shows more damages than what that did. But if you want t' make it bigger an' badder, fine, for that's what I'm sayin'—the railroad brings trouble. That, now this that you've come here about, and the track's still miles off. When it gets here, then you're gonna have what they got in Split Rock—booze tents and whore wagons and tinhorns, like Blake here wrote it up."

Judge Gerrish glared at Brandon. He had berated Abner Willson for running Calvin Blake's cleaned-up account of the lively doings on the far side of the tracks in Split Rock, maintaining that anything that painted less than a rosy picture of the railroad would undercut Spargill's support for it.

"I toned it down a lot, Judge," Brandon had protested. "Willson said it was good stuff, picturesque, like Bret Harte or Mark Twain." Brandon had thought so, too, and considered that for someone whose writing, up to a few weeks before, had been confined to letters and legal briefs and memoranda, he had developed a pretty good style.

"Bret Harte and Mark Twain weren't writing for a paper that was beating the drums to get a railroad in," Judge Gerrish said, "and you ought to have had better sense, Abner Willson, than to print that stuff. If you want to give your readers colorful glimpses of the seamy side of life, stick to Spargill, where it's at least real news people might want to know about. Anything away from here don't mean anything to them, so whatever you print about it, make it serve a purpose, or at least for God's sake don't let it undermine anything we're trying to achieve. Didn't anything better than debauchery and degeneration happen to you up there, Blake?" he asked Brandon.

The picture of himself and Jack Ryan lying on their backs,

desperately pumping the handcar with their feet while Indians showered them with bullets and arrows, came to his mind. An even worse advertisement for the railroad, that would be. "Not much," he had said.

Now, in the marshal's office, bathed in sunlight made watery by its difficult passage through the dusty windowpanes, Brandon saw that at least one reader of the *Chronicle & Advertiser* had taken the story as the judge had feared, as ammunition for a volley of complaints about the disorder the railroad would bring. He had to admit that there was some justice in the marshal's gloomy attitude; the railroad would bring change, and it had been clear from the start that change was something Tooley abhorred, except when it was a matter of changing the status of a good number of the respectable ladies of the town.

"We haven't had any trouble with Indians hereabouts since the town got started," the marshal said. "But they don't care for railroads at all, and any time you get railroad building, you get Indian trouble. And that's the thing, Judge—Indian doings ain't my business. The tracks are well away from Spargill, which is what I'm marshal of, and the army is who gets to deal with Indians. If I get up a posse and go out after them that's snipin' at the railroaders, then I am in federal trouble, which is nowhere for a lawman to be."

"That's nonsense!" Judge Gerrish said. "When there's a breach of the law it's up to any law officer to deal with it!"

"I ain't learned in the law, so I got to go on my own understandin' of it," Marshal Tooley said. "You bring me some statutes and codes and enactments as tells me I can go outside my jurisdiction and meddle in federal business, and I'll snap to attention and get at it."

The judge fumed a moment or so more, but Tooley was unmovable, and Gerrish and Brandon left his office. "The damn thing is, he's got a chance of being right in what he says," Judge Gerrish muttered. "Law out here's a crazy quilt of territorial and local statutes and federal regulations, and you can make out a case for almost any interpretation you favor. That's the same damn stuff he pulled when Parker was kidnapped, hiding behind the tangle the law's in. Usual thing is, you do what's needed and sort out the law on it afterwards, and any town marshal worth his salt would do that—at the damned least send Nason out to look into it—that's what a deputy's for, to do what the boss can't be bothered with. Tooley's all very well for Spargill the way it's been, but I don't know if he'll do after the trains start coming."

"Thanks for asking me along," Brandon said. "But I don't see there's much of a story to write up, the marshal declining to take action." No newspaper story, but certainly a couple of things to think about. For one, whoever was harassing the track crew, it probably wasn't Indians. Even if they were just being playful, Indians had the habit of playing hard, and it wasn't in their rules to knock a sentry out and leave him to wake up in the morning with his hair still on. For another, Judge Gerrish seemed to have an un-judicial impatience with the complexities of the law. In Brandon's experience, a judge would sooner lose himself in untangling a cat's cradle of statute and precedent than make up his mind outright.

"No," the judge said disgustedly. "Any honest story about Tooley'd break every law of libel, at least any I'd feel like writing."

And the obscenity statutes, too, Brandon thought. As far as he could tell, Judge Gerrish had not caught wind of Tooley's priapic progress through the bedrooms of Spargill, which spoke well of his detachment from the vices of gossip and prurience, less well of his grasp of what was going on in his town. It seemed to him that Gerrish's Spargill was a kind of impersonal mosaic of business and political elements, with the pungency of everyday human concerns and contrariness not getting much attention. His view of the town made it possible to manipulate matters as he had with ramming the increased bond issue through, but it could let him in for some surprises.

"I'll go down to the *Chronicle* office and breathe fire on Willson for a while," Judge Gerrish said. "It'll relieve my mind and won't do Willson any harm. How's he getting on with courting Julie Caldwell these days?"

"As usual," Brandon said. "Keeps trying to read her for

signs, sometimes finds favorable ones, sometimes unfavorable, but never makes any kind of move himself. I'm going out to Caldwell's in a while to look over how he's getting on with that car, and I'm to give Willson a full and detailed report on Miss Caldwell's temperature, humidity, and barometric pressure so he can make his next predictions for his personal almanac. What he ever expects to do with them, I haven't got a notion."

The wilderness of stumps around Caldwell's sawmill was a good deal larger than on Brandon's first visit. As Spargill grew the ancient woods around it retreated. Brandon wondered what the railroad's appetite for wood to fuel the locomotives would do to the forests. He supposed that if the trees along the right of way were felled to feed the trains, that would cut down on the danger of fires set by sparks from the smokestacks. There might be some kind of balance of benefits in there, if he troubled to puzzle it out.

"She is just about done," Jim Caldwell said proudly. "Upholstery for the seats, and apply and buff two more coats of varnish for the outside paintwork, and there we are, ready to turn her over to the DT and show the world what Spargill can do."

The passenger car was certainly impressive. Even in the shadow of the shed its green, gold, and red seemed to generate, rather than reflect, light.

"It looks about as good as that engraving Mr. Willson ran of it in the paper," Julie Caldwell said.

"Better," Jim Caldwell said. "That's a humdinger of a picture, all right, but it don't show the colors or give you a feel of her size."

"It was clever of Mr. Willson to find a way to have the engraving done," Julie Caldwell said. "It pleases me a lot that he did that and printed it. But of course, it was Mr. Vanbrugh that did the engraving, and just from seeing the *Spirit* once and making a couple of sketches. It's wonderful how someone can do that."

Brandon considered that those two comments would leave Willson poised between ecstasy and despair, and he was pretty sure that that was what Julie Caldwell, confident that they would be relayed to Abner Willson, meant them to do. It was about as certain as anything could be that she had marked Willson out as hers, provided he had the gumption to declare himself. Meanwhile, she would neither beckon him on nor slam the door on his toes, just leave him dangling until he decided to chance his luck.

"Thing I didn't understand about the picture," Caldwell said. "Wonderful delicate all over, but up in one corner it was kind of smudged and blurry."

With the aid of a hammer and a piece of lead foil, Brandon had brought the dent made by the arrow that hit him almost level with the rest of the steel plate, but not without some distortion of the engraved lines. He still did not feel inclined to go into what he considered a ludicrous misadventure, and said shortly, "Inking problem on some copies, I expect."

"Well, it was Auralee Conklin a while back, but none since," the man being shaved said.

"Marshal's losing his endearing young charms?" the barber said, sliding the razor along the underside of his customer's chin.

"Dunno," the customer said. "Either the lady's better at keeping things hid than the rest, or that chapter is closed. Any rate, Tooley's been visiting the girls up on Pike Street some frequent, which ain't been his custom, so he has been reduced to paying for it, and it ain't Tooley's way to do that if he can get it for free, like he used to."

"It will be a relief to me if all that's stopped," a man waiting for a haircut said. "There is half a dozen men I got to watch my tongue with so's I don't let the pig out of the bag about what their wives is up to, and I wouldn't care to add to the list. It is a wonder the husbands don't cotton on to what's up."

"All them men is busy about business," the man being shaved said. "Their stores and what, and the town council. They sees only what bears on that, plus which they ain't anxious to know about something that'd be shaming to them and oblige 'em to do something prominent and dangerous."

Brandon, leafing through a tattered *Harper's Weekly* containing an interesting article that proved conclusively that the southern states would never secede, nodded slightly. Conklin, Hardy, and the rest would be highly resistant to noticing anything inconvenient.

The barbershop door creaked open and slammed shut, and another candidate for a shave came in and took a seat next to Brandon. "Anybody heard of any emigrants comin' through?" he asked.

"No," the barber said.

"Well, I was out huntin' towards Happy Squaw Lake a couple days back, and I seen some smoke, so I worked around till as I could get a look without bein' seen myself, and I seen a camp with a kind of covered wagon and some fellows around a fire. Looked like they'd been there a while."

"Any women, children?" the man being shaved said.

"Not that I seen," the news-bearer said. "Got a look at one fellow, tall class of a man in a big hat, beard on him like a muffler knit out of horsehair."

Brandon continued to scan the magazine's praise for President Buchanan's enlightened policies, considering that the description of the campers' leader fit remarkably closely the man he had seen talking to John B. Parker in Split Rock.

Brandon emitted a strangled howl and came close to tearing the copy of the *Chronicle & Advertiser* he was reading across. He had proofread the sections Willson had told him to the night before, about half the paper, and was now, having helped the publisher distribute the day's edition, back in the office and reading it to see what else of interest it might hold. He had been rewarded far more than he had expected, or wanted.

"What the *hell* is this . . . this . . ." Words failed him, and he waved the crumpled paper at Willson.

"What is what?" Abner Willson asked.

"This . . . about Tooley," Brandon grated.

"Not Marshal Tooley, Morsel Toothsome, printed plain

for all to read," Abner Willson said cheerfully. "You have to be careful not to use real names in this kind of stuff. This is kind of a tradition in frontier newspapers, Blake—good, hearty joshing, see? You give somebody that needs it a kind of a jab, and he gets the picture, and everybody has a good laugh."

Brandon breathed slowly and deeply, forcing himself to keep from jabbering and groaning as he reread the piece headed "The Tale of Morsel Toothsome."

Morsel, a dainty young fellow, had the responsibility for keeping order in an unnamed village. He was, the story reported, a dab hand at keeping boys from rolling their hoops to the endangerment of the public, or stealing apples, and so satisfied the villagers, there being no other criminal activities. But when ruffians appeared on the outskirts of town and began throwing rocks and stealing horses, Morsel claimed that what went on out of the center of town was not his business and retreated from his responsibilities to playing blindman's buff and other games with the girls, and hiding in their beds when called to duty.

"Maybe a little heavy-handed," Abner Willson said, "but you don't want to go for subtlety with the kind of readers we get. I figure it'll prod Tooley into doing something about whoever's giving the railroad people a bad time. That about getting into girls' games might be a little broad, but it's so wide of the mark, he won't take offense—one thing Tooley isn't is girlish."

Brandon closed his eyes for a moment. It would be nice not to have to open them again, but there was no way out. He did so, and looked at Abner Willson. "Boss," he said, "you are right about Tooley not being girlish, I am sorry to say. He is so damned male, in fact, that he has been playing games with the girls and jumping into their beds every chance he gets. The girls in the main being the wives of prominent businessmen and town councilmen."

"You're joking, Blake," Abner Willson said after a moment. He looked at Brandon's face. "No, you're not joking." He listened with growing dismay to Brandon's summary of Tooley's career as Casanova. "Oh, damn, damn, damn, dear me and damn," Willson said when Brandon finished. "And I don't carry a gun. The pen is mightier than the sword, I always figured, but a sword won't ventilate you from twenty feet away, will it? You got a gun you can lend me, Blake? If you do, I can decide whether to defend myself or blow my own brains out before Tooley does it for me."

Brandon fished the .38 from his trousers pocket and gave it to Willson. It was probably a bad idea, but Willson needed a weapon right now, if only to keep from shaking apart like an engine speeding without a governor.

Willson held the revolver awkwardly, but with a renewal of confidence. "Maybe Tooley won't be all that mad," he said. "It's kind of public, but a man like that might take it as a sort of compliment that his, ah, amours are raising comment in the papers. A kind of advertisement, you might say."

Brandon shook his head. "Not any more. Why isn't known, but the ladies cut Tooley off a while ago. So what you wrote's going to look to him like the worst kind of mockery, both about what he did and about not getting to do it any more."

Abner Willson's shoulders slumped, and he inspected the barrel of the .38 with gloomy interest, as if wondering what it would taste like. "I wonder if Miss Caldwell would put flowers on my grave. Probably wouldn't take the time off from being painted by that popinjay Vanbrugh, not even to pick a bunch of daisies."

Brandon heard distant shouts and cries and a sudden pounding of feet on the plankwalk. A bulky shape, moving too fast to be identified, flashed past the *Chronicle*'s street window, and the front door burst in, kicked almost off its hinges.

Though everything was happening in an instant, Brandon seemed to see it clearly and slowly, as if in a series of pictures revealed by constant flashes of lightning. Tooley stood in the wrecked doorway, bellowing with rage, raising his revolver to bear on Abner Willson. Willson goggled at the marshal, making no effort to raise the .38 that dangled at his side.

Brandon clawed the tiny .30-caliber single-shot from his vest. Flame and noise sprang from Tooley's pistol, and a case of type next to Willson scattered leaden slugs over the table and floor; another shot, fired while Brandon was raising his pistol, spun Willson's hat into the air.

Brandon took time to aim, trying for the marshal's gun hand. Tooley howled but did not drop the gun, though he clapped his left hand to his right forearm. He turned the gun on Brandon and fired, but the shot went wide, his wound being enough to throw his aim off at least temporarily. Brandon threw the empty gun at Tooley's face and jumped toward him, wincing at the blast of another shot. Then he was grappling with Tooley, trying to twist the revolver from his hand.

Tooley suddenly grabbed the weapon with his left hand and jammed the muzzle against Brandon's abdomen. Brandon was quite sure that the last thing he would ever see was the whites of Tooley's glaring eyes and his distorted face, then the whites vanished under sliding lids and the face relaxed.

The marshal slumped to the floor, hands dragging at Brandon as he went down. Judge Gerrish stood facing Brandon, breathing heavily, his stubby revolver held by the barrel, the butt that had felled Tooley still facing upward.

16

If he'd given me a chance, I'd have explained that I didn't mean anything by it," Willson said. "Or anyways not what he thought I meant."

"'Marshal, all I wanted to do was tell the readers you're a sissy who hung around with the girls because you were scared to do your job'—if he worked out that was what you meant, sure, he'd have slapped you on the shoulder and had a good laugh," Brandon said sourly. His contacts with newspapermen in St. Louis had been slight, but enough to convince him that they assayed a richer vein of idiocy than the usual run of people, and Willson seemed to be running true to form. Maybe there was something in the ink that got to them after a while.

Of course, what Cole Brandon was doing would, in some eyes, mark him as ready to be outfitted in a straitjacket, but if so, it was a cosmic kind of madness, the lunacy of a Lear or a Hamlet, robbed of sanity by the malice of fate, not a piece of lackwit zaniness. It was almost twelve hours since Tooley had burst in shooting, been clubbed down by Judge Gerrish and carried off to jail by his deputy and acting replacement, Nason, with the aid of a couple of drafted loafers, but Brandon was still jumpy over it. The muzzle of Tooley's revolver had left no lasting mark on his belly, but it seemed to him that the point of its contact burned as if he had been branded there. A pound or so finger pressure on the trigger and Cole Brandon's bowels would have been spread over the office floor, and Calvin Blake would have had a black-bordered eulogy in the *Chronicle & Advertiser*.

Brandon and Judge Gerrish sprawled in chairs in front of the main worktable, watching Willson compose a story directly on the form, his fingers blurring with speed as they snatched slugs of type and set them up along the wooden guides. His lips worked slightly; Brandon supposed he was reciting the story as he invented it, word by word, as he snatched at the lead letters that built it up in the form.

"Can't blame him, in a way," Abner Willson said, bizarrely continuing to form words he was not saying aloud in the intervals between the ones actually intended for his hearers as his fingers moved with machinelike speed. "Must have seemed I was out to spill his secrets to the whole town and make fun of him while I did it."

"And you did it a lot more neatly out of ignorance than you would have on purpose," Judge Gerrish observed. "Kind of thing you should have known, Willson." He looked speculatively at Brandon.

"Willson sends me out to get stories he can use," Brandon said, "preferably with lots of names in them. What I learned about Tooley's tomcatting, that wasn't a story we'd ever print, even though it had lots of names of ladies who usually like to see themselves mentioned in the paper. So I didn't consider it was my business to tell Willson everything I learned or heard, when there wasn't anything he could do with it just now."

"You seem to have a way with getting hold of a story, even writing it up," Judge Gerrish said. "But if you don't have the burning urge to tell everything you hear, and paint it in primary colors, I don't know that you'll ever make a newspaperman. All the same, Willson should have known about Tooley, just on his own; and so should I. It's nothing but a squalid scandal, I suppose, but there's something about it that frets me some. I don't know the ladies very well, and it may be that they have their own, um, urgencies, for women get up to surprising things as they get along. Frankly, they wouldn't have struck me as the kind of women Tooley would have pursued."

"Maybe they kind of made it worth his while," Abner Willson said. "Tooley always seemed to have more money than he got paid."

"That's a disgusting thought!" Gerrish snapped.

"I know," Abner Willson said. "That's what makes me afraid it could be true. That's that one done." He twisted the locking clamps into place on the page form and carried it back to place it next to the press.

He returned and took a chair facing Judge Gerrish and Brandon. "Now that I've got most of the paper out of the way," he said, "there is the question of what to do about Tooley. Not the law stuff—that's your department, Judge, but what goes into the paper, which is what the public is going to pay a lot more attention to. 'Mad Marshal's Shooting Spree! Attempts Murder When Exposed as Lecherous Lothario,' that's kind of what it calls for. But it don't make the town look good, does it? Could make the DT people wonder if it's sound enough to run the tracks to."

Judge Gerrish nodded his head. "I doubt John B. Parker would be swayed in matters of business by a scandal, except to look for a way to gain some advantage out of it, but I don't think we want Parker to be sniffing around for any more edge than he already has, and the less said about this the better. You get into Tooley's reasons for this and the whole town goes into a turmoil, with the ladies denying everything, or, worse, admitting it. The business community would go all to hell."

"Likely to come out at the trial," Brandon said. "Defense counsel'll have it out of him in no time, and he's bound to use it in court."

"True enough," Judge Gerrish said. "You'll doubtless have observed some of St. Louis's more adept trial lawyers in action during your days on the *Dispatch*." Brandon stirred uneasily, but the judge did not seem to have given any special significance to his mention of St. Louis lawyers. "Best we don't have a trial, certainly not a local one. I believe I'll work out something with him—guilty plea, sentence suspended on condition he leaves Spargill and is never seen here again. In fact," the judge said thoughtfully, "if so many people hadn't seen him go crazy and start shooting, I'd be inclined to paper the whole thing over and keep him on as marshal. Nason'll have to take over, at least for a while, and, difficult though Tooley was, I don't think Nason could handle the job as well."

"No, he couldn't," Abner Willson said acidly. "I can't see Nason expressing his criticism of something he read in the paper by killing the publisher and reporter. He ain't the man Tooley was, and I don't object to that one bit. Out of sight, out of mind—out of our sight, out of his mind, I suppose that'd be—that's the ticket for Tooley, as far as I'm concerned."

Brandon halfway agreed. At the moment Tooley had been jamming the gun against him he would cheerfully have seen the marshal struck by lightning or bitten by wolf-sized tarantulas, but once the danger was past he was indifferent about what happened to the man who had caused it. Since his unbroken presence on the job for two years showed that he hadn't been part of the gang that had ridden with Gren Kenneally that autumn day, what happened to him was unimportant.

Brandon listened silently to the other two men discuss the matter and carried his reflections further. Given more thought, the notion of sending the marshal on his way with instructions to go and sin no more, at least not anywhere near Spargill, struck Brandon as off the mark in some way. There was a lot left unexplained about Tooley, such as his determined amorous forays in unlikely territory and his clear animosity toward the railroad. Spargill might feel that it was finished with Tooley, but was Tooley ready to be finished with Spargill?

If he really dug his heels in, demanded a trial, and made it clear that trial would implicate the wives of the most prominent men in the business community and town government, he might be able to cut a deal that would in fact get him his old job back, and maybe a seat on the town council thrown in.

Or, of course, get him an accidental death or suicide while in custody, not an unusual exit for an embarrassing prisoner. Tooley, though, seemed to have done his job well enough so that there was not, as in many towns, a pool of criminal talent to draw on for a discreet killing. There were some unemployed freighters, let go by Ben Stoddard as he reduced his freighting business in preparation for the loss of half of it when train service would connect Spargill with the world that lay to the north. For the moment the freighters preferred to hang around and drink up what they had left rather than head out and try to find work. The most likely prospective assassin was returning his elements to the earth at the bottom of a gulch south of Spargill. Brandon frowned. Sut Liebwohl would have been a good candidate for any job of murder going, by what Brandon had seen, but he could not somehow convincingly visualize Liebwohl killing Tooley. It seemed to him that there were a lot of discordant elements in the picture of the situation he had built up, and, maddeningly, that looking at it from a slightly different angle would make sense out of it, like turning a kaleidoscope and seeing a new, symmetrical pattern emerge as the jumbled pieces of glass shifted position.

"A nervous breakdown brought on by the cares of office and unremitting faithful service, that might be the line," Abner Willson said. "Condolences of community, magnanimous refusal of publisher to press charges, and so on."

"Expression of confidence in Acting Marshal Nason," Judge Gerrish said. "Plus a hint that the council'll be hunting someone halfway competent to do the job and boot Nason back down to deputy, in case nobody believes in the confidence part."

"That's all very well," Brandon said slowly, "if Tooley wants to go. I'm not sure that he does."

Brandon's explanation of why Marshal Tooley might not care to leave Spargill was interrupted and, as it proved, exploded by the entrance of Nason, his flannel shirt sagging under the weight of what had been Tooley's star of office. Brandon was not sure that Tooley had had enough of Spargill, but Tooley seemed more certain.

"When I come back from supper," the acting marshal said, "I looked in on him to give him a sandwich I'd brung, since there ain't no provision for feeding prisoners regular, which the marshal says is 'cause the town council cain't see—"

"You're the marshal now, Nason," Judge Gerrish said irritably. "For God's sake act like it and tell us what you came to tell."

"Bars sawed right out of the window, wide open, nobody in the cell," Nason said. "Before you go on at me," he added, raising a hand defensively, "I didn't put him in the cell with no hacksaw blade on him. I was tryin' to work it out on my way up here to tell you, and what I come up with was that he was doin' some work there a while back, left the blade by mistake, and remembered where it was whenas he was put there today."

After a long pause Judge Gerrish said, with effortful calm, "That doesn't seem all that likely, Nason."

"No, it don't, not one bit," the acting marshal said. "But if it ain't that, then someone on the outside cut them bars and loosed him. And that means we got to ask around town, ask all sorts of folks about who'd want the marshal away from here before the law's handled his case. Why they'd want that. What the marshal done to make 'em want it. And so on. So it seemed to me that the saw left behind by accident was the best explanation to go on with."

The pause before Judge Gerrish spoke this time was reflective rather than stupefied. "So it is, Nason, so it is. Clever of you to think of it."

It seemed to Brandon that Nason was turning out to be better qualified than Tooley at one prime function of a town marshal: seeing to it that those who pulled the levers of power got what they wanted. But unasked or not, the question remained: Who wanted Tooley out and why? And more important, what was Tooley going to do now—put as much distance as he could between himself and Spargill, or, if Brandon had been right in his guess, see to unfinished business?

After a week Brandon had seen no evidence that the departed ex-marshal had left loose ends behind him that he meant to tie off. His horse had vanished from the livery stable, and a few possessions from his rooming house, presumably at the time he had escaped; whether removed by Tooley or by the well-wisher who had cut the bars in his cell window could not be determined. Nobody had reported seeing him in the hills near town, and nobody had behaved suspiciously enough to suggest they were hiding him closer by. Nason, displaying more activity than Brandon—and for that matter than most people in Spargill—had expected, had gone out to check on the mysterious party led by the bearded man Brandon had seen talking to John B. Parker at the Split Rock station, and he'd discovered that they were naturalists from an eastern college combining a vacation with a survey of the plant and animal life of Colorado. They had neither seen nor heard anything of Tooley.

Nason seemed to be turning out to be a satisfactory replacement, Brandon thought as he stopped in his morning rounds to take a look at the site where the train station would be built when the tracks reached here—in not too many days, if the schedule was to be met. Disorder had not overtaken Spargill, and there were no more mildly troublesome drunks showing how much they were enjoying life by fighting or shouting than there had been before—fewer, in fact, since most of Stoddard's laid-off bullwhackers had left town. When the railroad got here, it would be a different picture, Brandon thought. The crowd that livened things up around Split Rock would be coming in when Spargill became the railhead, and it would take more than Nason to keep them in line.

That stretch of flat land beyond the station side, he thought, that's where the yards and the roundhouse would be, probably, and beyond that the saloon and gambling tents and the whores' carts would mushroom.

Brandon walked toward the center of town and turned down Main Street. Ben Stoddard hailed him from the freight office. "Any news of the marshal, Blake?"

"Marshaling away down at the office when I passed, 'bout twenty minutes ago," Brandon said.

"Tooley, I mean," Ben Stoddard said. "It'll take me a while to think of Len Nason as anything but a kind of tail dragging behind Tooley."

"Not sighted, as far as I hear," Brandon said. "Expect he's a long way off by now." He considered that as a probability, kept short of certainty by the nagging feeling that Tooley still had something to do in Spargill. "How's business?"

Ben Stoddard shrugged. "Some of the merchants that can do it are holding off on having stuff sent here until the railroad comes and the freight rates drop by about half, which is what they're bound to do. But there's not too many do that, so the income isn't down all that badly, and the cash isn't draining out so fast these days."

"Cut the payroll some when you paid off those bullwhackers," Brandon said.

"That and . . . some other economies," Ben Stoddard said. "That load that vanished on the way to Denver last month, that cost some, though the loss hit the shippers mainly, since we can't afford to guarantee arrival—if stuff gets broken along the way, we'll pay up for that, but disappearances of wagon and goods together, we don't cover that. Look on it more as an act of God."

Brandon, who knew that it was an act of the less highly regarded Sut Liebwohl, and that it had nearly included his own permanent disappearance, said nothing and continued on his way.

Outside the building that quartered the Businessmen's Club on the ground floor and Judge Gerrish's chambers on the second he saw a sleek yellow-brown dog tied to a post. It looked like the animal he had seen Tobit Conklin, the butcher, leading around Spargill. It thrived on scraps from the butcher block, and waggish customers would sometimes insist on seeing that it was alive and intact before making their purchases.

Brandon poked his head in the door and saw Judge Gerrish in conference with Conklin, sign painter Sam Hardy, dry-goods merchant Charley Pratt, and George Parsons, the bank president. He knew them as the most influential members of the town council, its informal executive committee. At least two of them—all four, he suspected —had been cuckolded by Marshal Tooley. But he expected that that was not what they were conferring with Gerrish about. He wondered if in fact they, like most of the rest of the town, knew of it, and he supposed that they had worked pretty hard not to.

Pratt looked up and saw him. "Private meeting, Blake," he called. "No story yet, but there's likely to be in a while, and you or Willson will be let know of it." From his tone it did not sound as if the story would be a cheerful one.

"Gentlemen," Judge Gerrish said, "I suggest we admit Mr. Blake to our deliberations. As we find ourselves confronted with a wall we don't know how to scale or dismantle, it might be useful to have another pair of eyes look at it. Blake might see something we don't."

"What's there to see?" George Parsons asked morosely. "We've outsmarted ourselves, and there's no way out of it."

"Mr. Blake has an original mind," Judge Gerrish said. "I have known him to look at an equally unpromising situation and come up with a highly inventive yet effective solution."

"What situation?" Parsons asked.

"It is still a matter of some confidentiality," Judge Gerrish said smoothly, "and not suited for public discussion, but you may take it from me that it saved the day." Brandon admired the deft way in which the judge recommended to the council members the talents of the man who had given the judge the inspiration for the scheme he had used to bamboozle them into passing the railroad bond issue.

Brandon pulled up a chair and joined the five men at the table. The problem was simple and dire: There was no prospect of the DT tracks reaching the Spargill city limits before the August 1 deadline.

"If they don't, then the subsidy's off," Parsons said. "And if the subsidy's off, then so's the railroad. John B. Parker's back in Split Rock, keeping an eye on progress, and if the deadline's not met and the subsidy's forfeited, he'll pick some other route south for the DT, pull up some track if he has to, pass the loss on to the stockholders, and Spargill dries up and blows away. Damn it, Gerrish, if you didn't have that forfeiture clause tied to the subsidy, we wouldn't be in this fix!"

"Without that clause you fellows wouldn't have gone for the extra fifty thousand Parsons demanded, and you know it," Judge Gerrish said, "and the townspeople wouldn't have voted for the bond issue either. We had to have that in to get the bonds through."

"And there wasn't any reason to think there'd be this kind of delay," Charley Pratt cut in. "Shooting into the track crew's camp, thefts, and so on. Can't even tell if it's Indians, the way Tooley claimed."

"We've got all the damn money for the subsidy down in the vault," George Parsons said, "and God knows how we'll sort out handing it back if the whole thing falls through."

Brandon listened to a few minutes of bickering and recrimination, then said, "Where's it look like the tracks'll be by the deadline?"

"Not far off," Sam Hardy said. He shoved over to Brandon a map he had been studying. "About eight miles north of the town limits, but the stretch from there on in's pretty troublesome, so it'd take 'most a week to get track through."

"Could we kind of stop the clock?" Charley Pratt said. "You know, just not turn the calendar page over, kind of keep it July thirty-one till the tracks get in?"

A brief silence fell, during which Pratt's fellow councilmen looked at him closely, as if wondering, Brandon thought, whether some prankster had substituted a quantity of canned tomatoes for his brains. After a moment Tobit Conklin said, "Charley, if you eat a couple of pounds of my best beefsteak tonight, you are for damn sure going to be visiting the privy before a week or ten days has gone by. There is clocks you do not stop."

"True enough," Brandon said. "But there could be another side to that coin. Where do the tracks have to be laid to?"

"North Road," Sam Hardy said. "Not that there's a road there now, but there will be, it's laid out on the map right at the town line."

"Does it say North Road in the forfeiture clause?" Brandon asked.

Judge Gerrish searched papers in front of him, held one up, and inspected it. "No," he said. "Not as such, just 'the northernmost limits of the municipality of Spargill.'"

"Same thing," Sam Hardy said. "Why're we—"

"And these limits are set out how and where?" Brandon asked.

"In the charter of incorporation," Judge Gerrish said, looking at Brandon with some interest. "Some specifics of minutes and seconds of north latitude, plus some landmarks—line runs straight east from that needle kind of rock in the river, as I recall."

"The charter's bylaws provide for amendment?" Brandon asked.

"Well, naturally you'd have to . . . oh. Oh, yes, indeed." Judge Gerrish looked sharply at Brandon. "That's something I should have seen, isn't it? And it took a newspaperman to spot it. Blake, it seems to me your talents are wasted in your line of work."

"Maybe, Judge," Brandon said, pushing back his chair and rising to his feet. "But I'd best get back to it anyhow. Good day, gentlemen." He gave them a sketchy wave of the hand and walked toward the door.

The four councilmen gaped at him and set up a gabble of confused inquiry and expostulation. Gerrish slammed his hand on the table with something of the effect a gavel, and they fell silent.

"As Tobit pointed out so colorfully that I, for one, will never forget it, we can't do anything about the matter of time in this," Gerrish said. "The tracks have got to be at the city limits by the first, and there's no way around that. Mr.

Blake reminds us that there's another aspect to the business, and that's location."

Gerrish paused a moment and looked around at his audience, now mesmerized. "Gentlemen, we can't move the track work along any faster—but we can by God move the town limits to where the tracks'll be by August first!"

17

As the tracks snaked closer to Spargill, keeping pace with the remorseless advance of the calendar and clock toward the end of the month and the deadline, railroad fever had grown in the town, with more and more Spargillers making the steadily shorter trip north to see the track gangs in action. Brandon had ridden out twice, each time impressed by the implacable movement forward of the iron rails, slammed into place on the ties by running workmen, then spiked down and levered into exact alignment. He was also somewhat shaken by the alteration in the land that the tracks made. First there was the area of flux and change, the ground dug out level for the right of way, then the steadily advancing rails and the yelling, hammering workers; and behind them, stretching north, the lines of track, looking as if they had been there forever, taming and binding the land.

Each time he had written pretty much the same story, which never contained any mention of cut trees, scarred earth and vanished birds and animals. "The town's bet a lot on this, and they're caught up in it worse than baseball, 'most as bad as gold fever," Abner Willson said. "So everything we write about the railroad's going to be a big hurrah, or it don't get printed."

The stories were illustrated with steel engravings of track-laying, not made on the spot but sent down by Nelson Vanbrugh. "Did these up near Split Rock," the note to Abner Willson accompanying the plates said, "but who's to know? All are 1 or 2 columns, lines are a touch broad for better reproduction on your paper. Feel free to use with my compliments."

"The bastard," Abner Willson said, holding the plates up for inspection.

"No good?" Brandon asked.

"They're great," Willson said gloomily. "The skunk's coarsened the engraving just enough so's the lines won't blur on the cheap paper I use. He's a dab hand at it for fair, God wither his fingers."

Brandon's amused snort at this self-contradictory comment prompted Abner Willson to explain. "He figures Miss Caldwell's train-crazy, like her pa, and so anything he can do that boosts it will put him in good with her, and I don't have a choice but to run his stuff, since I got to admit it makes the paper hum. It is a torture when the calls of a man's profession and livelihood contend with those of his nature and inclination, Blake."

"But she's not, is she? And so you can run all his engravings you like without putting up his stock any," Brandon said.

Abner Willson brightened. "There is that. I will use the serpent's stuff and benefit from it, leaving him to crawl about with nary an apple to bite on."

Brandon found that he did not mind writing what amounted to puffery for the railroad. When he composed his stories he found that he was as avid as any genuine resident of Spargill for the trains to start, for the life, growth, and prosperity that would inevitably ensue. After all, it had taken two of his most bizarre inspirations to bring this about, and he felt a certain responsibility—perhaps that of a man who has seduced a woman while blind drunk or crazy and feels a guilty paternal interest in the by-blow, but there all the same. He found this odd, then reflected that he had been there close to two months, and that the town had become a real place to him, not just a stage set for his mission—not that there had been any indication of forthcoming action on that score—and that Calvin Blake was becoming as real as Cole Brandon. As the old actor, Edmund Chambers, had told him back in Kansas, making yourself believe the part you were playing was the key to doing it successfully; but what happened if the belief grew stronger than the awareness that it was a part?

Now it was the last day, with the sun just past its zenith and starting its slide toward the rim of the hills to the west. Some hours after it had sunk behind them, the track crew, working by the light of flaring torches, would drop a pair of rails on a row of ties, sledges would spike them to the ground, and an invisible line on the earth would be crossed, and John B. Parker, or one of his companies, would be entitled to the eighth of a million dollars resting in the Spargill Trust's vaults.

Judge Gerrish hailed Brandon in front of the Chapultepec. "It's cutting it pretty fine," he said, "but the last messenger brought word that the tracks should reach the new town line between ten and midnight. I expect about everybody's going to be out there from sunset on, whooping it up and giving the track-layers three cheers every three minutes and free whiskey oftener than that. John B. Parker's coming down to drive a silver spike or something, and then come right on here to pick up the subsidy money."

"He didn't see anything out of the way about shifting the town limits?" Brandon asked.

"Sam Hardy took my letter about it up to him, and told me he laughed till he almost had an apoplexy. Said it gladdened his heart to do business with people who thought like that, and that he might have expected it from that old fox of a lawyer." Gerrish gave Brandon an amused look. "But it wasn't me that thought of it, was it, Blake—not a lawyer at all."

"No," Brandon said. "Newspapermen get to see all kinds of shifts people get up to, just as much as lawyers do."

"So they do," Judge Gerrish said. "As the inspirer of this great event, I expect you'll be out there at sundown, waiting for the climactic moment."

Brandon shook his head. "My experience, anything that's meant to happen at a set time comes on a good bit later. Also, with so much riding on it, there's going to be a lot of bets on whether the deadline gets met, and those gamblers I saw up in Split Rock are bound to have got at the crews and worked something out with them. It's going to be a real drama, with everybody betting for and against, stakes getting higher as the clock runs out, and they'll likely get the tracks across the line with a minute or so to spare at most. So I'll have a nice, quiet late supper, likely have the Superior mostly to myself, and amble on out so's to get there about eleven. Won't miss anything much, and I can always get any spare facts from the folks who were there from the start."

"Just what you'd expect from an experienced newspaperman," Judge Gerrish said.

"How about I leave the coffeepot on the table and light out?" the waiter said. "You already paid, so you're welcome to set as long's you like, but I am in a sweat to get out to the track-laying shivaree. That is doings like we ain't had in or near Spargill before, and I would admire to see it while there's still some meat on it. Plus which I got a bet that the tracks'll come acrost the line before eleven-thirty."

Brandon nodded and put two silver cartwheels on the table. The waiter's eyes widened at the sight of a hundred twenty-five percent tip. "When you get out there, get this down on the quarter of twelve-to-midnight spot," Brandon said, "any odds you can get. I'm wrong, we'll give you a free ad in the paper."

The waiter slipped the coins into his pocket and looked thoughtfully at the table top. "Might could advertise for a lady friend," he said. "Describe myself, or near enough, and say I'd like to make the acquaintance of a refined but game lady, replies to 'Stalwart,' care of the *Chronicle & Advertiser*."

Alone in the dining room Brandon savored the coffee, a cigar, and the unaccustomed solitude. Often enough, riding on some errand, he was alone, but an unpeopled room—for all he knew, an unpeopled building or town—was a novelty. He grinned at the memory of the waiter's proposed advertisement, though it might not be a bad idea, a column of ads for personal needs. If the waiter's ran, "Stalwart" might attract replies from some surprising people. The ladies of the Browning Society, and whoever else had been receiving Tooley's attentions, might well consider themselves "refined but game," and be ready to play again. He frowned: There was still a lot about Tooley and the ladies that didn't make sense.

But, Counselor, he told himself, it's lawyer thinking to suppose that things have to make sense. You're a newspaperman now, and you know they're as likely to be totally preposterous. More.

Spargill was by no means a ghost town, but Brandon met only a few people on the street, and only about half the houses showed light in their windows, and the others looked all the darker for the weak illumination of the irregular ovoid of the moon climbing in the eastern sky. Most of those he passed were riding north, kicking their horses into faster motion as they responded to the fact that something was going on at the railhead; probably nothing much just yet, but it was there, their fellow citizens were participating in it and they *weren't*, and might be missing out on something absolutely amazing.

Brandon decided to allow himself an hour for the trip, which was getting progressively easier as steady horse-and-vehicle traffic beat the trail into a wide, nearly level road. He consulted his watch, saw he should leave in about half an hour, and decided to see what a deserted Spargill looked like at ten o'clock in the evening. Not as lively as San Francisco or St. Louis, and not as dangerous, either—not, anyhow, with Sut Liebwohl and Marshal Tooley off the scene.

Liebwohl and Tooley . . . both had tried to kill him, for different reasons. But why was he sure they were different?

As if by a piece of obvious stagecraft, Tooley's successor materialized and raised a finger to his hat brim. "Evening, Mr. Blake."

"Hey, Marshal. Not out keeping order at the track shindy?"

"No," Nason said. "The railroad people'll be keeping what order there is, and about half of anything that goes on'd be past even the new town line and no business of mine, and it'd be an almighty mess to figure it out, so I'm best here. Spargill ain't much of a trouble to police, but it deserves somebody taking at least that trouble, and I got the star, so it's me."

Brandon fell in step alongside the marshal as he walked up a darkened Main Street, then turned a corner. "I never figured I'd get this chance," Nason said. "Marshal Tooley was kind of like a rock, or a waterfall, something you figured'd always be there and couldn't do nothing about. When I come to the *Chronicle* office and had to cart him off to the jail, that was like seeing buffalo run acrost the sky, all strange and wrong. And then I put him in the cell and turned the key, and by damn, it come to me what a prime bastard he was, and that seeing him jailed was like Christmas when I was a kid, good's a new toy or knife. I never really wanted to be marshal till then, but when I saw I was and he wasn't, why, it made me swell out like a poisoned pup, I was that proud. So I am going to give Spargill as good marshaling's I can. Stop dead, don't move or make a sound."

The last sentence came in a lowered voice, riding a soft exhale, less carrying than a whisper. Nason stopped Brandon's forward progress with an outstretched arm. "On the right. Horses," Nason breathed.

In the block of shadow behind a building Brandon saw dark masses that, as he looked, resolved themselves into three, possibly four, horses. They weren't near the livery stable, he knew, and then realized that the building was the bank, and the horses were waiting in the alley to its rear. Without talking, or even particularly thinking, he and

Nason eased themselves out of the faint moonlight and into the shadow of a store across the street.

"Someone," Nason breathed, touching Brandon on the shoulder. Brandon could now see an upright figure standing next to the back wall of the bank building. An indistinct motion of the upper part suggested that the man was looking around from time to time.

"You'll help me take him. No noise," Nason said, neither requesting nor ordering but stating a fact. Brandon nodded.

Nason touched him on the shoulder and gave a push. Brandon retreated down the side of the building until the sentry at the rear of the bank was out of sight, then crossed the street with Nason. "I'll shy a pebble past the corner," Nason muttered. "When he comes to look I'll silence him as best I can. You armed?"

Brandon slid the .38 out of his jacket pocket and held it up. Nason nodded. "Good. I'll pull him forward, you knock him out. Don't hold back, we're going to need him sound asleep. He'll have friends inside, and best they think all's serene out here."

Nason stooped, reached something from the unpaved street, and flicked his arm. A scrape and rattle came from the plank walk across the way, and one of the now-unseen horses stirred and blew through its lips.

Nason edged up to the corner of the building, sliding a long piece of something from his pocket. A kerchief, Brandon supposed, and wondered if Nason had done some garroting in a darker part of his past. Brandon followed, almost as close as a dance partner. The dark vertical of the corner was broken by the silhouette of a head topped by a broad-brimmed hat, peering across the street toward the source of the sound.

As it came more into view Nason struck, crooking his arm around the man's throat and stifling all but a protesting grunt with a jab of the wadded kerchief into his opening mouth. Brandon plucked off the hat with his left hand and rapped the exposed head with the butt of the .38. He tried to imitate what he recalled of Judge Gerrish's pacifying blow to Tooley's head—not forceful enough to crack the skull, not gentle enough to leave any trace of consciousness—and it seemed to work; the man slumped in Nason's grip, dropping a revolver he had been holding. Brandon stooped and picked it up. There were, he saw, three horses, which indicated that there were two of the gang left to deal with.

Nason inspected the victim's flaccid face and lowered him to the ground. "Out for a bit," he said. "Now let's us ease ourselves into the back door here and see what's—"

The ground gave a gentle shake under them, and a muffled kettledrum beat seemed to strike their ears and the pits of their stomachs at the same time.

"Blown a safe with nitro or dynamite," Nason said. "Gimme that fellow's gun. We'll go in, advise 'em they're under arrest, and shoot 'em to rags if they so much as cough."

Brandon handed over the captured weapon and slipped the single-shot .30-caliber sleeve gun out of his vest. With four guns—or three and one-sixth, if you were talking in terms of firepower—between them, they ought to be able to take on two unsuspecting bank robbers.

Nason eased open the unlatched back door of the bank and stepped in. Behind him Brandon could see a faint glow coming from what looked like a closet. He had never been in this part of the bank but supposed it was the entrance to the vault, in what would be the cellar of another type of building. A bitter smell hung in the air and stung his eyes, and he could now see wisps of smoke eddying in the dim light.

"We get to the top of the stairs," Nason muttered, "we'll have the drop on 'em, like shooting fish in a barrel if they cut up rough." He was probably right in this estimate, and the robbers appeared to have considered the possibility also. At any rate they had supplemented their sentry with a couple of steel cash boxes balanced on on-edge ledgers which, being below his line of sight, Nason bumped into and overset with a clatter of metal.

He and Brandon sprang toward the vault stairs. A hand holding a lantern appeared, swung the lantern, and let it go as Brandon and Nason fired two shots each at the stair entrance. The lantern smashed to the floor, and the flicker of burning oil spread around Brandon's and Nason's feet, illuminating them and leaving the rest of the scene dark.

Brandon hurled himself to one side and into a crouch, firing at indistinct forms that dashed through the circle of flames; Nason's weapons blazed from the other side of the room, and the scene was lit by action-stopping lightning-like flashes as the fleeing robbers in turn fired on their assailants before vanishing through the back door.

Nason cursed and jammed cartridges into his empty revolver, then ran to the door. The way was easier to see now, as the flames from the smashed lantern began to feed on the wooden floor. Brandon heard a drumroll of hoof-beats dying away rapidly, counterpointed by the rimshot staccato of Nason's pistol.

Brandon whipped his jacket off and flailed the spreading flames. Nason reappeared through the black square of the doorway. "They got away, slung that sentry on behind one of 'em, and took out. If my horse was—"

"If it was here, we could get it to piss on this fire and put it out," Brandon panted. "As it is, help me with it, or the damn bank'll burn, and that's worse than letting some hardcases get away. Come *on*, man!"

Nason dropped his guns and got out of his jacket and vest, blanketing the largest patch of flames with the jacket and using the vest to beat out less established colonies.

As the last of the flames died, darkness refilled the room. Brandon fished in a pocket for matches, found one, thumbed it alight, and held it like a candle till he found an intact lamp on a desk. The match burned down to his fingers, and he dropped it, causing a brief puff of blue flame from some evaporating coal oil at his feet. Operating by touch, he tilted the chimney, wheeled the wick up, struck a new match, and lit the lamp.

In the warm circle of light the rear room of the bank looked, except for the absence of broken glass and blood, as if a severe brawl had taken place. Furniture, scattered by the recent combatants as they dove out of the sudden firelight or dashed for the door, lay around the room, one chair having lost a leg. An irregular circle of char about ten feet across lay on the floor like a badly handmade black rug. Gouges and splinters in the floor and pockmarks on the walls marked where the dozen or more shots fired in those few crowded seconds had hit; it seemed as if none of them had found a human target.

Nason moved around the room, lighting lamps until the level of illumination reached normal nighttime standards. He picked up one lamp and moved to the vault entrance. Brandon joined him and looked down the short flight of stairs.

Smoke still eddied in the room below them, but thinly enough so that the lamplight clearly showed the door of the vault, hanging by its bottom hinge, and heavy bags stacked inside. Behind the door, on the floor, lay a sheet of dark metal, strangely distorted.

"Damn," Nason said. "The railroad bond money. John B. Parker near as anything found the cupboard bare, I guess."

The fumes had a foul odor Brandon knew from an experience in a mine in Arizona that he preferred not to remember. "They used dynamite," he said.

Nason nodded. "Cut a stick down to get a small charge, stuck it against the lock, and held that sheet iron over it to keep it in place and force the blast in. Not too much noise and pops about any lock, but you got to be careful about the charge. Too much and it knocks the iron back and makes you sandwich meat."

Brandon, feeling drained and tired, and in advance dismayed at the idea of writing the account of the events of—he checked his watch disbelievingly—the last seven minutes, found his curiosity piqued. "You told me you didn't have much ambition about law enforcement work," he said. "But you seem to know a lot about safe blowing and how those fellows work."

Nason sighed. "Read about all that in *The Police Gazette*. Marshal Tooley made me read it cover to cover, every issue. Said a deputy should be educated, if nothing else. His idea of a joke, I guess, showing me he didn't think I could amount to much. I expect he could be right, me letting him get away."

"From jail?" Brandon said. "But that wasn't—"

"Just now," Nason said. He looked at Brandon glumly. "Gun flashes ain't much to see by, but I got one good look. He was one of 'em, Marshal Tooley was."

18

. . . escaped on horseback, leaving the bank ablaze. Marshal Nason and Mr. Tremayne quenched the fire, then made the happy discovery that the funds produced by the recent bond issue were still intact within the shattered vault.

Brandon squinted at the paper. "Within the shattered vault" had an Edgar Poe tone that he hadn't intended. Oh, well, the rest of it worked pretty well. By no means the complete truth, as the identity of the principal robber had been omitted and that of the marshal's helper had been changed to that of one Arthur Tremayne, a traveling man recently arrived and quickly departed. The temporary triumvirate of Judge Gerrish, Abner Willson, and Marshal Nason had decided that no good purpose would be served by revealing that Tooley was at large and criminally active, that the news would cause alarm without enhancing safety, and that the fact of an attempted bank robbery was all the bad news Spargill and the Denver & Transmontane Railroad needed to be fed just now.

Brandon had firmly held out against serving as a character in the story he was writing, and maintained that an imaginary substitute who could not be checked on would serve quite well. "If Tremayne had been here, it's just the kind of thing he'd have done, so it's not misleading," Brandon said.

"But there is no Tremayne," Judge Gerrish said. "You invented him."

"That's how I know what he'd do," Brandon said blandly. Now he continued reading the paper, its ink still damp, as Willson folded and piled the morning's run.

Mr. John B. Parker, president of the Denver & Transmontane Railroad and general manager of Occidental Contracting, the firm laying the line to Spargill, arrived with Judge Quincy Gerrish and other notables shortly before one o'clock in the morning, coming to the bank directly from the celebration of completion of track to the municipal limit (described elsewhere in this number), in order to take immediate possession of the funds raised by the bond issue.

Apprised of the attempted robbery, Mr. Parker's gratitude was nearly indescribable.

Brandon frowned at the page. The way he'd put it, it sounded as if it was Parker's gratitude that had been informed of the crime, not Parker. It was a demanding business, keeping track of what had to follow what. "Indescribable" was a nice touch, though. Parker had turned a cold glance on Nason and said, "If there's a dollar of mine missing from those sacks, I will have your guts for fiddle strings. If you'd been doing your job and not boozing or whoring, they'd never have got in to the bank. That oaf Tooley wasn't much, but if he was still marshal, you can bet this wouldn't have happened."

Brandon had been surprised that Nason's only response was a tight grin and the comment that Parker was probably right; Nason later told him that it was then that he saw that linking Tooley to the robbery would create more problems than it would solve, and that it was better for him to take what passed for a mild reproof from John B. Parker than to let a crazed wildcat out of the bag.

He assured the citizens of Spargill who had gathered to inspect the damage to the bank that he would use the funds to promote the rapid progress of track to the center of town, and that work would begin immediately upon a new depot, a ready-constructed building manufactured by Montgomery, Ward & Co. of Chicago and shipped in sections. See elsewhere in this number for an account of the proposed celebration of this historic event.

Brandon leafed through the paper. There was hardly anything unrelated to the advent of the DT tracks. Carpenters and helpers were being sought for the construction and fitting out of the station; the town band urged any Spargillians possessing an instrument and, with any luck, musical ability, to turn out for practice for the festivities. The telegraph line was moving ahead of the rails, and a heavily headlined notice, embellished with one of Vanbrugh's engravings, proclaimed that the Spargill office of the Occidental Telegraph Company would open within a week.

"That'll be a help to you, the telegraph coming in," he called to Abner Willson.

Willson shook his head. "Not much. Convenient for ordering paper and such a bit faster, that's about it."

"But you'll get news from all over the country, all over the world, right away," Brandon said. "With the Atlantic cable, something could happen in London now, and you'd know about it in an hour."

"I know about it in a couple of days or a week, and that's good enough for Spargill," Abner Willson said. "The *Chronicle*'s on top of what happens in Spargill, and tells the readers all about that, in large part thanks to you, Blake, and that's what they want. Even Judge Gerrish, as long-headed a man as you'd want to meet, he wants to know what goes on in Spargill . . ."

At least that part of it that can be printed, Brandon thought, recalling the judge's unawareness of Tooley's harem.

". . . and don't care a fig for doings in London or Lisbon or Leghorn, and not much more for how things are in New York or San Francisco. Spargill's the judge's world just now, like it is for most of the folks here, and if I was to run a story about Queen Victoria eloping with the Emperor Francis Joseph and it squeezed out an item about Mrs. Daveney's nephew Eldon visiting from Denver, where he has a prominent position in the gas works, I would be in trouble. And rightly so."

Abner Willson straightened up from the pile of papers and looked at Brandon. "Reminds me. Jim Caldwell's prettying up that car of his for the great day, means to present it to John B. Parker in his capacity as president of the DT on behalf of the people of Spargill."

Brandon asked, "How's he going to get it down here?"

"That's what you're going to go up there now and find out." Willson flipped two copies of the paper to Brandon. "Give these to Jim Caldwell and Miss Caldwell."

"Sure," Brandon said. "Met Miss Caldwell in the street a couple of days ago, and she told me what a great job you were doing with the paper."

"Really?" Abner Willson straightened up and beamed, looking like a crow cheered by the discovery of an appetizing piece of carrion.

"Yeah," Brandon said as he stepped through the front door. "Said the way you were using engravings now dressed it up a lot."

Willson's snarl followed him into the street. Julie Caldwell must be both patient and determined, to keep using Vanbrugh as a goad to prod Willson with such meager results. Some day the goad would dig in enough to prompt him to action, and it would be interesting to see what it was.

* * *

"I had hoped and expected that the Denver & Transmontane would think enough of *The Spirit of Spargill* and what it stands for," Jim Caldwell said, "so's they'd lay a spur line up here and let her roll down to the main line, but it's not to be. The secretary to an assistant of an associate of John B. Parker himself wrote me that they would be happy to accept delivery if no cost would be incurred, but otherwise they would have to be content with thanking me for the thought."

"But Pa hasn't given up, Mr. Blake," Julie Caldwell said. "Not Pa. Something like that doesn't discourage Pa." Her tone seemed to waver between affection and vexation, as if her father's perseverance struck her as admirable but wrongheaded.

"No, I don't give up easy," Jim Caldwell said with simple satisfaction, casting a fond glance at the gleaming shape of the passenger car, now apparently finished to his satisfaction. "Here, come along and I'll show you what I'm doing."

He led the way to a space by the river where two men were busy knocking together a shallow, oblong box of heavy pine timbers about half the thickness of railroad ties. Thick wooden wheels and iron fittings lay on the ground. Beyond them was an example of the finished form of their project, a wagon about seven feet long, four wide and two high, carried on six iron-rimmed wheels perhaps six inches thick, three to a side. Three heavy eyebolts protruded from the front, or possibly the back.

"Front and back wheel trucks go in those carts," Caldwell said proudly. "Twelve extra-wide wheels in all, that's enough to bear the weight, which is a hair over seven ton. Ben Stoddard's promised me the use of some teams of mules to haul her, and some laid-off bullwhackers that'll be glad of a day's pay. Start off with half the mules hauling from the front, rest of 'em hitched behind, ready to slow her when we get to the downslope. Whereas it gets steep, we'll put 'em all on the back, a twenty-mule team brake, you might say. All my own invention."

"No one but you could have done it, Pa," Julie Caldwell said.

Later, walking with Brandon to the beginning of the path back to town, she said, "You told Mr. Willson what I said about the engravings?"

Brandon assured her that he had.

"How'd he take it?"

"Ground his teeth, tore his hair, and chewed on some lead type till he felt better," Brandon said.

Julie Caldwell smiled. "Good."

Ben Stoddard stood beside Brandon and watched the freighters unloading huge panels of joined planking from the wagons and carrying them to the open spot where the Spargill depot of the Denver & Transmontane would, in surprisingly few days, rise.

"There's a newspaper story for you, Blake," Stoddard said. "Men cheerfully helping build their own tomb. Brought all that down from where the train left it at Split Rock, saw to it that it was delivered without damage. Ironic, wouldn't you say?"

"Freight's freight," Brandon said. "They got paid for it."

Stoddard grinned. "So they did, and handsomely. I charged double rates for oversize pieces, and the DT had to stand still for it. They could send it by train a lot cheaper, or no cost at all if they don't want to charge themselves for shipping their own stuff, but not till the tracks get here, and they're set on having the station up by then." He looked north, along the now well-trodden roadway that the tracks would follow, and sighed.

"I don't expect I can complain much," he said. "Everything out here seems to grow fast and die soon, as big as those sunflowers back in Kansas for a while, then dried-out stalks. I did fine in freighting for a few years, but it works out that not long after there get to be enough towns and folks wanting things in them to make freighting an area worthwhile, then the trains come along, and the freighters move on or go into something else. Expect it's the same with other things, in not too long the mining towns'll be played out, the big Texas cattle drives'll be over, whatever's making big money'll go bust someday."

"What'll you do?" Brandon asked.

Shouts drifted up to them from where the freighters manhandled the building sections into stacks under Sam Hardy's direction.

"Stay here until the line goes through to Denver," Stoddard said. "I can get along on half the business for a time, specially since when I lose business I lose a lot of costs—payroll and so on. And"—he looked sidelong at Brandon—"this isn't to go in the paper, and for God's sake don't tell Nason, but there's something you might want to know if you'll be discreet how you use it. Okay?"

At Brandon's nod he continued. "Right now, in spite of losing the northern trade, I'm in better shape than you might think. I had a partner, what they call a silent partner, and he bled a lot more than he should have out of the business, and for a couple of reasons I couldn't do much about it. He helped me get set up here, roped in some of the businessmen who backed me, and his payoff was a piece of the business. Not too bad, though he held out for a larger slice of the pie than I wanted, but he kept demanding his end in cash, right off the top, instead of keeping some in reserve for when income went down and the expenses stayed the same. So a lot of times it was a damned close-run thing whether I could make the payroll or pay a creditor, and it got worse the more the business dwindled."

Brandon was beginning to understand quite a lot that had puzzled him about Spargill since his arrival. "Likely this partner would have felt pretty sick about the train coming in."

"As a skunk-eating dog," Ben Stoddard said.

"After a while not totally sane on the subject, maybe. Capable of doing things to stop the railroad coming in, or slowing it, anyhow."

"Well, yes," Ben Stoddard said, looking uneasily at Brandon.

"Could have teamed up with some out-of-work freighters to do things to harm the railroad and those that supported it, that's a possibility?" Brandon had last used that tone, like a syrup-coated scalpel, on a witness in a fraud case, who only then realized that he had made a bad mistake in saying anything at all.

"Ah . . . " Ben Stoddard said huskily.

"For example," Brandon said icily, "conspiring with that walking dog turd Sut Liebwohl to kidnap and kill a pro-railroad reporter?"

Ben Stoddard stared at him in genuine surprise. "Sut drifted out of town about the time that wagon disappeared. If he did anything, it had something to do with that, not what you were talking about!"

Brandon studied him a moment, then said, "What it comes down to, you knew Tooley was up to some strange stuff, but you didn't know the details, didn't want to know, in case it was something you'd have to do something about."

"I didn't mention Tooley," Ben Stoddard protested.

Below them, the last of the station sections had been stacked, and the freighters were walking toward the empty wagons with their patiently waiting mules.

"If you're talking about something big and gray, with flat feet, tusks, and a nose like an anaconda, you're not going to surprise anybody when you tell 'em it's an elephant," Brandon said impatiently. "You were screwing up your nerve to split on Tooley, and you wanted me to know something about it so maybe I could ease the word into Judge Gerrish's ear and let him work out what to do about it without you getting in too deep."

"You got it," Ben Stoddard said morosely. "I've been worried since that try at robbing the bank. Nason didn't see who it was, but I've got a feeling Tooley was involved. He knew the bank layout, and he'd know how to do the job. And if Tooley's around still, and clear off his head, the way it seems, there's a hole in the pit of my stomach tells me he might come after me to take what he'd claim is his share of the business. If I go to Nason and ask direct for protection on the grounds that Tooley's my sleeping partner, he's as likely to think that I'm in cahoots with him and jail me. But if you could kind of let a word drop here and a word there, maybe something could be worked out."

Brandon ignored the implied plea for reassurance and said, "You have any idea why he went crazy and tried to kill Willson and me?"

"Um . . ." Stoddard said. "Well, that piece said some things that he could have misunderstood."

"Thought they referred to the women he was bedding," Brandon said.

"So you know about that."

Brandon ran a hand across his clean-shaven chin and smiled thinly.

"Oh, yeah," Ben Stoddard said. "Abner Willson shaves himself, and Gerrish trims his own beard, I expect; they wouldn't be soaking up barbershop gossip. Well, it wasn't all that much of a secret, except to Sam Hardy, Tobit Conklin, and them, and it might be they chose not to know about it. What Tooley told me, some of those fellows used themselves up in their business, so to speak, and if there was someone came along that kept the little woman from wanting the full platter of their marital rights, why, that wasn't entirely unwelcome."

Brandon was interested. "So Tooley confided in you about that? That sort of surprises me, but maybe you can tell me what he was up to. Those ladies aren't the kind that a man like Tooley usually goes after."

Ben Stoddard gave him a weak grin. "Plump, painted, and perfumed, that's more Tooley's style, I'll agree, though a lady of a certain age can show a man a better time than you might think, being clearer in her mind about what's what and what she likes. But you see, this was a matter of business."

Brandon stared. It sounded as if Abner Willson's cynical suggestion that the women had "made it worth" Tooley's while had been on or close to the mark.

"Most of 'em were wives of men on the Town Council," Ben Stoddard said. "Tooley'd get 'em to talking when the doing was over, as you might say, and that way he'd get a good idea of what their husbands were up to about the railroad—whether they'd vote the bond issue through or not, say. The marshal had it both ways, the good time a grateful woman can give you, and information he could use."

Brandon was appalled at this casual recounting of cold-blooded (as far as was possible, given the nature of the enterprise) seduction for self-interest, but thought for a moment and wondered if it hadn't been pretty much an even trade of favors, given the husbands' preoccupations.

He remembered Tooley's uncharacteristic cheerfulness on the morning after the council got word of Parker's demands for an additional $50,000. Right up to the council meeting the next day it had been close to a sure thing that the bond issue would fail, the railroad not come to Spargill, and Stoddard's freight business continue to give Tooley the flow of money he wanted. And no wonder the marshal had been so taken aback to see him the next evening: Tooley had to be the man who had helped Liebwohl knock him out and bundle him into the departing wagon.

"He must've been too plain about what he was after with Auralee Conklin," Ben Stoddard said. "He told me she gave him the gate a couple days before that piece came out, and I guess put the word out to the other ladies, for there wasn't any of 'em would give him the time of day after that, and he was pretty much more 'n half crazy from then on, shamed by being turned down, cut off from information—not that anything he'd learn would change things by then—and to top it, having to pay the Pike Street girls for what he'd been getting for free."

The freighters were seated in the empty wagon bed and on the driver's seat, passing a bottle among them.

Stoddard passed his hand across his mouth. "He came into my office that morning to try to get some money, and he seemed no more 'n usually mean when I couldn't give him any, and then he picked up the paper, that I hadn't seen yet, and looked through it, and then he made a noise I ain't heard the like of since a wild boar I was hunting in Texas one time tore the bowels out of one of the hounds. Thought he was going to die on the spot, then he pulled out his gun and I thought he was going to kill me, but he ran out and on down toward the paper."

Brandon studied Ben Stoddard for a moment, then nodded. "I'll find a way to let Nason know Tooley might have been involved in the bank robbery, and try not to involve you." The "try" was disingenuous, given that Nason knew for the best possible reason that Tooley had tried to rob the bank, but Brandon felt like letting Stoddard sweat a little. Anybody who'd been in partnership with Tooley deserved some uneasiness, on general principles.

The wagon driver bawled to his team and snapped his long whip over the lead mules' backs; the wagon creaked into movement, headed down Main Street. The new lumber of the panels that would be the railroad station gleamed pale gold in the sun.

Two days later, the walls of the station were standing roofless, giving it the look of a dollhouse in the process of assembly—which, questions of size aside, in effect it was. Painters and carpenters swarmed over it, covering the bare wood and inserting windows and doors. Sam Hardy and three of his helpers stood over some long panels of shingling, presumably the roof, and seemed by their gestures and frequent consultation of a large sheet of folded paper to be trying to figure out how to get it onto the building.

A piece of board lay on the ground next to the roof sections, painted a vivid red with gold lettering: SPARGILL. Brandon wondered how much Sam Hardy was charging the DT for this example of his craft.

Next to the unfinished station red-glinting wires snaked down into a green tent from a line of poles that ran along the right of way until they vanished into the woods. The last poles had been dug into the ground, set up and tamped in place yesterday, and the wire brought in only a few hours ago. The telegraph office, which would also serve to dispatch and keep track of trains on this division, would be in the station when it was completed, but for now would operate under canvas. Spargill was now connected with the world.

Brandon realized that he could, if he chose, send a telegram to anyone he knew in St. Louis, a guaranteed surprise to any who received it. By now Cole Brandon would be a fading memory for most of those who'd known him, and only a few wondering when or if he would return. Elise's sister Krista, yes, probably. A little before he'd left St. Louis she had let him know that there was a chance for them to make a life together if he should come to want that. And it wasn't out of the question that, if this hunt ever had an end—one that he survived—he might return and . . . Yet every time he considered the idea, it seemed unlikely.

Or he could telegraph Jess Marvell in Split Rock. If, that is, he had anything to say to her. Brandon shook his head. Where he was and what he was there for had nothing to do with Krista Ostermann or Jess Marvell, and the less either of them was on his mind the better.

The tent flap opened, and a man in shirtsleeves stepped out and called to a lounger who had been studying the men at work as if he wanted to get some pointers if he ever decided to try working himself. The lounger came over, received an envelope and a gestured directional instruction from the telegrapher, and ambled toward the center of town.

Brandon walked over to the tent and poked his head inside to address the telegrapher, who was again sitting in front of his instrument, looking at a newspaper.

"Calvin Blake, from the local paper," he said. "It looks like Spargill has received its first telegram, a historic moment I'll have to write up. Anything you can tell me about who it's for?"

"Hardly confidential, since that fellow'll probably tell everybody he meets, and they'll hold up the envelope to see if they can read through it, which they can't, and it wouldn't matter if they could," the telegrapher said. "Judge Quincy Gerrish, Main Street."

Brandon jotted the judge's name on the folded sheet of paper he took from his pocket. "What did you mean about it not mattering if the messenger could read the telegram?"

"Nothing but number groups," the telegrapher said. "Three pages of 'em, sent twice for checking."

Brandon was surprised. "Number groups?"

"Stand for words or letters. Your town's first telegram's in cipher. Best way to send confidential information."

As Brandon walked away he decided that the first-telegram story was not worth doing. No color, and the judge wouldn't be happy to have the fact of his coded message splashed in the paper. After all, since he'd gone to the trouble of having the information sent to him in cipher, he was entitled to privacy in his business affairs.

Whatever the hell they were.

19

The din was beyond anything Brandon had experienced. It battered his eardrums and hammered at his gut. It should have been somewhere between irritating and unbearable, but in fact he was enjoying it and could identify and relish its clashing components:

. . . the constant yelling of the crowd;

. . . the sharper yells of the track crew as they ran forward with the iron rails and slammed them onto the ties—the very last row of ties, now ending at a massive buffer;

. . . the clang of the sledges pounding spikes into the ground, securing the rails to the ties;

. . . the steady, pulsing scream from the whistle of the locomotive that puffed with a dragon's heartbeat as its drivers turned over slowly, moving it and the cars it drew down the newly laid rails;

. . . the tootling and thumping of the suddenly enlarged town band, which had settled on "Sweet Betsy from Pike" and "Oh, Susannah" as being the only tunes all the instrument-owners could play, or nearly play;

. . . the intermittent explosions of fireworks set off by

boys and guns shot off by older boys and men—women and girls, too, for all Brandon knew, since they also seemed determined to enjoy the day as noisily as they could;

. . . and, like mud and moss daubed between the logs of a cabin to make sure no chink was left for the wind to come through, the hysterical barking of dogs, filling in any instants of potential silence.

The cheers from the crowd swelled even more as the last pair of rails was laid, spiked and aligned, and the engine chuffed ahead, bringing the two passenger cars abreast of the station and the new platform that had been finished only that morning.

The locomotive gave a resigned belch of steam and one last shriek before shuddering to a halt.

John B. Parker leaned from the tender and waved his tall hat at the crowd, then stepped down and was surrounded by most of the Town Council, all of whom shook his hand vigorously and began moving as a group toward the temporary platform that had been built at the edge of the open space beyond the end of the tracks. Parker looked uneasy, and Brandon wondered if he had apprehensions that a dedicated garroter would spring out of the crowd and choke him; not an unreasonable fear if you conducted yourself as John B. Parker was well known to do.

Now the passengers were getting down from the two passenger cars behind the locomotive, some of them Split Rock–based friends or relatives of Spargillers, now free to drop in or be dropped in on with almost no effort and small expense; some of them merely curious sightseers or inveterate excursioners, four of them known to Brandon.

He pushed his way through the crowd to where Jess Marvell, Rush Dailey, Jack Ryan, and Nelson Vanbrugh stood, looking around with a mixture of confusion and interest.

After an exchange of greetings they moved out of the crowd and to a comparatively quiet space to one side of the station. "Good to see a familiar face, Mr. Blake," Jess Marvell said. "I've come down for a few days, with Rush and Jack, to see about setting up a Marvel Hall here. I'll want to come down to your newspaper office and look through some back numbers to get an idea of what Spargill's like. There won't be enough train passengers coming through to support a Hall for quite a while, so it'd have to attract the local people, too, and it's been my experience that each town is just enough different so you have to pay attention and fit your business to it."

"Spargill's a pretty nice burg," Nelson Vanbrugh said. "Good combination of straight lines and curves in the streets, and they got the stores and houses massed about right, nice irregular roof lines, so you don't get that stupid-looking straight line of shadow down the street. And the hills are amazing, some of 'em straight up and jagged, some of 'em rolling like waves, the way you get in Pennsylvania sometimes. I believe you'll find lots to interest you in the paper, too, Miss Marvell. Willson, the fellow that runs it, knows what he's doing, all right. Say, there he is now. Hey, Willson, hello!"

Vanbrugh waved vigorously at Abner Willson, some distance away in the crowd beginning to gather at the platform on which John B. Parker, Judge Gerrish, and four members of the town council stood. Willson glanced in their direction, stiffened, and looked away. "Guess he didn't see me," Vanbrugh said. "Have to call on him, see what use he's getting out of those engravings I sent on."

"He'll want to thank you, I'm sure," Brandon said.

"Do you think we ought to stay to hear Mr. Parker's speech?" Jess Marvell asked Jack Ryan and Rush Dailey.

Rush Dailey cocked his head thoughtfully, which appeared to put him in danger of being garroted by his high collar, and said, "As it's to the folks in Spargill, and we ain't them, I don't see the need."

Jack Ryan said, "For once I agree with young Mush; we've had enough of John B. Parker's gas to float us as it is."

"Well, now," Rush Dailey said hastily, "on the other hand, you got to consider that he might look on it as disrespectful. So maybe . . ."

"Put it that way, you've got something," Jack Ryan said

cordially. "Probably best we set ourselves for some of Parker's painful pearls of palsied prose."

Rush Dailey glowered, finding that there was no way to keep from being in agreement with Ryan, a state Brandon could see he found offensive. Brandon calculated that Rush Dailey had a couple of years of growing to do before he learned not to be manipulated by slickers like Jack Ryan; but perhaps the exposure to Ryan would season him fast. As far as he could tell, Jess Marvell didn't favor one above the other and certainly wasn't within a country mile of letting Jack Ryan get into any kind of romantic involvement with her. He was glad he felt certain of that, and faintly uneasy that he felt glad.

"I've got ashes in my eyes and up my nose," Jess Marvell said, "and I'm going on to the hotel to wash and get my things into my room. Rush, please carry my valise; Jack, you can tell me what Mr. Parker says."

Jack Ryan looked ruefully after them as they made their way through the crowd, then grinned at Brandon and Nelson Vanbrugh. "Ain't nice of me to devil the kid, and he's a real workhorse, but it's so easy to poke him and watch him hop that I can't resist it. Now, what the patent quick-firing sulphuretted hell is *that?*"

He pointed, and Brandon and Nelson Vanbrugh turned to look in the direction he indicated; the crowd stirred like a wind-whipped stand of wheat as it began to turn to see what the cries and shouts to one side heralded.

Up Main Street plodded three pair of mules hitched in a team. Behind them, gleaming in red, green, and gold, its roof a dozen feet or more above the ground, an ultimately splendid passenger car glided toward the crowd, the station, and its destined companions, the cars and locomotive of the Denver & Transmontane's first train into Spargill.

On the front platform Jim Caldwell and Julie Caldwell stood, waving at the crowd.

"The car I told you about," Nelson Vanbrugh told Jack Ryan, "the one I did the engraving of."

"The one that crazy old coot was building up in the hills?" Jack Ryan said. "Called it *The Ghost of Spargill* or what?

Damn, if it isn't the dumbest play I ever saw or heard of! But I suppose it makes the name fit, it's stupid enough to really be the spirit of this place!" He shook his head, grinning in amazement.

Brandon felt a rush of heat around his eyes and temples and narrowed his eyes. True enough, Jim Caldwell's monomania had its ludicrous side—but damn it, he thought, where does Ryan get off knocking my town?

When he realized just how he had framed the thought, Brandon took a deep breath. Counselor, you are starting to get in trouble when you think that way. This is not your town, you have no town. You have a job, and that's it.

He looked down Main Street, at *The Spirit of Spargill* emerging from the clustered buildings of the town, and saw that it had become familiar to him, known in detail . . . his town indeed, if he wasn't very careful.

"You don't usually think of a railroad car as an art gallery, but it don't make a bad one, does it?" Nelson Vanbrugh observed.

Brandon agreed that Vanbrugh's paintings, engravings and drawings showed to advantage, propped against the velvet seats of the *Spirit of Spargill* or up on the window sills. The sun striking the east-facing windows was filtered by shades, and the whole interior of the car was filled with a nearly shadowless light. When Julie Caldwell had heard Vanbrugh inquiring yesterday about a vacant store where he might show his pictures and, with any luck, sell some, she had both let him know that nobody had gone out of business yet in Spargill and suggested that the *Spirit* would serve the purpose. The paragon of passenger cars had been accepted for the Denver & Transmontane by John B. Parker and rested temporarily on a siding by the train that had brought him to Spargill. On the first regularly scheduled trip, two days hence, it would be incorporated into the train and carry the name and fame of Spargill to Split Rock and points beyond.

Vanbrugh looked at his watch. "I announced the opening

for noon, and I'll let the public in then, if anybody wants to come. You think there'll be much of a market for my stuff here, Blake?"

Brandon looked down the car, to where Judge Gerrish and Julie Caldwell were taking advantage of Vanbrugh's invitation to have an early look at his work and inspecting some large landscapes leaning against the windows. He had hoped Jess Marvell would be there, but he had seen her driving around town in a buggy hired from the livery stable, getting a sense of her future customers. The paintings were nearly the size and shape of the windows, looking at a hasty glance like scenes observed through them. As one painting depicted a crag-topped mountain glen, another a vista of prairie, and a third a dense forest, the effect was unsettling, as if the car were passing through three different worlds at once. Vanbrugh's smaller work, on the seats, included meticulously engraved prints of aspects of life and work in the West—detailed, accurate, and replete with color, incident, and useful information; worth studying, but somehow unexciting.

The drawings, whether finished or rapid sketches, were another matter. The one Brandon had seen Vanbrugh working on in the tent saloon at Split Rock was there, the skeletons at play; and there were equally lively and disturbing scenes of groups and individuals. There were some portrait sketches like the ones Vanbrugh had sent Julie Caldwell, vividly idiosyncratic, though Brandon did not know the subjects and could not judge if they conveyed character as sharply as the ones he had seen.

Except one. It was rapidly drawn, as if the artist had realized he had only an instant to capture what was in front of him, with such life and vigor that it seemed to hang above the paper in front of Brandon. The first impact it had was of surpassing charm, the kind the poets claimed for Helen and Cleopatra; the second was his recognition of the subject as Jess Marvell.

He detached his attention from the sketch with an effort and said, "I guess there should be something for about everybody here." He saw movement outside the car and focused on it: Abner Willson approaching, apparently making for the rear door.

Nelson Vanbrugh lifted one of the engravings and inspected it. "I hope they go for these," he said. "The paintings and drawings are fun, but this is what I'm really best at. If I could make my living at these, I wouldn't have to do splashy tourist-trappers for the railroad."

Brandon pondered the paradox of Vanbrugh's determined preference for the least original and striking of his work, one more instance of the near-axiom that most people were the worst judges of what they were or did.

Down the car Julie Caldwell said, "This is interesting." Brandon and Nelson Vanbrugh walked to where she and Gerrish were inspecting a small painting. It showed a pool in a forest stream, with a woman—Indian, to judge by skin color, with dark, braided hair, and some buckskin clothing on the stream bank—bathing. She was substantially submerged and facing away, so that nothing that most would consider improper could be seen, but the effect was undeniably pagan.

"There's a pool like that upstream from the sawmill," Julie Caldwell said. The car rocked gently and the steps creaked as Abner Willson entered the far end of the car. "Nice to swim in."

"I'm glad you like the painting," Nelson Vanbrugh said, taking it from her.

"Now, just a minute!" Abner Willson said. "You take your hands off of Miss Caldwell, Vanbrugh! That'll be enough of that, you hear!" He looked at the painting. "Have you no shame, man! Showing a lady indecent pictures, and as much as asking her to let you paint her that way! Put that picture down and step outside and we'll settle this!"

He fell silent as the four others in the car looked at him: Brandon and Gerrish with exasperated amusement; Vanbrugh with appalled dismay; Julie Caldwell with, it seemed to Brandon, a certain satisfaction.

"Abner," Judge Gerrish said patiently, "you have vacated

your attic and it has become the haunt of bats and owls. Calm down and get it clear in your mind that Mr. Vanbrugh offered no insult to Miss Caldwell, she herself chose to examine the picture, and it is not in any detail indecent."

"Oh." Abner Willson looked around uncertainly and sank into one of the seats, from which Vanbrugh moved swiftly to remove a sheaf of drawings. "Oh, my." He looked up defiantly at Vanbrugh. "I might have been wrong on this, but you can't blame me, forcing your attentions on Miss Caldwell like you've been."

This evoked an exasperated snort from Julie Caldwell and an uncomprehending stare from Nelson Vanbrugh. "Well," Abner Willson said, "you sent her those sketches. And you sent me that engraving of the *Spirit*. And the other railroading stuff."

Nelson Vanbrugh sighed. "I told her about my sketching when I was down here before, and she said she wanted to see some of them, particularly the one I did of her. I was kind of uneasy about that one, but she was a good sport about it." Brandon remembered the sketch's amiable but distinctly feline appearance.

"Good sport about what?" Abner Willson said. "That was the prettiest picture of a woman I ever seen in my life." Julie Caldwell smiled demurely.

"And the engravings . . . I can't work out where you'd figure that Miss Caldwell would be pleased by my giving you pictures of track gangs and rolling stock to run in the paper, but however you arrived at that, you're wrong. Ah . . ." Nelson Vanbrugh paused and cleared his throat. "This is a hell of a time—excuse me, Miss Caldwell—a rotten time to bring this up, probably, Willson, but . . . Well, the fact is, what it comes down to . . . I am looking for a job."

Nobody found anything to say to this, and after a moment Vanbrugh continued. "I am sick as mud of doing pretty paintings to sell railroad tickets, but it's paid well enough so I don't have to make a lot of money for a while. What I really want to do is engravings for magazines and newspapers, it's what I do best, and I want a spot on a paper where I can do that—go out and see what's happening, draw it and engrave it and slap it in the paper while it's still news—for whatever you want to pay. I like your paper, Willson, and I think this town's going to grow and provide enough things to draw so that I'd be busy, and your paper'd look twice as good as any in Colorado or even Wyoming. Those engravings I sent you to use were kind of like a salesman's free samples."

Abner Willson looked intently at Nelson Vanbrugh. "Oh, my," he said. "I surely got that wrong, didn't I? Well . . ." He took a deep breath, and the process by which his mind was rearranging the image of a horned demon into that of, if not an angel, at least a fellow human, was almost visible. "Why not? Your stuff's good, I never said it wasn't. Come on around to the office later on, about—"

"Perhaps after three. Mr. Willson has some matters to discuss with me, I think," Julie Caldwell purred.

When she and Abner Willson had left the car, Nelson Vanbrugh said, "You know, seeing those pictures looking like what you'd see through the window gave me an idea. Imagine the whole side, both sides, of a passenger car painted with a landscape. It'd be like countryside moving through countryside, just amazing! I wonder if Caldwell'd be agreeable to that if I could work out the time."

"I doubt it," Judge Gerrish said. "He put in a lot of work to make this the way it is now, and I don't expect he'd want it changed around like that."

"Maybe," Nelson Vanbrugh said. "Hey, you know, Willson had it wrong about me wanting to paint Miss Caldwell bathing in the river, but it'd make a darn good picture, skin tones, sunlight on the water. D'you suppose . . ."

"Why not ask?" Judge Gerrish said smoothly. "It's some time since I've refereed a duel."

John B. Parker and the bearded man with the broad-brimmed hat were once again standing and talking, but this time on the veranda of the hotel, not at the Split Rock station. Brandon paused in his passage down Main Street to wonder what would bring Parker and an academic naturalist together for a second time. As he watched Parker nodded, turned, and strode away, up Main in the direction of the railroad station. Which, Brandon reflected, was also the telegraph office.

The bearded man looked around and drew a deep breath. He had the look of someone who had spent a lot of time lately living rough, topping the experience off with a talk with John B. Parker, never known to be an enjoyable activity for any human being. Brandon calculated that in about three quarters of an hour it might be worth his while to look in at the Chapultepec, or perhaps the Mountain Goat, if the naturalist meant to unwind quite rapidly.

"Blue-eyed Innyans," Dr. Fitch said. "Woon expeck that, Innyans being brown in the eye mainly, but these fellows were blue. In the eyes, that is, not all over. Might've thought I was drunk, but we didn't carry liquor with us, so I wasn't. But gimme some time and I will be."

Brandon considered that Dr. Myron Fitch—"Doctor phlossphy, not medicine, don't ask me to lance your boils," he'd explained—of Linglestown College in Pennsylvania was past the destination of being drunk already and moving on down the line at a good rate. Brandon had joined him at the Mountain Goat's bar about ten minutes ago, and Fitch had adopted him as a lifelong friend immediately if somewhat blurrily, and was telling him of the recent expedition. His account, not entirely to Brandon's surprise, was singularly short of the information on the animal and plant that inquirers had been told was the party's object.

"Innyan hunters came through," Fitch said. "Brothers, half-brothers, sommin like that they said they were, four, five of 'em, all blue-eyed and beak-nosed, damnedest strangest Innyans I ever saw, not that we have many back in Pennsylvania anymore. Wonner what tribe they're from?"

"The Mountain Goats, probably," Brandon said. "This bar's named for them." He raised his glass to the trophy on the wall, as proxy for Ned Norland, who seemed to have left a perpetual reminder of his presence behind him. "See anything else interesting, you and your friends?" he asked. "New animals, trees, plants, things like that? Heard that's what you were looking for."

Fitch gulped his whiskey and gazed owlishly at Brandon. "There's animals and plants, and there's animals and plants," he said slyly. "Some's where you can see 'em, and some's where you can't, if you take my meaning."

"I don't," Brandon said.

"Juss as well," Fitch said. "John B. Parker'd garrote me with my own beard if I was to let the cat out of the bag. Not cat, though, more fishes and snails and such, d'you see?"

"Not clearly," Brandon said.

"Well, it's, uh, whaddyou know about gelology? Thass what my doctorate's in, gelology."

"Geology" seemed a fair guess at what Fitch was essaying, and Brandon said, "Study of rocks?"

"Right!" Fitch said. "Buy you another drink, Blake, pleasure to meet a fellow gelologist this far from home, but not so far as all that, look at it one way, eh?"

"If you say so," Brandon said, sipping at the fresh drink the bartender brought while Fitch gulped again at his.

"As you will recall, Professor," Fitch said with surprising precision, though his eyes seemed completely unfocused, "when areas of forest and swamp were covered by succeeding layers of deposition during the passage of eons, the animal and plant forms were compressed by immense forces, becoming in time wholly mineral, though organic in origin, and the imprints of these forms may often still be seen as fossils."

"Interesting," Brandon said, considering it as truthful a statement as he had ever made.

"What is?" Fitch said, once again slurring his words.

"What you just said about fossils."

"Never said nothing about fossils," Fitch said firmly. "John B. Parker'd have my toes for toothpicks if I said anything about fossils before he's ready. You can't make me say anything about fossils or anticlines or synclines or coal seams or anything like that."

"I wouldn't dream of trying," Brandon said. "Nice talking to you, but I've got to be on my way."

Outside the Mountain Goat, he wondered whether the information that there was almost certainly an area rich in coal where Fitch and his party had been exploring should go first to Abner Willson or Judge Gerrish, and he decided on Gerrish. The news seemed to call for some kind of action, though he had no idea what.

He found the judge in his office, whittling viciously at a chunk of wood. "If I'd studied to be an Indian medicine man instead of going into the law," he said to Brandon, "this'd hold the spirit of John B. Parker, and I'd be slicing him into kindling and lighting the fire with him. Maybe I'll persuade that idiot Willson that Parker's after Julie Caldwell and Willson'll challenge him to a duel and blow his brains out. I'd like that."

"The honeymoon is over?" Brandon said.

"Rape is more like it," Gerrish said sourly. "And that's going to go on for a long, long time."

Brandon dropped into the chair facing the judge's desk. His news would wait, and he was beginning to see that it might be more welcome than he had thought.

"You remember when Parker upped the tax assessment from ten thousand a mile of track to eighteen, to sweeten the bond deal?" Judge Gerrish asked.

"Said he'd recommend to the DT board that it be raised, yes," Brandon said.

"Well, it seems that John B. Parker, the Killer Elephant of Wall Street, master of the Iron Horse—that same John B. Parker is helpless as a babe when it comes to handling the board of directors of the Denver & Transmontane Railroad, a pack of bootlicking toadies he picked from the cellar he grew them in. No, sir, John B. Parker appealed to their better nature, their sense of fairness, but they were implacable, turned him down flat. Anyhow, that's how he tells it."

"And you got the bond issue through on the basis of eighteen thousand a mile," Brandon said thoughtfully.

"So I did. And that means that I bear direct responsibility

for an arrangement that's going to leave Spargill in debt till somewhere past 1900, for there's no way those taxes'll pay off the principal and interest on the bonds. I've let the town down badly, and I don't expect they'll be happy about it, and why should they? I worked like hell to make an honest deal here that'd have something for everybody, and look what happened. Maybe I'd have been better off . . ." He glanced at Brandon and stopped. "Well, it's one damned mess, isn't it, Blake? You came to see me about something; tell me what it is, and maybe it'll take my mind off John B. Parker."

"It's about John B. Parker, Judge," Brandon said, and recounted what Fitch had told him in the Mountain Goat.

"Coal," Judge Gerrish said softly. "Spotted the formations when he was riding with us, damn, yeah, said they reminded him of Pennsylvania, so he did. And then got hold of this Fitch and the others and sent them prospecting, and it's there, no question. So John B. Parker'll have a perpetual supply of fuel for his trains, more efficient than wood and ready to hand. And not a word of it to any of us here. My, my, you have to get up pretty early in the morning to get ahead of John B. Parker, don't you? Well, as far as I'm concerned, it's about three A.M. right now. Let's go, Blake."

Gerrish snatched up a long pad of paper from his desk, clapped his hat on his head, and strode down the stairs and onto Main Street. Brandon caught up with him and matched his pace; the judge was muttering under his breath, and Brandon caught a "whereas" and an "insofar." Gerrish appeared to be mentally drafting some kind of legal document.

At Tobit Conklin's butcher shop he put his head in and called to Conklin, "Council meeting right now—if you can't make it, give me your proxy."

"You got it, Judge," Conklin called, bisecting a fowl with a cleaver. "Can't leave my trade in the busy part of the day."

Sam Hardy, Charley Pratt, and George Parsons were equally unprepared to leave their establishments and equally agreeable to giving Judge Gerrish their proxies, though

Gerrish did not trouble to explain to each of them that the others would also be absent.

"That's a quorum, then," Gerrish said with satisfaction. They had left the bank and were walking briskly up Main Street. "I've got four proxies, so I can move and pass the resolution myself, and tell them about it later on."

"Resolution," Brandon said with a lift of his eyebrows.

"Your inspiration, Blake. You saved the day by pointing out we could move the town limits north. Well, we can do the same thing now—move 'em west, right up to where those fellows were looking for coal and, the way it looks, found it."

"Parker was heading for the telegraph office right after he talked to Fitch," Brandon said. "He'll have wired his agents or the territorial government or whoever, and have got a lock on the mineral rights by now. Don't see any way you can forestall that."

"I don't mean to," Judge Gerrish said. "Parker can have the mineral rights, and welcome to them. But the council is right now going to pass two resolutions. One to extend the limits to the west. And the other to construct a toll road over the only route down to the railroad. I think it'd be a nice idea to set the tolls according to tonnage passing over it, don't you?"

Brandon stood beside Gerrish at the telegraph counter as the judge scribbled away at the drafts of the resolutions, grunting and chewing on the end of his pencil as he sought for the right phraseology. At a couple of points Brandon forcibly restrained himself from helping or pointing out a detail it seemed to him Gerrish was bypassing.

"The resolutions go to the county clerk, other messages to the territorial clerk and some fellows I know in the mine and land offices, summarizing what I'm doing," Gerrish explained to Brandon as he gathered the scribbled sheets of paper together and approached the telegrapher. "That way Spargill'll be on the record with the new limits before Parker's claim to the mineral rights gets recorded, so there won't be any nonsense about easements." He handed over the papers to the telegrapher, who began scanning them for legibility and counting the words.

"It sure helps to have connections in government," Brandon said.

Judge Gerrish said, "It helps to have connections everywhere."

20

Passing by the livery stable in midafternoon, Brandon heard a familiar voice and looked into the stable yard. Rush Dailey and Jack Ryan were standing by a buggy, which Brandon recognized as the one Jess Marvell had hired for brief excursions around Spargill during the two days she had been there.

"That ain't right," Rush Dailey said.

"Right or wrong don't come into it," Jack Ryan said. "It's the way business is done."

Brandon decided to hear more of the conversation and edged back so he could do so without being seen.

"You hired the hack for Miss Marvell, and it's your job to get the best price for her you could," Rush Dailey said stubbornly.

"And that's what I did. And it happens that the best price included a little something for me from the liveryman. That's how it goes, Mush, the ox that treads out the corn gets to chomp some of it up, like it says in the Bible. Now you've found out about it, you planning to peach on me to the boss? Wouldn't do you any good. She knows how things are in business."

"No," Rush Dailey said slowly, "I wouldn't do that. That's the work you do for Miss Marvell, and how you do it is for Miss Marvell to judge. What I do is what I do, and if that was to cover keeping tabs on what you do, why, then, I'd take care of it myself and not go bothering Miss Marvell with it."

"So long's you keep your nose out of what I'm doing, we'll get on fine, kid," Jack Ryan said. "I am doing my job like a whiz, don't you forget it, and Miss Marvell's projects wouldn't move as fast as they do without me. And it ain't a good idea to get on my bad side, either, if you want a future in Marvel Halls. There is some turns in the track that could make me the conductor on that train, as you might say, with Miss M. as engineer, or even the other way round. You may think you're sweet on her, but forget that. She needs a man, not a kid, and Jack Ryan could damn well be that man."

Rush Dailey gave a chuckle that seemed to Brandon strangely mature. "Miss Marvell don't *need* a man, nor a kid neither, if you want to put it that way. Miss Marvell decides what she wants and goes after it. And you don't have to be smart as a horse to see that she's not gone after you any more than she has after me. Man or kid, she don't treat us as different, one from the other."

Rush Dailey's voice had grown louder during his last comments, and Brandon realized that he and Jack Ryan had left the buggy and were walking toward where he listened. He moved away briskly from the stables and onto Main Street.

He had arranged—he was not quite sure why—to join Jess Marvell on the hotel veranda for a glass of lemonade or so in the heat of the afternoon. They had settled the business about the reports up in Split Rock, so there was nothing of substance for them to talk about. He decided against mentioning what he had overheard between Rush Dailey and Jack Ryan.

But he remembered the freighted atmosphere of their last talk, in the dusk in Split Rock, and was glad that their meeting today would be in the open and in the light.

Darkness could lead to errors in judgment, especially with someone who looked the way Jess Marvell had in Vanbrugh's drawing.

She hailed him from a long padded bench on the veranda, and he walked up the steps and joined her, glad to be out of the still-strong sun.

"I ordered your lemonade when I saw you down the street," she said, and handed him the cold glass.

"Thanks." He leaned against the padded backrest and seemed to continue settling, sinking into a relaxed comfort enhanced by the familiar townscape stretching in front of him and the familiar woman seated beside him. He frowned slightly. Why familiar? He had seen Jess Marvell only a few times, an hour or so altogether in Kansas, not much more than an hour in Split Rock, so she was a virtual stranger. No, she wasn't; hours had nothing to do with it. Something stirred in him that he didn't recognize for a while; then knew he'd experienced it in the past, then was able to put a name to it: happiness.

They talked of the Marvel Halls, of Nelson Vanbrugh and John B. Parker, of Kansas and Colorado, of weather and railroads, of mountains and magazines, drifting from one topic to another with unhurried ease, drifting in the light, constant breeze of happiness that played on them.

"The regular train service to Split Rock starts tomorrow, early afternoon," Jess Marvell said. "I'm going up on it. I don't know when I'll be back to Spargill."

"I'm taking it, too," Brandon said. "Willson wants me to try to sell some of the merchants there on advertising in the *Chronicle*. Now that the trains'll run, it'd be worth the trip from one place to the other if there's something terrific on sale."

"I'll enjoy that, riding up with you," Jess Marvell said.

Like figures on a medieval clock marching out of the works to demonstrate a parable and then disappearing, Brandon saw first Abner Willson and Julie Caldwell walking arm in arm down the street and into a shop; then Rush Dailey and Jack Ryan talking or arguing as they entered the provisions store; then Auralee Conklin of the Browning Society, last of Marshal Tooley's informant-lovers, carrying a basket into her husband's butcher shop.

The two pairs and the single, each demonstrating a different facet of what could go on between a man and a woman: Willson's simple-minded jealousy and single-minded devotion; Rush Dailey's ideal of service and Jack Ryan's calculating assessment of benefits; and Auralee Conklin's . . . whatever it was, but maybe the strongest of all.

Jess Marvell could have no notion of what Brandon was noticing on the street, or of what significance he was finding in it, yet it seemed to him that she knew his mind and his mood as if she shared it, as if they floated on a single sea of awareness.

"I think I will ride up tomorrow, not take the train," Brandon said after a while.

Jess Marvell looked at him with serene inquiry, as if not expecting what he had said, but not surprised by it.

"On horseback's a good place to think," he said.

"Yes," Jess Marvell said, not asking what it was he proposed to think about.

"I'll start early, probably get to Split Rock not too long after you do," Brandon said. "When I do, I'll call on you at the hotel, is that all right?"

"Yes," Jess Marvell said.

The route north was the same as he had taken only a few weeks before, but it might as well have been in a different world. The old trail was still there, kept open for riders and the last freight wagons, but the tumbled rocks and gravel of the roadbed, the assertive striping of the cross-ties, and the gleam of the rails dominated the view, making the original roadway seem like a useless vestige of the past. The telegraph poles with their short crosspieces looping copper wire from one to the next in shallow wave shapes marched ahead and out of sight around the next curve. Trees that had shaded Brandon on his rides to and from Split Rock lay in untidy heaps by the cut-back edge of the forest, and he rode in a broad, sun-washed avenue, assailed by the heat from the sun and that which seemed to radiate or reflect from the stone ballasting and the rails.

With such constant abrasive reminders of change— change for which he had a good measure of responsibility— Brandon found it harder than he had expected to sort out his thoughts but kept reapplying himself to the task. When he got to Split Rock he would be tired from the ride, and that might be all to the good; it seemed to him that he was over-packed with energy, that his thoughts fizzed and darted about like bubbles in soda water, hard to capture. Maybe fatigue would let him go flat, allow some of the curious agitation he felt to drain off.

Circle around it how he might, it came down to: what to do about Jess Marvell? There were any number of reasons to do nothing, starting with the task that fate, or Cole Brandon's self-will, or the ghost of his wife—it didn't by now matter what—had imposed on him. That did not admit of any involvement, certainly not the profound sort that anything with Jess Marvell would have to be. And then, if things ever sorted themselves out so that Cole Brandon could reappear and lead the life of a normal man, and share that life with a woman, there was Krista, known for years, the closest kin he had left, and far more woven into the fabric of his life than Jess Marvell could be. . . . No. There was no gauging the limits of how close Jess Marvell might become in time. Krista could perhaps become as close as Elise had been, perhaps more; even the memory of Elise was becoming ghostly, and he could not precisely remember what he had felt when they were together. But he knew that Jess Marvell could become more than close, that if he let it happen, they could in some measure become each other.

"I am not ready for that," he said aloud. And that was it, finally. Not that he did not want it, not that it wasn't infinitely desirable. But this day, he was not the man for it. Another day, another turn of the wheel of time and circumstance, and he might be. Whether it was his hunt after the Kenneally gang or who he was just now did not seem to matter much; the fact was clear.

When he knew this he felt a sense of clarification—almost, but not quite, satisfaction. It was best to be sure, even if what he was sure of was an immense loss. Brandon had learned to live with loss.

Brandon paused at the edge of the bridge stretching across the gorge. Though it was finished, with the twin rails stretching across, it still looked flimsy, but it had obviously supported the train that had brought John B. Parker, Jess Marvell and the rest to Spargill.

He contemplated the tracks running across the bridge but decided against urging his horse onto them. He would have trusted a mule, too unimaginative to do anything but put one foot in front of the another and keep upright under all conditions, but a horse could find five ways to commit suicide and manslaughter upon finding itself a couple of hundred feet in the air with only ties less than twelve inches wide for footing.

This one had already negotiated the journey into and out of the gorge coming and going and handled the descent confidently. As he neared the bottom Brandon heard the repeated *chunk* of an axe and wondered if the bridge builders were doing some final shoring-up.

Right under the bridge the river ran fast and noisily, and Brandon's descent was unnoticed by the two men working at the bridge until after he had them in plain view. One was wielding the axe Brandon had heard, cutting deep notches into a supporting timber. Brandon saw other timbers, hewn through, dangling above the stumps. An axe lay on the ground beside another man, and he cradled a heavy-caliber rifle on his chest.

Just as the significance of what he was seeing hit Brandon the man with the rifle saw him, sat up, and raised the gun. Brandon flattened himself on the horse's back as the gun boomed.

The horse screamed and reared back, standing up almost straight. Brandon threw himself to one side, landing in a clump of woody bushes that had a pungent, medicinal smell.

The horse screamed again, wheeled, and scrambled back

up the way they had come down. A spray of blood drops marked where it had been hit; Brandon hoped that the wound was not serious.

He heard one man call, "He's gettin' away—go after him and finish him off!" and realized that his fall had not been seen. He crouched deeper in the bush until he saw the man with the rifle pound by, uphill bound. He could still hear the clatter and frenzied whinny of the wounded horse's upward progress.

He wriggled over to a ledge looking down on the area where the men had been working. The man who had been chopping had laid his axe down and was looking anxiously after his companion. Brandon eased the .38 out of his jacket. The chopper was about twenty feet away, an easy shot. But the report would bring the rifleman down, forewarned and ready to finish the job.

Brandon calculated time, distance, and needs. It would be highly desirable to find out from these men what they were up to and why. But only one was needed for that. And the best chance of getting hold of that one was to make sure the other wasn't around. Brandon was alone, not with Nason, and the chopper was a good bit farther away than the sentry at the bank had been, and it was broad daylight instead of deep night, but the general idea was the same: take the victim by surprise, don't let him make a noise, and put him to sleep immediately.

Brandon settled into a crouch, holding the .38 by the barrel, butt projecting like a gavel, waiting for his chance and hoping it would come before the rifleman came down the hill again.

At last the man turned to look across the river. Brandon tensed his thighs and made the strongest leap he had ever managed, crashing to the sand and pebbles only four or so feet from the startled man.

As if mounted on springs, he gave another bound, slammed into the man, and rode him to the ground, holding his mouth with one hand.

The impact knocked some of the fight out of the man, but not all; he eeled madly beneath Brandon. Brandon struck at his head with the revolver butt, managing only a glancing blow. The man wriggled from under Brandon, rolled up and into a crouch, and dove for Brandon, now also, if unsteadily, on his feet. Brandon jumped backwards, hoping to get a chance to employ his gun, whichever end would do the job best by now, since the original plan had failed.

"Wally! Down!" the man with the rifle called, appearing at the mouth of the trail with his weapon raised. Wally was already launched at Brandon again; Brandon lunged to meet him, grabbed him, and turned as the gun boomed.

It felt as if someone had hit Wally in the back with a twelve-pound sledge. The impact drove Brandon back, with the instantly dead man still clutched in front of him. He raised the .38 and fired over Wally's limp shoulder as fast as he could work the trigger.

The rifleman dropped his gun and sat down slowly, as if very tired and deciding to rest, but when Brandon got to him he was on his back, staring at the sun with unseeing eyes. There was a bloody mark on one trouser leg, and his left cheekbone was a mass of red pulp and white splinters. Brandon was glad that the back of the man's head was not visible.

Breathing heavily, he staggered over to the bridge supports and looked at them. Six had been cut through, and two were undamaged. The ones on the far side of the river looked as if they had not been tampered with, but it seemed to Brandon that ten supports were not going to do the work of sixteen. A light train with only a few cars might get across it without collapsing, and then again it might not.

A light train like the one due along here at somewhere around 4:30 this afternoon if, as he recalled, the bridge was about two-thirds of the way toward Split Rock.

He looked at his watch, blessedly still ticking after the fall, the leap, and the fight. He cursed and began scrambling up the hill.

At the top he paused for an instant and looked across the bridge. It seemed as sound as ever, like the deceptive apparent firmness of quicksand. He wondered why, if Wally and his companion had wanted to wreck a train here, they hadn't simply torn up the tracks at the end or even in the middle. A train going at any speed wouldn't be able to stop in time and would just spin ahead into empty air and eventually crush itself and everybody inside on the rocky floor of the gorge. Everybody, this time, including Jess Marvell. Then, as that weird drunk Syrian in the tent at Split Rock had made so vivid, the consuming fire.

Then he saw it. Section crews routinely patrolled the track, and the odds were that one of them would come across any such visible damage before a train came through. But a crew-carrying handcar could go back and forth across the weakened trestle and never cause a tremor.

He looked at his watch and shuddered. He couldn't be sure of just how far from Spargill the bridge was, and depending on that, the train would be here in anything from thirty seconds on. He sprinted southward on the track, wondering how a man on foot stopped a train. Standing in front of it seemed like a poor idea, especially as the stretch of track just before the gorge formed a sharp S curve so that nothing on the track would be seen until the train was almost upon it.

Sweat blurred his eyes, and it took him a second to realize that he was about to run past his horse, which was standing by in the shadow of some trees, breathing heavily, with its head down. There was an oozing furrow on one shoulder, but it didn't seem to be severely damaged. Humane as he generally was toward horses, Brandon did not much care at the moment how this one was, so long as it could move for the next few minutes. As he vaulted into the saddle he heard the whistle of the train—at what distance he could not tell, but certainly not far.

The whistle grew steadily closer, and he could hear the rhythmic noise of the locomotive, then the clatter of the car wheels, then the clicking of the rails as their butted ends transmitted the power of the oncoming train.

Then there it was, rounding a bend no more than a hundred yards away. Brandon came to an instant decision, swung the horse around, and slapped and kicked it into its fastest gallop, as if entering a losing race with the train.

The whistle screamed desperately and constantly; the engineer had caught sight of Brandon and the pounding horse as the train overtook them.

Brandon saw the slatted shovel of the cowcatcher, the steam-spouting cyliders, the gleaming black curved wall of the boiler, the spinning drive wheels and the thrashing fury of the pistons slide by him, then the engineer's cab, red-lit from within by the open firebox, with a blue-capped head goggling at him. Brandon goaded the horse to a last burst of speed that slowed the train's movement past him and jumped for the ledge on the tender that served as a step to the locomotive. He grabbed at the cab window post, was convinced that his arm had been jerked from its socket, then fell forward into the cab.

The soot-painted fireman jerked him to his feet, then stepped back as Brandon drew the .38.

"Not a robbery," Brandon gasped. "Just listen. Trestle's cut ahead, less than half the supports left, train'll go into the gorge, you've got to stop right now!"

The engineer gaped, then said, "I pull the throttle all the way up and signal the brakeman to twist the wheel's hard's he can, it'll still take half a mile to stop, this speed—still, best do what I can. Start praying, mister."

He reached for the signal cord with one hand and the throttle with the other. A flash of memory came to Brandon, the other thing that the drunk Syrian had said. . . . He struck with the pistol barrel at the hand that now almost touched the cord. "No! If we can't stop, then the only thing's speed—go as fast as we can, we might make it across."

As the engineer hesitated Brandon pushed the throttle all the way down and felt the train surge ahead, swaying as it took the curves.

"You're risking a boiler explosion," the engineer said, eyeing Brandon's revolver.

"Faster way to die than falling off the trestle onto rocks," Brandon said.

Then they were out of the curving track through the woods and into the open, with the straight line of track aimed across the gorge beckoning them with a deceitful assurance of security.

Now that they were almost on it, the bridge was hidden by the bulk of the boiler, and it seemed to Brandon as if they were launching into empty air, which might at any moment prove to be the fact.

The noise of the engine and the cars changed, becoming less intense as it was no longer reflected from the roadbed and escaped into the void through which they were traveling. It seemed to Brandon that the locomotive's headlong rush was becoming tentative, not that it was losing speed but that it was slowly moving its nose from side to side as if uncertain of a scent it was following. When he looked out the cab window at the rapidly nearing far side of the gorge it seemed to shift back and forth, then to tilt a trifle as well.

Brandon pushed hard on the throttle, hoping to squeeze a last ounce of power out of the boiler; then the swaying motion stopped, trees flashed by them, and solid earth surrounded them. The engineer said, "We're across, by God!" He gently loosened Brandon's clenched hand from the throttle, eased it up, and pulled the signal cord.

The train lost speed, and the locomotive's bellowing died down to a stertorous grumble; Brandon heard the squeal of the brakes.

When it stopped, Brandon, the fireman, and the brakeman climbed stiffly down out of the cab. The fireman bent double and began ridding himself of lunch, breakfast, and yesterday's supper.

Brandon looked down the train and saw passengers stepping down, some sinking to the grass, some following the fireman's example, some staring ahead or behind.

The gorge was well over half a mile behind them, but in the clear air the dissipating cloud of dust over it could be easily seen, as could the dangling length of track at the far side, hanging down the precipice like a forgotten end of rope. It was as sharp as one of Nelson Vanbrugh's meticulous engravings, framed by the expanse of meadow or prairie that stretched to the east and a line of woods that approached to within twenty yards of the track on the west.

Then a knot of passengers and a severely upset conductor surrounded the engineer and demanded to know what had happened. Brandon, not being in railroad uniform, seemed not to be expected to contribute anything and stepped aside.

"Mr. Blake," Jess Marvell said. She studied Brandon's torn clothes and scratched hands and face, glanced back at where the bridge had been, and said, "How nice that you were able to take the train after all."

21

"I know enough about railroad travel to make sure of having a good meal with me, even if I'm in the business of providing off-train food," Jess Marvell said.

Brandon prowled in the basket set out on the seat—one of the three-passenger ones, not the narrower two-thin-person type—of *The Spirit of Spargill*, on its first run. He found a generous chicken sandwich and bit into it. He had had a good breakfast in the morning, but that now seemed like sometime during the Johnson administration.

A quick inspection had shown that the snake imitation the train had done on its way across the trestle had not damaged the cars, and the engineer had satisfied himself that the boiler and its plumbing had sustained Brandon's extraordinary, though brief, demands on them without injury. Jack Ryan and Nelson Vanbrugh came back into the car and sat behind Jess Marvell and Brandon. Two people he had expected to see on the train were not present, Rush Dailey and John B. Parker. "I've left Rush to look after things in Spargill for me for a while," she said.

"The boss couldn't do without me at her side," Jack Ryan said, winking at Brandon, to his irritation.

233

Jess Marvell ignored him and said, "And Mr. Parker was going to make the trip, but something came up he had to deal with—some new business with the Town Council, he said."

"Getting steam up again," Nelson Vanbrugh said. "We should be on the way to Split Rock without much time lost after all."

Aside from a wrecked trestle that's probably burying two dead men in the gorge, and a hurt horse that's trying to find its way home, and a few score lives shortened by a minute or so of stark terror, we seem to have come through this all right, Brandon thought as he chewed on the succulent chicken and generously buttered bread. But it would be nice—no, not nice, but a damned good idea—to find out who's behind this. There's more than Wally and his pal into it . . . Huh. I've killed a man and never knew his name, that's odd somehow. But they didn't know mine, either. . . . Got to be a gang of some sort. Kenneallys? Cold-blooded enough for them, sure, but out here that's not much of a distinction.

A gang, though. Ready to swoop down and poke through the wreck and loot the dead. Ready . . . somewhere near where the wreck was going to take place.

Before he was fully aware of what he was thinking, Brandon had put down the half-eaten sandwich, pulled the .38 from his jacket, flipped the cylinder open, and begun jamming cartridges from his pocket into it.

"What . . . ?" Jess Marvell said.

"Do you have a gun with you?" Brandon asked Jack Ryan.

"Always. Why?"

The locomotive chuffed explosively and gave a few peremptory tugs at the cars, which shook but did not begin to move ahead. Then from the front came shouts and shots, the clang of a bullet hitting metal, and the cut-off protest of the whistle. All attempts at forward motion stopped.

"You passengers!" a voice called, seemingly from the woods. "Outta the cars in three minutes, valuables ready to hand over. Do that, nobody gets harmed!"

"Ryan, Vanbrugh," Brandon said urgently. "Scoot into the other cars, keep down so those outside don't see you moving, and tell the passengers on no account to leave. Any with guns should get ready to use them."

"You don't think they mean it about not hurting us?" Jess Marvell said.

"They near as anything sent everybody on the train down to smash or burn to death," Brandon said. "And from what we heard and the fact that the engine's not moving, I'd guess they've shot the engineer, probably the fireman. For us to go outside'd be like a chicken offering to pluck, disjoint, and fry itself, save them trouble."

"That's what they'd do, all right," Jack Ryan said. "Fellows that's set enough on what they want to cut a bridge aren't going to stop at a few throats. Let's get on and rally the troops, if there are any." He and Nelson Vanbrugh left the cars, walking in a crouch and scuttling across the car platforms as quickly as they could.

"We almost died back there," Jess Marvell said after Brandon had explained the situation to the other passengers in *The Spirit of Spargill*. "And now we could die here."

"Yes," Brandon said.

Jess Marvell smiled faintly. "Then there wouldn't be anything to think about, would there? I wouldn't even ever have to know your real name, would I? It'd all be complete, not the shape we might have wanted or expected, but complete."

Brandon was not at all sure what she meant, but it did occur to him that he might well be spending the rest of his life with Jess Marvell—a whole five or ten minutes, say—and maybe that was what she meant.

Jack Ryan slipped back into the seat behind Brandon and Jess Marvell. "Five guns in one car, four in the other. With yours and mine, six here. Loads, not so good. Most six-shooters with five or six in the chambers, but only five fellows have extra cartridges. One fellow took charge in each car, 'll tell 'em what to do when."

"No express or mail car, the conductor tells me," Nelson

Vanbrugh said. "They'd be carrying shotguns, which would be a comfort."

Brandon looked out the window. "They can hide in the trees and shoot at us and do damage, but they can't rush us while we can still shoot, twenty yards of open ground to cover."

"But keep an eye on the open ground to the right," Jack Ryan said. "Not likely they'd find a way to get around and come at us from there, but they seem to be in the business of doing the unlikely thing."

"You people!" a voice came from the woods. "You coming out? Yer last chance!"

No reply came from the train. Brandon motioned everybody in the car to duck below window level and behind the metal support of the padded seats, and hoped that somebody was doing the same in the other cars.

A Fourth-of-July popping came from the woods, and glass shattered in the windows and sprayed the crouching passengers.

An hour into the siege, nothing much had happened. Single shots came from along the edge of the woods, and an incautious passenger who tried stepping down the stairs was driven back by a flurry of shots that holed his jacket and chewed up the stair frame.

Then a battlefield-like volley of musketry slammed into the sides of the cars, splintering wood and boring into padded cushions but not, going by the absence of outcries, into flesh.

Brandon eased his head up and peered over the jagged edge of glass in the bottom of the window frame. A man dove from the woods, running toward the train, evidently hoping the fusillade would have discouraged the passengers from looking out immediately. Brandon slid his .38 onto the sill, steadied the sight on the middle of the running figure, and squeezed the trigger once. The man's feet skidded from under him, and he fell flat on his back, his pistol a few feet from his outflung hand. He clutched his midriff and writhed slowly, and Brandon pondered giving him a finishing shot. He decided against it. The man might not be mortally wounded, and in any case he was out of the fight. If he was suffering, his friends could decide how to deal with it; Brandon couldn't afford to waste the ammunition.

A figure darted out of the woods and ran in a crouch toward the fallen man. "Get him, Blake!" Jack Ryan called.

"He's just getting the wounded man out of the way," Brandon protested.

"He's a fool, then, and if you won't do it, I will." Jack Ryan stood up, aimed his revolver carefully, and squeezed off a shot that sent the second man face down by the first. "One less—"

Three or four lights winked at the edge of the woods. Brandon heard Jack Ryan grunt and saw him slammed to the far side of the car before he heard the rattle of the pistol shots and the boom of a heavy rifle.

It was probably the rifle that had punched the finger-sized hole in Jack Ryan's jacket, vest, and chest, but either of the smaller-caliber wounds in his throat and forehead would have achieved the same result.

To Brandon's dismay, all the armed passengers in the car were firing as rapidly as they could at the trees; he could understand the impulse, but in a few moments the only ammunition in the car was the four shots in his revolver and an uncertain but small number of cartridges in his pocket.

When he looked back at Jack Ryan's body he saw that Jess Marvell had placed a napkin over the face and was looking down at Ryan somberly. "That didn't have to happen, did it?" she said.

"No."

"He wanted to kill that man, and he got careless, and so . . ." Jess Marvell looked down sadly and wonderingly at Ryan's body.

"Hey!" Nelson Vanbrugh called. "Listen!"

They heard a whistle, then the gradually swelling noise of an approaching locomotive.

"Well, yes," said the conductor, who had come into the

car when the word of Ryan's death was passed to him, "this train's overdue at Split Rock, plus which the telegraph wire snapped when the trestle went, so they knew something was wrong and sent a train out to check. There'll be armed men on board, so our worries are over."

Ryan's, too, Brandon thought. Mine and Jess Marvell's go on.

A drumming of hoofs from the woods suggested that the failed train robbers agreed with the conductor's view of the approaching train.

Brandon joined four or five men who went to look at the fallen bandits. The one Brandon had shot lay face upward, and the face was faintly familiar. After a moment he was able to place it in a setting, flourishing a whip over a team of mules pulling a loaded wagon out of Spargill, probably early on in Brandon's residence there. One of the freighters put out of work by the railroad, doing something to strike back. If he had chosen to garrote John B. Parker, Brandon would have felt some sympathy, but as things were, no.

The other dead man lay face down, a bulky shape on the ground. Two men took the shoulders and turned the body over. Brandon was not surprised to see the vacant but still truculent face of Marshal Tooley.

He turned away and walked back to where Jess Marvell and Nelson Vanbrugh stood outside *The Spirit of Spargill.* The paint and gilding that Jim Caldwell had applied so lovingly were scarred and splintered. "Be a job to do that over," Nelson Vanbrugh said. "Say, d'you suppose, if I did the job for free, Caldwell'd agree to that idea about landscapes on the sides? If I could figure how to make the windows look natural, that car'd be the ninth wonder of the world."

There is a monomaniac for you, Brandon thought. Men shot dead around him minutes ago, his life and everybody else's in danger, and he's thinking about how to do a damned moving mural. And Caldwell's no better, making that passenger car some kind of idol, the way those folks in India do, juggernaut, they call it. And Charley Pratt, hipped on turning every blade of grass or tree into money. And John B. Parker . . .

And Cole Brandon. Lunatics all.

"There's something I have to do in Spargill," Brandon said. "A man I want to talk to some things about. He's older and I don't know if he's any wiser than I am, but he's the kind of man who'll listen, and when I hear myself talk to someone who's listening, maybe I can figure out what I really think."

Jess Marvell did not say, "I'm a good listener." Brandon knew that she knew that if the time ever came for her to listen truly to him, a lot of things would have been settled permanently between them. The brief exchange in the car before the robbers opened fire had changed something between then, more than if they had made love. Jess Marvell would never be more naked than when she had said, "It'd be complete." Whatever came of it, everything or nothing, each was a presence in the other's life for good now.

He looked toward where the crew from Split Rock was working at the gorge. "They'll have the wire working in a little while and be able to call Spargill for a handcar, though probably one's on the way already. I'll get to the other side and go on down, maybe have my talk tonight. Then . . ."

"Then is then," Jess Marvell said. She held out her hand. "Then is when you'll have something you'll find you want to say to me. And then is when I'll hear from you, and not before, I think. Till then, Mr. . . . Blake."

Her grip was firm and cool, and it amazed him that he was able to let her hand go.

22

"Good of you to come, and, no, it's by no means too late," Judge Gerrish said. "I've had a garbled version of your exploits at the bridge—somewhat different from those of the late Horatius, but quite as epic—and I'd admire to hear the true version. And in any case, there are one or two matters it's been on my mind to talk to you about, and this is as good a time as any."

Brandon settled comfortably in the chair in Gerrish's warmly lamplit study. It was different in many ways from the offices at Lunsford, Ahrens & Brandon, but it was still the same kind of place—a law office, with the fustiness and dust and quirkiness of such places, but with the comforting sense of being part of a universe of rigorous, if sometimes twisted and bizarre, logic. It was a world he had chosen to exile himself from, and it was pleasant to drop back into it, if only as a visitor.

Gerrish listened to Brandon's narrative with interest, facilitating it from time to time with a judicious lubrication of bourbon. "Well, that shows you what having ears and hearing not, and having eyes and seeing not, can lead to. I knew Tooley was strange, but not that he was a secret businessman, an extortionate investor. And that led him inevitably to robbery, murder, and a sudden and ignominious death, and at the hands of young Ryan, too, very curious. It seems we never know what will happen, do we, Blake?"

"Well, no, Judge," Brandon said.

"Yet we never give up trying to know, or even more futilely, trying to make things happen, which shows how little we learn. I suspect that we will never know if there are any truly wise men among us, as they'll never say anything or do anything. But I suppose I'm not ready for wisdom, nor are you, Blake, because we do seem confoundedly caught up in doing things and finding out things."

Judge Gerrish beamed at him cheerfully, and Brandon tried to figure out why.

"I said I had a couple of things to talk to you about, Blake, and here's one of them. You've only been in Spargill a short time, but you've had a profound effect on it. Without your distinctly unethical but effective suggestions the railroad would not now be a presence here. And without your bump of curiosity turning up the coal business John B. Parker would be bleeding the town dry for the next thirty years, and he's mean enough to live long enough to extract the last drop of blood."

Judge Gerrish looked at Brandon over the tips of his fingers in almost an actor's rendition of a lawyerly gesture. "You are therefore a citizen of considerable value to Spargill, both proven and potential. And, as you know, the fortunes of Spargill are what I have chosen to devote most of my energies to. Yet I do not have a capable associate to share that devotion with. It has come to seem to me that you could be such an associate."

"But . . ." Brandon said. "A partner. You'd, ah, need a lawyer for that. . . ."

Judge Gerrish shrugged. "Out here it's not hard to become a lawyer. Work with an established attorney for a while, read a few books, have a few friends among the examiners, even bribe someone—any number of ways to do it, and pretty much anyone can do it, and has." He looked at

Brandon with a slight smile. "I imagine you'd find it easier than most, Blake. But no, I am not talking of a law partner, though it's not out of the question if you should ever feel so inclined. Your position on the paper is a prominent and respectable one and could very well lead to other situations, either professional or political or both."

"Ah . . ." Brandon said after a moment of considering what the judge had said and deciding that it was not yet interpretable.

"Yes, I *am* a windy old bastard," the judge said cheerfully. "In plain terms, if you'll stay in Spargill, settle here, work on the newspaper or at anything that comes along you like better, you can count on getting on the Town Council, having a hand in running things, be elected mayor if we ever amend the charter to provide for one. You'd be the second most important man in Spargill, most important in the course of time, which means you'd have the most chance to make things happen the way they ought to, or the way you think they ought to. It's the most fun in the world and may even do some good in the long run, and how many jobs can you say that about?"

Brandon pondered for a long time, sorting out his confused thoughts. This, though unexpected, was the perfect introduction to what he had come to consult Gerrish about. Spargill was nothing special in the way of towns, but it had insinuated itself into his consciousness strongly, and staying there would mean that he would be sited—and occupied— in a way that would allow what there might be between him and Jess Marvell to grow and, if the force was in it, flower.

And all it would take was abandoning the hunt for the Kenneally gang, turning his back on Elise's ghost, on Aunt Trudi's, on the others . . . and on Cole Brandon.

He looked hard at Gerrish and took a sip from the tumbler of whiskey in front of him. Well, he'd come here to spill his innards to the old fox, and Gerrish had, by accident, met him more than halfway. All it took was the fast jump into the water, and he'd be swimming.

"There is something you could help me with," Brandon said. "I am . . . there's something I'm kind of sworn to do, and it isn't really within the law. . . ." Manhunting and murder isn't, in most jurisdictions, Counselor—you're right about that.

"I am an officer of the court, Blake, and sworn to report any wrongdoing whatever to the appropriate authorities, and I don't care squat about that when it comes to helping a friend, so fire away," Judge Gerrish said.

Cole Brandon and St. Louis did not come into Brandon's narrative, but he gave the basic facts of the story, of the murder of his family and of his hunt, now spanning two years, and the three kills it had produced so far.

"It hasn't come yet to finding a man and executing him, Judge," Brandon said. "Him-or-me situations twice, and one that killed himself with fear when he got stuck in a well he thought had treasure hidden in it. But it could—I suppose it's bound to—and that's murder in the eyes of the law. Not mine, not any more. And I don't suppose that's sane, don't suppose the whole idea's sane. If I want to be sane, I'll take up your offer, I suppose. Yet something in me says I can't let this go, can't rest while Gren Kenneally and the rest are alive and walking."

Judge Gerrish sighed. "There's more to life than sanity, Blake. Some lives are meant to run in a mad riverbed, rocky and twisted, and they'll never be anything else. Sanity'd be wasted on them. Others have a mad stretch in the course, and when it's mad time, that's it, and then maybe it's straight and smooth and sunlit to the sea. I expect you're one of that kind, and only you will know when you're out of the mad part. Gren Kenneally's one of the other sort."

Brandon was surprised. "You know about Gren Kenneally?"

Judge Gerrish smiled thinly. "The Kenneallys are a topic of considerable interest out here, as, indeed, in several other parts of the country. Gren is of particular interest. You know, I think, of the origin of the Kenneally clan?"

Brandon nodded. Jake Trexler had told him of the criminal dynasty founded by Peter and Quint Kenneally in the Ozarks, of its spread through Missouri and the Border states and territories, of its links to the most vicious guerrilla bands of the war—that was where Gren Kenneally was fledged—of its rumored shift of headquarters to the Neutral Zone in Indian Territory, where no government whatever had jurisdiction and no human law applied.

"The Kenneallys illustrate what happens when crime becomes successful," Judge Gerrish said. "When the robbers and thugs prosper, something must be done with the money. More and more these uses are legitimate, as, while you can use money criminally, it's easier to invest it or buy things with it. At first the attraction is that legitimate people can be induced to act as screens for illegitimate activities, but then it becomes apparent that the energy and planning put into robbing a train or a bank will pay a lot more if it's put into land sales, stock promotion, or railroads. Criminality is in many ways a matter of definition, and definitions aside, the Kenneallys are men seeking power, to exert their wills. The same must be said of many we regard as pioneers, ranchers, and so on, who built their holdings by grabbing public lands and killing Indians. John B. Parker ought to be enough inspiration to make the James brothers consider turning in their masks and learning to make real money."

The judge grinned at Brandon, the warm lamplight reddening his beard and accentuating the resemblance to a fox that Vanbrugh's sketch had shown.

"So the Kenneallys, many of them, in the second and third and fourth generations, went forth and sinned no more, so to speak. Crime is an excellent way to build up capital fast. They took the fruits of crime and used them to become merchants, speculators, manufacturers, land promoters . . . even lawyers."

Judge Gerrish paused, sat back in his chair, and laid his hand on the desk. "And sometimes, Mr. Brandon, judges."

Brandon's darting reach for the .38 stopped when Judge Gerrish slid aside a sheaf of papers on the desk to reveal a revolver, on which his hand now rested casually.

Brandon sat back and waited for whatever was to happen next. "You weren't in the robbery with Gren, were you?"

Gerrish shook his head. "Do I look like a madman,

Brandon? When I was Quint Kenneally the Second, I did some things around Fort Smith that the statute of limitations hasn't run out on. But the Honorable Quincy Gerrish, with as good a law license as money can buy, is a reasonably upright citizen, and more useful than most."

"Name change or not, you're still a Kenneally," Brandon said.

Gerrish nodded. "True. And some of my kin are in the halls of government, and some are in the hills of the Badlands, and I'm connected to them on both sides of the law. There are times when my cousins of the dark side call on me, and there have been times I've called on them. That's how it is, and I'm not going to apologize for it. After all this time, criminal or not, we are, as it were, an old, established firm, us Kenneallys, and if there are going to be criminals, they might as well be ones who know how to do it right."

"Nowhere in that is anything that sounds like Gren Kenneally," Brandon said.

"As I said, Gren Kenneally is mad," Judge Gerrish said. "Mad in the worst way, loathsome and vile, worse than a killer and thief. And he is a Kenneally, that's the worst of it."

"He gives your family of crooks and murderers and robbers a bad name, is that it?" Brandon said, stifling a bubble of what felt like laughter rising in his throat.

"Precisely so, if journalistically put, Mr. Brandon," Judge Gerrish said. "All of us do what we do, and if it incurs a penalty, those who are caught at it will pay the penalty or use standard means to evade it. But what Gren Kenneally has done and will yet do if he is not stopped adds unacceptably to the risks of doing business. If I were ever exposed as the son of Quint Kenneally, I might live it down and even, in some quarters, gain credit. But to be known as a relative of Gren Kenneally would damn me everywhere."

The judge's third use of his real name crystallized some of Brandon's more scattered suspicions. "You've known who I am for a while, haven't you? Two or three weeks, anyhow. Known I was after Gren and the others."

Judge Gerrish nodded.

Brandon leaned back and whistled softly.

"Yes," Judge Gerrish said. "That was the second thing I wanted to speak to you about. I'd have preferred the first alternative, helping me run Spargill, and if you'd taken me up, it'd never have come to this. But it's clear you're past that. Gren Kenneally and the stupid or misguided or extremely unlucky louts who robbed that train with him and murdered your family at his command, those men are a thorn in the sides of the real Kenneallys and their associates. They have to be got rid of, and frankly, we haven't been able to find them to do it. A professional gunman we might hire to hunt them and go after them couldn't be trusted to do the job, and if he did, he couldn't be trusted not to use it against us. You came into our ken last year, when that oaf Oscar turned up dead in Arizona after some ambiguous association with a gambler called Beaufort Callison, a gambler no other gambler or saloon keeper appeared to have heard of. Charles Brooks, briefly of Bascom, Texas, where another of Gren's playmates died, also came to our attention, and both were soon convincingly connected with Cole Brandon, Esquire, late of St. Louis. You were not expected here, but once you had appeared, it didn't take long to identify you."

"So," Brandon said. "You people are about as thorough as the Nationwide Detective Agency, that I hired to hunt . . ." He stopped and looked closely at Gerrish.

"Well, they did all they could," Gerrish said. "Didn't hold back at all, and in fact found that wretch Casmire for you. Bad luck that Gren prevailed on old Peter to come through with those false witnesses and get him acquitted. And if they ever get hold of Gren, you can't imagine what a bonus there'd be in it for them."

Brandon looked up at the paneled ceiling and at the red-and brown-bound law books on the shelves, solid and staid-looking as ever, and carrying no conviction whatever of the certainty and sanity of existence. "You've picked me as your cat's-paw, evidently," he said. "Crazed enough to go after your madman and his crew, not caring if I commit murder or suicide. How would you help make that happen?"

Judge Gerrish lifted a paper from his desk. "This has taken a long time to put together, and it only reached me a few days ago—that mysterious telegram you politely made a point of not asking me about. The names, either real or false, of what we believe to be the remaining men who were with Gren Kenneally in that robbery, and what is known of their most recent whereabouts. There is nothing, unfortunately, about Gren Kenneally himself in it, and the rest of the information is not up-to-date enough to give you a clear course, but you have made more of less. As your journey to Spargill shows."

Brandon frowned, unable to make sense of the judge's last comment, then looked hard at the paper. He could refuse it, and walk away from the chance to let a criminal dynasty retain him as a mad dog with permission to kill selected quarry. That would not now, probably, result in bestriding the narrow world of Spargill with Judge Gerrish like a pair of colossi, but it would allow him to reject the obsessing burden of vengeance, to explore what there might be between him and Jess Marvell.

Between who and Jess Marvell? Not Cole Brandon, not now. If Cole Brandon, then a Cole Brandon who had seen the job through, mad or not.

He said a silent good-bye to a long road that seemed for a brief while to have opened before him, reached for the paper, and scanned it. Seven names, or sets of names, for some of them fancied a small arsenal of aliases, apparently; seven notations of latest known locations. Six meant nothing to him. The seventh did.

"Jack Ryan," he said wonderingly.

Judge Gerrish nodded. "New York street boy, sent west to a farm family, ran off from them and fell in with Gren and the rest. I can tell you, I was pretty shaken when I saw his name on the list, for I'd rather liked him. But he was one of them, no question about it, and I hadn't any idea what to do about him. But Marshal Tooley's friends solved that, didn't they? That's one you don't have to feel any responsibility for."

Brandon remembered his refusal to shoot Tooley as he performed his last, perhaps only, heroic action, and Ryan's response. "You can credit him to me, Judge."

THE TRACKER

✦ D.R. BENSEN ✦

☐ **#1 MASK OF THE TRACKER**.......73834-8/$3.50
He lived by the law until it failed him—
then he went hunting for justice.

☐ **#2 FOOL'S GOLD**.......73835-6/$3.50
The hills swarmed with men tearing
riches from the ground. The Tracker
aimed to put one man in it...six feet deep.

☐ **#3 DEATH IN THE HILLS**......73836-4/$3.50

Available now from Pocket Books

**And coming in December 1992
#4 THE RENEGADE**
